James W. Carr

Plainfield

Illinois

ELLA LINCOLN;

OR,

WESTERN PRAIRIE LIFE.

An Autobiography.

BY

MRS. E. A. W. H.

JAMES FRENCH & COMPANY.
BOSTON.
1857.

Entered according to Act of Congress, in the year 1857, by
JAMES FRENCH & CO.,
In the Clerk's Office of the District Court of the District of Massachusetts.

Electrotyped and Printed by
W. F. DRAPER, ANDOVER, MASS.

PREFACE.

In presenting this work to the public, the author is aware that it may find some readers who will be shocked by the seeming boldness and peculiarity of her style. She is aware that the daughters of prosperity, as they turn over its unpretending pages, may be "disgusted" with the homely faces and undraped outlines of the stubborn facts before them.

"Coarse" — "unlady-like," may be the indignant language of many a city lady, whose ideas of life and manners have been formed amidst the luxuries which have never disappeared from around *her*; — who has never been called upon to fling aside the beautiful dependence of womanhood, and battle alone with the ruder spirits of a cold, cold world.

In reply to such, we quote the language of another:

"It is well, too, that they who have objected to the representation of 'coarseness,' and shrunk away from it with repugnance, as if such conception arose out of the writers, should learn that not from the imagination, — not from internal conception — but from the hard, cruel facts pressed down by an external life upon their very senses, for long months and years together, did they write out what they saw, obeying the stern dictates of their consciences."

The style of Ella Lincoln has, in a measure, grown out of the circumstances which have surrounded her. She has *felt* too deeply to tell the story of her life in a *whisper*.

Nursed in luxury; and afterwards doomed to such vicissitudes as seldom fall to the lot of any human being; it were hardly to be expected that in describing the past, she should mellow its roughness with a gauzy veil.

ELLA LINCOLN.

INTRODUCTORY CHAPTER.

> "All the world's a stage,
> And all the men and women merely players;
> They have their exits and their entrances;
> And one man in his time plays many parts."

The world *is* a stage; the expression not the less true for its frequent repetition.

When we turn, in retrospection, to the first up-rising of the curtain of life, considering all the circumstances and influences under which we made our debut to the world, we are constrained to acknowledge the wisdom of the omnipotent Director of all, who has allotted to each one of us an individual "part," saying only, "Perform it well."

One wears the ermine or the crown; another, the brown frock of the peasant. The serf is not required to ape the dignity of the feudal lord, or the lord the humility of the dependant; but each is admonished to study his "part," and let his dress and carriage be in perfect keeping with his character. An indiscriminating or prejudiced audience may not always award just praise to the performers; but He who watches from behind the scenes will justly remunerate every one of them for their services.

The great stage of life is also divided into countless lesser stages, upon which we play our minor parts; diversifying the one grand drama with farce or song, dance or pantomime.

Alas that there should be times when we are loath to play at all, and long to hide ourselves in some darkened corner, to turn our back upon the world and weep — to weep for the stage-lights of our own happiness, burned low, and flickering in their sockets; while the cold-hearted audience chides *us* for the shadow which is cast upon their own selfish enjoyment!

It has fallen to the lot of Ella Lincoln to have acted many minor parts. She has paraded in the gay habiliments of wealth and fashion; has worn the dun drapery of meagre competence. She has been guilty of the wildest freaks of comic humor, and danced in her heart while her steps were as steady as the march of time. She has bowed to the audience when its levity forbade her respect, and pronounced her epilogue with a smile, then stolen away to weep.

From the reminiscences of a life made up of both tragic and comic acts, I have selected *a few* scenes. For the manner in which I present them to you, reader, I ask your kind indulgence.

CHAPTER I.

The demon Change hath stalked
Along the well known street,
And blasted as he walked
All whom he chanced to meet.

WOODVILLE is a thriving town in Eastern New Jersey. The eye of the traveller rests upon its beautiful homes as he descends the eastern slope of Scollay's Mountain; and then his attention is arrested by the smoking nostrils of the iron horse, as he speeds through its western suburbs, dashing away over the plain, until finally lost in the distance; and now his weary vision rests upon those unpretending scows which glide so lazily along the canal, heavily laden with coal and iron ore.

The mountain is thickly wooded with oak, hickory, and chestnut trees; their sturdy trunks encircled with laurel and grape-vines, sweeping the rider as he bows himself to the saddle-bow. On its top is a ledge of bare, brown rocks, difficult of access, which from time immemorial has been a place of resort for the pleasure-seeking pedestrian.

It affords an extensive view of many miles of beautiful country, traversed with brooks and flecked with rural homes.

Woodville, as it was long ago, was the home of my childhood.

The mountain is the same; the brooks have not changed their courses; here and there I recognize a familiar tree. But those old white cottages are overshadowed with fabrics of bricks and stone; and the eyes of the stranger gaze curiously out at me, as I pass *my own* latticed window.

I miss those ancient poplars that stood up like soldiers in battle array along the highways, and the lordly oak that shaded the gable end of the old homestead — gone at last, after wrestling with the winds and storms of a hundred winters.

I miss the long row of willows whose foliage swept gracefully over the brook; the stranger's hands have planted the young elms in their stead. The old house is rejuvenated and improved, but not to my eye; even the old well-curb is superseded by a stiff, ugly pump.

The old gray stone church, where my mother worshipped, stands alone in the suburbs, deserted at last. There, when a mere infant, I looked up wonderingly into the face of the hoary-headed minister, and again into hers, awed by the solemnity of his tones, and the meek thoughtfulness of her countenance. There *her* mother, too, led her toddling footsteps up the ancient aisle, and taught *her* baby-lips to keep silence.

Relic of the past! I gaze upon it now with somewhat of the same reverent awe I felt for its square windows and unornamented doors when my child-shadow fell upon it, scarcely larger than a pigeon's wing.

The genuine Yankee "meeting-house" was plain to severity in its architecture — a mere shelter from the sun and storm for the convenience of true worshippers; not like the modern "church" — a pillared, frescoed pile, with cushions so soft and rich that honest poverty almost fears to lean his head upon them. The old steeple, so long and tapering, seemed to loom upwards as we gazed, until we fancied it lost itself in the robes of the angels that hovered there continually to bear up to their Father the prayers of the penitent. It elicited no speculative remarks concerning its cost, or encomiums upon the architect who designed it. It simply seemed to say, "There is rest beyond earth's clouds and storms; strait and narrow is the path which leads thitherward; blessed are they whose faith shall not waver, nor their feet slide."

They are all gone now. As often as the shadow of that ancient pile walks over the graveyard, from morn till sunset, it touches the grave of the designer and the builders, and lingers awhile upon the lowly roof of every member of that buried choir, the melody of whose voices first filled its solemn aisles, and floated away in silvery cadence, circling along its galleries.

Earth has no preacher so eloquent as the ancient church, — its solemn spire forever pointing upwards, fitting emblem of the life to come; its shadow resting on the memorials of mortality beneath and around it.

Our Academy was a long, narrow, white building, with as many windows as a cotton factory.

"Ding dong,
Come along,
Juvenile throng,"

said its sharp, penetrating bell at nine o'clock, A. M.; and away went Ella Lee to school.

That venerable pile has also yielded to the hammer of modern improvement, and become a railroad depot, full of trunks, porters, and people who travel without errands, because it is "fashionable." Out upon such desecration!

And away in the suburbs of the town there is a high, imposing brick fabric, with a cupola handsomely ornamented; and over the carved entrance is inscribed, in golden letters, "WOODVILLE INSTITUTE"—a place where parents who live like kings at home send their children to live like beggars.

All those old, "cheap, cash," "variety," "Boston," and "New York" stores, are superseded now by aristocratic blocks, where impertinent clerks look slyly at each other, and smile, if an honest mountain-girl asks for "calico." They have all "prints" now; "calico" reminds them of "Helen McGregor" or "Meg Merrilles."

The stores are not unlike the new churches which have usurped the places of the old "Methodist" and "Baptist," for which I had scarce less reverence than for the old stone.

Fault-finding Ella! are not the stores and the churches all stylish, and Woodville improved by their erection?

Yes, but *I* liked the old-fashioned store, with the plain pine shelves, and one clerk at the counter; and, when I enter the new-fashioned church, my mind reverts to the gorgeous temple of that ancient king, who, with all his "wisdom," is a sad example for modern Christians, and the less we say about him, the the better.

Woodville, as it is, I admire: Woodville, *as it was*, I loved. Often — oh, how often! — since my own weak hand has rowed my life-bark over the waves of misfortune and change, I have sighed for a haven like that! — Woodville *as it was*, before the din of the great world came thundering hourly through its mountain passes, and the weary traveller reined up his horse at the door of one of our quiet hotels, secure of rest, undisturbed by a hurrying, jostling crowd of strangers.

I can hardly recognize the home of my childhood in the "smart" railroad town, where successful speculation metamorphoses the loafer into the gentleman, and the man whom poverty induced to sell *his lot* before "the nick of time," has become a mere myth in society.

A good old-fashioned village spoiled by a railroad is like a poor girl lately married to a rich nabob, bewildered with vanity, and incessantly rustling her own silks.

Friends of my childhood, you have not forgotten Ella Lee, the doctor's daughter, with whom many of you learned your "A B C's" at the old Academy? Ella, with the blue eyes and light-brown curly hair? noisy, laughing Ella, whose feet never seemed to grow weary, whose lips were never at rest? You knew the story of her outer life: come hither, sit down, and read the story of her life's deep *under current*, upon whose changeful waves hitherto but One has gazed. "Ella

Lee," "Ella Lincoln." Throughout her strange, eventful history, memory has, at times, recalled your forms as vividly as if she had but drawn her portraits yesterday.

You remember my father, Doctor Lee, who followed his profession faithfully and successfully for many years? Unlike some of our modern "doctors," he never forgot *his "patients"* to speculate in town lots or trade in horse-flesh; never left a "patient" at the door of death to attend a party or political meeting. When he had "calls," he attended to them; when he had leisure, read medical works, "keeping up" with the improvements of the age in the healing art.

Mrs. Lee, too — kind, affectionate, free-hearted Mrs. Lee! — pious without bigotry, charitable without ostentation. You partook of her hospitalities, were happy in her sympathy, and loved to look upon her pleasant face when she said, "I am glad to see you," because you knew she *meant* every word she uttered. She was always neatly attired; always ready to welcome her friends, her own happiness springing out of the satisfaction of her guests.

Doctor Lee's house was a pleasant home for all. It was a neat white cottage, with green blinds, and a piazza in front and rear. There were tall maples in the wide green door-yard, and lilacs, seringoes, and roses, all along the fence; and the brick walk from the gate to the door was bordered with the more delicate blossoms of the garden

There was also a little forest of fruit-trees behind the house; and rich luxuriant vines encircled their thrifty branches, and played with the zephyrs that sighed in their leaves.

Oh, in all the world there is to each of us but one father's house! throughout time's tangled labyrinths we meet no second mother. "Home, sweet home!" How oft in later life the weary heart looks back to its innocent joys! how the poor victim of selfishness yearns for a mother's soft caress, a father's care, a brother's unselfish love!

"Home is where the heart is," and God hath sanctified and blessed the home of wedded love; but ever, among its dearest comforts, nestle cares and griefs, unimagined, when, careless as the birds and bees, we sported about the grounds of the old homestead.

Memory, make me not again a child. Lead me not back to the old garden, to sit in its pleasant shades, to climb the old pear-tree that stands up like a sentinel by the gate, to pluck the currants and raspberries, and shake the bright dew-drops from the morning glories into my mother's face, as she smiles upon me in the bed-room window. Those bluebirds and yellowbirds that built their nests under the eaves; the robins that gathered our cherries — I see none so beautiful now! Fancy's veil is rent asunder by the chafing cares of time, and the maturer eye rests mournfully upon undraped reality.

I have called our house "a cottage." So it was. But I did not say it was not larger than a martin's cage. It was large, with a dozen rooms, and any number of closets. It was furnished handsomely. Doctor and Mrs. Lee were prone to the pleasures of good living. Reaping the profits of a fine farm and lucrative profession, they were able to buy it, and had children and servants to enjoy it. Somewhat fewer than a dozen of us — little brown-haired, blue-eyed creatures, laughing generally, sometimes crying for variety's sake — looked up to them for "gingerbread" and "good example;" and four hired persons helped to "train us up in the way we should go." There was "Harry," a respectable white man, who was a kind of overseer-general; "Peggy," the cook, as black as my shoe; "Hannah," a mulatto; and "Stephen," colored. "Harry" was honest and true, one of nature's aristocracy, misplaced in the cradle; "Peggy," was worthy to have been the Queen of Africa; "Hannah" was a good girl, a little spoiled with *white blood;* and "Stephen" — well, he was a convenient little imp, who passed the bread at dinner, killed young chickens for amusement, spoiled the *ballast* of the carriage horses to get "hairs for fish-lines," and spoke the truth, *not as a rule*, but an exception.

Both my grandfathers owned slaves, some of whom are yet living, and remain as slaves in different branches of their families. They were born before the passage of that law of New Jersey which rendered colored children free at twenty-one years of age. The present owners, if they should free those, some of them aged blacks, would be responsible for their support, in case they did not do well, as long as they lived.

I often asked my mother, when a child, to "call the roll" of her father's slaves. The names were short, as "Bill," "Sam," "Jack," "Gin," "Cate." Pity all white babies were not as lucky as blacks at the christening; for not the least of the burdens of life is a name long enough to span a pumpkin.

In childhood, I witnessed an affecting scene between my mother and one of her father's runaway slaves.

It was evening, and she sat knitting. Her children gathered around her, her calm smile telling of a heart at peace with all the world.

The door opened gently, a black face thrusting itself inside.

"How do you do, Miss Clara?"

"If old Joe is alive, he is here!" she exclaimed, rising, and clasping both his hands in hers, while a throng of memories crowded upon her heart, and tears fell thick and fast.

"O Miss Clara, *I am old Joe!* It was *I* that dandled you upon my knee; *I* that took you to the meadow, lifted you up on the old black horse, and led him around with you upon his back. *I* gathered nuts for you; made you rush-baskets. They were all here then — master, mistress, and all the children. I took a notion to do for myself, and ran away. But *he* was a good master, *she* a good mistress. Great changes, Miss Clara! great changes! *My* head is as white as wool — I am seventy-six. *You are grown wonderfully;* and these little boys and girls — all *yours, Miss Clara?*"

"All mine, Joe."

Joe was my mother's guest for a month, during which time he visited my uncles, and wept at the graves of his old master and mistress, and my mother's only sister. Then, laden with presents and good wishes, he was suffered to "depart in peace."

Next to mothers, the servants of families have the greatest influence in forming the characters of the children. Parents should be careful not to surround their little ones with the vulgar or vile. Many an adult is indebted to a conscientious servant for those better influences which follow him into scenes of temptation with a restraining power. Much has been said and written of the influence of the pious mother; much should be of that of the *pious servant.*

Heads of families are apt to estimate the worth of servants by bodily activity and capability. They should see to it that there be also a moral soundness. Better might they surround their offspring with those poisonous vipers which only kill the body, than those moral monsters who infuse into their higher nature the poison which destroys the soul.

That family servant who performs his duty cheerfully and well is more deserving of praise than the good master, because, without the same stimulus to good behavior which may influence the superior, with no other eyes constantly upon him than those of the Master in heaven, he goes his quiet round, expecting no earthly preferment as a reward for his double service.

"Well, Miss Ella, to-morrow will be Sunday, *if you and me live to see it,*" said our good Peggy every Saturday night, "and you must learn your catechise, and not play with your dolls; for it is the Lord's Day, and them that doesn't keep it will be sorry, forever and ever." "Good night, dolly; to-morrow will be Sunday, *the longest day of the whole week;* but you must lie there, right still, in that play-house; and, *if ever Sunday is over*, I'll see to you." Dear, good Peggy! It is many a year since I have heard her pious lessons; but just as regularly as the week rolls round, and my heart says, "To-morrow will be the Sabbath," just so regularly comes back the recollection of that voice; that sentence commencing with "Well, Miss Ella," ending with "*forever and forever.*" Peggy, Ella has never forgotten you! Your face and form are daguerreotyped upon the tablets of her heart of hearts. Yours — the first to hail her when her baby-boat was launched upon the sea of life; the last to bless her, when, in later youth, she launched upon the waves of care — there in health, rejoicing in all her happiness; there in sickness, holding the cup to the parched lips, and turning the feverish pillow. I thank the good Father that the veil of distance has long hidden Ella's fate from thee.

> Thy kindly words would be too late;
> I could not bear them now.

CHAPTER II.

A noble brute is a nobler thing
Than a brutish man or a soulless king.

Doctor Lee visited his patients on horseback. He owned a beautiful, graceful bay, whose name was "Cesar." Cesar's step had become as stereotyped in the village, on the plains beyond, and in every path where horse could go upon the mountain, as Ella hopes the words she is now writing will be upon the minds of her readers.

"There he comes! that 's Cesar's step!" exclaimed some member of the family, as he paced leisurely into the lane leading to the barn, and, "I am so glad!" responded our mother; "the evening is extremely dark, and I have been somewhat troubled about your father's absence. But Cesar is sure-footed; he is worth *to us* almost his weight in gold!"

Dear old Cesar! he deserved to live a hundred years. He did live twenty-one; and was as sleek and beautiful three days before he died as he was at five years old. So said the Doctor; and I am sure he did not change at all from the time that little toddling "Ella" first ventured out to the gate to see him, until a tall girl she stood beside him, wondering that beneath that comely exterior there was hidden so much spirit that if any other person than his master ventured to mount him, he was pretty sure of an unceremonious *hint* to get down speedily. Even his mistress, a most accomplished horse-woman, rode him at the peril of her life. She risked herself in the saddle a few times; and then the result of her temerity was a broken arm, and almost uncounted bruises. When the Doctor rode, he went pacing along like a lady's jenet; when others asked the same favor of him, he started off like a whirlwind.

I doubt if the customers of Doctor Lee ever separated the idea of the man from the horse. A strong attachment had grown up between the two; and when at last a murderous blacksmith, in setting a shoe, drove a nail clean through the hoof into the flesh of the foot, inducing the lock-jaw, of which he died, the Doctor mourned for his favorite as he would have done for a long tried friend. He never became attached to another; never acknowledged again that he had "an easy saddle horse."

Upon "Cesar's death," "Ella" composed the first rhymes that ever flowed from her inkstand. Here they are:—

"Oh stranger, pause! behold this corse,
Tis Cesar's own—our good old horse."

There—she will spare you the remainder of that poem, if you will please to say she has improved since then.

Doctor Lee's outward seeming was that of a cold, stern man. Whatever he thought necessary for the best good of his family, was freely lavished upon them; he spared neither himself nor his purse. But there was such a repulsive gravity in his usual manner; such an apparent want of interest in domestic affairs; such an imperative, "*do this*," or "*do that—it is my will*,"—that he almost cancelled an obligation by his abruptness in bestowing it.

Mrs. Lee spent money, visited, dressed, employed her time and entertained company agreeably to her own taste, her husband never interfering; but there was a something in his manner that seemed to say, "no farther." As if always fearing that he might not approve, she never dropped the bridle of the "unruly member," or gave full play to an exuberant fancy when he was present. She seemed rather to look up to him with a degree of reverence, as a child to a superior in years and knowledge.

He was indulgent and kind; in one sense, a good husband and father; but he ruled *through fear;* not an agreeable though a convenient agent.

Never kiss your wife before your children, nor take a little prattler upon your knee before your wife, and you will not need to issue "ten commandments" every morning.

Is there any "perfection under the sun?" Now that I look back through the mists of time; and behold that honest, self-denying man, toiling early and late; educating a large family of children; surrounding them with all the comforts and luxuries that reason could expect, and demanding for all this kindness only obedience in return, I *know* that he must have assumed that outward coldness, and that very sternness originated in a mistaken judgment concerning our best good.

We never know the true value of friends so long as they are with us. I acknowledge, with a repentant and grateful heart, that if "Ella Lee" had never broken over the restraints imposed upon her by paternal love, "Ella Lincoln" would not now be writing her own history, — at times, with a trembling hand, through blinding tears.

It is the duty of every child, and paramount to all others, to obey the known wishes of a parent. And he or she who wrings the bosom of a kind parent, to take refuge in the affections of *the stranger*, will, sooner or later, reap the price of such unfilial conduct in some overwhelming calamity. The duties between parents and children are mutual, however, and in some instances the obedience of the child ceases to be a virtue.

Let parents remember that they are in a measure accountable to the Great Father for the happiness of their children, and the children, that the commandment to "honor" both "father and mother" is not qualified thus: if no other one claim all your love and reverence.

My mother! no sternness marred the expression of thy calm, sweet face! It seems but yesterday since I climbed upon thy knee, and poured into thy sympathizing ear the story of some little grief, or ran shouting into thy presence with an apron-full of flowers; but *yesterday*, since a taller child I enjoyed thy sweet companionship; yesterday, that I saw thee lying white and speechless upon the pillow of death; *yesterday, yet O how long!*

CHAPTER III

"She had a mind
Deep and immortal; and it would not feed
On pageantry."

Doctor Lee believed in educating *women* moderately. He could not see the use of crowding a young girl's brain with "too much learning," which "makes even *men* mad." He thought the whole world going crazy upon the subject of female education, and "*knew*" that none except women of the stoutest physical organizations could bear protracted mental labor. So he felt; and of course he considered it his duty to crush in "Ella" what he believed to be a wild, speculative ambition—for she was a frail, sensitive child, apparently doomed to an inert, uneventful future; to hang like a mill-stone about some poor fellow's neck, and look for happiness only in the heaven of his smile.

It was a cruel, though well-meant kindness, to wish to keep a daughter shut up forever and aye, like a piece of white satin in a milliner's bandbox, thereby incurring the danger of her becoming silly and uncompanionable.

When "papa" supposed that Ella knew enough "for a girl," he set the foot of his authority down upon the neck of her ambition, and said, "no farther;"

and with a grieved heart, but a *will more determined*, the natural consequence of oppression, she left school.

My time was my own, however; he did not interfere with my manner of passing the hours in my own room, which were hours of leisure, to speak only of physical employment.

In my own quiet chamber I continued to study for two years, uncheered by his approving smile, unsustained by the consciousness of any one's earnest sympathy in such pursuits.

My mother did not openly encourage those aspirations which he condemned, but sometimes expressed to her friends a regret that my father did not foster that fondness for literature which seemed a part of my very being; for, said she, "our different tastes are the gifts of God, and my daughter's passionate thirst for knowledge cannot be quenched in the frivolities of fashion and show."

"Studying again — I would it were otherwise!" she would say, laying her hand affectionately upon my head, and brushing back the clustering curls from my pale, thoughtful brow; "for the path of literature is steep and thorny, and even the few who gain the long-wished for goal of success arrive there with weary hearts and broken health."

And then I gazed inquiringly into her sweet, blue eyes, hoping to read there another meaning than that her words expressed, and fancied I detected in their mystic depths, "It is your lot — go forward."

I persevered. When the house was thronged with visitors, young, gay, companionable; often, upon some slight pretence, I begged to "be excused," turned a deaf ear to the music and laughter below, and was soon absorbed in my studies.

Two years had glided away since I left school; and then outward influences won me imperceptibly from the chosen path.

Arrived at woman's most frivolous age, with the means at my disposal for gratifying a fondness for dress, I longed for admiration and the eclat of being a belle.

Both parents seemed pleased with this new phase of their daughter's ambition, and did not discourage her from attending balls and parties at home, and visiting prominent cities and watering places, always elegantly attired.

You know, reader, rich men's daughters pass at a high per cent in this money-loving world. "Ella Lee" was *called* witty and beautiful. I do not give it as *my own* opinion that she was. I am writing "an Autobiography," and must not speak of such things. I will say, however, that "Ella Lee" was a vain girl. Her father should have fostered in her bosom that more rational ambition which she strove to stifle by indulging thus in idleness and folly.

Even then, within the heart's sanctuary, she despised herself at times, and longed for higher, holier communings.

It is a fearful risk for a parent to attempt to eradicate the love of any certain object of ambition from the heart of a child; to bring her down from her high dreams of distinction into a sphere of more practical usefulness. The time will come when the current long restrained will burst its feeble barriers, and rush wildly on, bearing away with it health and peace.

Parents cannot change the innate structure of a soul, and, do what they may to amuse the truly ambitious child, they fail entirely in their aim by an injudicious or unsteady discipline, which renders doubly irksome to a sensitive spirit the commonest duties of life.

CHAPTER IV.

I heard, let down by reverent hands,
  The grating of the cords;
And shuddered, as the pattering sands
  Fell on the coffin boards;
I said, "a gem of rarest worth,
  Christ, to thy crown is given:—
She's left her place of prayer on earth,
  To join the choir of heaven.

JUST as stern winter melted into Spring, and the blossoms and green grass sprang up everywhere, making the whole earth beautiful, my mother died.

In society she had been an ornament and leader; the poor had hailed her as a benefactor; all who *knew* had loved her.

Suddenly, as if death had come to her in the whirlwind or the lightning, she was called away.

Oh! the utter desolation of that hearthstone from which death has swept the Guardian Spirit,—the utter loneliness of the children when they sit there, comfortless for the first time, gazing at her "vacant chair."

Then they realize *all* her worth; *all* her self-denying love. They *think* of her tireless care, her patience with all their waywardness; that, though sorrowful when they erred, she never frowned. They recall to mind her sweet smile of approbation when *all was well*, and regret that they ever caused a solitary tear to moisten those eyelids, now closed forever upon the scenes of earth.

"Will our mother never — never in all the world come back again?" sobbed out my little brother Edwin, as he hid his bright curls in the folds of my dress, — all wet with the rain drops of grief.

"Never, Eddy!" replied little Carrie, clinging yet more closely to my neck; "didn't you hear the minister say she 'd gone home to God's house, where all the angels live? and he said we would all go there too, sometime, if we would be good, and love our father, and each other, and God. But how *can I love* papa as I did *her*, when *he* never takes me on his lap and kisses me as she did; nor you either, Eddy."

Then for the first time the stern man melted into tears, clasped the little ones to his bosom, and spoke of our great loss.

"I will try to be as a mother to you all," he said; "but I have not her gentle, Christ-like nature. You will miss *her* still, as if *I* were not here. Oh, heaven, why this stunning blow?"

"Be still, and know that I am God!" said the white-haired minister, in low, solemn tones, for he had entered unperceived as my father ceased speaking; "let us pray."

Even the mere babes hushed their sobbing and folded their little hands as we knelt together — that broken family circle!

And then *he* poured out his own beautiful petition in our behalf into his Heavenly Father's ear; and we all felt comforted, and arose with sealed lips and more perfect resignation.

Time, the great healer, — the mourner's friend, — slowly uplifted the cloud which had settled dark and heavily upon our home, and let in again the light of happiness.

My father sat not so often musing alone, with his hand pressed upon his forehead, his moistened eye fixed upon the corner where her smile had always welcomed him; the little ones shouted again as they played, speaking less often of their "dear departed mother!" The heart cannot always grieve; there must be reaction or death.

It is well that we *can* in a measure forget; that sorrow's first keen edge becomes blunted by time, for if the intenseness of the first suffering caused by bereavement remained unabated, the heart would break under the accumulated weight of the numerous bereavements of years.

In the domestic arrangements of the family there was no important change. Peggy studied to have everything done in the good, old way, and if any intruding adviser ventured to say, "Why do you thus?" she answered with dignity, "So my mistress, that's gone, learnt me to do it; I am not as wise as she was."

We all looked up to Peggy as an oracle and benefactor. Like her departed mistress, she was never weary of duty, selfish, or ill-natured.

Home was yet *home* — friends coming and going; the children as neatly clad as before, and all their little wants attended to; no discomfort, no confusion there. Home was the same picture — from it the most perfect figure of the family group had been dashed out by the rude hand of death.

After the usual time had elapsed, we laid aside our mourning dresses, and resumed our cheerful colors. "Ella" returned into gay society, not recommencing her studies, for there was *no one to encourage her now.* But she often yearned for rational occupation, and wished a hundred miles away some arrant flatterer, and in his stead *a book.*

Ella tried to be happy, to be always gay; but memory would not sleep; and as often as the exciting festivities were over, she turned away from the glare of the stage, the voice of the flatterer, and found herself alone — dismally alone! Her father was kind and indulgent; her brother a companion and friend; but into their ears she could not pour unreservedly her tale of hopes and fears; upon their bosoms she could not pillow her head and weep — those April showers of wayward girlhood!

"I miss thee, my mother, thy image is still
The deepest impressed on my heart;
And the tablet so faithful in death must be chill,
Ere a line of that image depart."

CHAPTER V.

"Love looks not with the eyes, but with the mind,
And therefore is winged Cupid painted blind."

WOMAN puts a strange, wild faith in the being preordered by Heaven to be her guardian and guide through life. Few marriages are the result of prudence, few of convenience. I despise that sickly sentimentality which feeds upon "sighs," and prefers "a moonlight serenade" to a substantial supper; but I believe love *is*, was, and ever will be, while humanity exists. I believe, however, that, like the wild colt, it may be bridled and governed; and if, after all our trouble, we find it still running away with our better judgment on its back, we had better discard the mad creature at once, and forget it.

Love is *one* of many passions; and it is not any more pardonable to indulge in an *extravagant* admiration of any of the erring children of Adam, until that passion works our ruin, than it would be to indulge an unreasonable *hatred*, until we grew mad and slew its object. We may *hate* hundreds; some (*profess to*) *love* half a dozen.

O, Ella Lincoln, you plain matter-of-fact creature! you apostate! what are you driving at now? Do *you* believe in third, fourth, and fifth marriages? That a man may actually love a woman, and *vice versa*, seventeen times?

Well, my uncle Lemuel certainly *loved* his wife, Ida, the choice of his youth. When the hectic fever burned upon her check, her blue eye shone with unnatural brilliancy, and her prim, elastic step waxed feeble and slow, he said to her, mournfully,

"O Ida, my first and only love, how *can* I lose you? Long, and cold, and dark, will be the life-journey without you, — alone! alone! I shall never wed another! never!"

One year from the date of *her* decease, he stood gazing through the open lattice at the moon, with his arm clasped lovingly around the fairy figure of Ellen Bruce, his bride. I stepped on tiptoe, close up to his side, and heard him say to her, in a low, lover-like tone,

"Ellen, dearest, I am happy. We were surely made for each other!"

"Ahem!" said Ella, at his elbow.

"Why, Ella, you little chit! are *you* here? Ellen, my love, this is Ella Lee, my brother's daughter — a little pet of mine. I hope you will love each other;" and the lady kissed me.

Of course I thought it would be very uncivil in me not to make an appropriate speech on so grand an occasion; and I stammered out,

"I shall like *her*, if she's a bit like my dear, dead aunt Ida, who was so beautiful and good."

"Ella, you'd better run home," he said, in a quick, nervous tone; "your mamma will be looking for you. See! the moon has risen — time *you* were in bed."

About three years from that date, I asked my

mother "if I might go over the way to Uncle Lemuel's, to see my new aunt Caroline, who had invited me to visit her."

"Yes, dear, if you will be very careful about your manners, and not say any improper words while there."

"No indeed, mamma."

"So, here you are, Ella! come to see your aunt Caroline for the first time. I hope you may be charmed with her, and she with you," remarked my uncle, as the new aunt kissed me and put away my bonnet.

Then I seated myself as "properly," and was as "womanly," as I supposed the occasion required, and began to consider what kind of a remark would be most "proper" for a child like me, as I gazed upon the countenance of the interesting new comer.

"Well, Ella, what think you of your new aunt's style of beauty?"

"O, she is very beautiful, with those long, black curls, and such bright eyes! I hope *she's* had the *measles;* for my aunt Ellen (who had light hair and blue eyes) forgot to have 'em when she was little, and so, when she got 'em, she died."

"Ahem! hem! I have a little business around the corner, my dear; excuse me."

Uncle Lemuel *loved* "Ida," and "Ellen," and "Caroline," — no doubt he did.

If I should be asked to write a "Chapter upon the Loves of Ella Lee Lincoln," I should say but little; and the story would run thus:

First of all, there was my little cousin Paul Smith,

about twelve years of age, with light-brown curls and a blue roundabout. I *loved him*, because he always carried my books for me, and gathered flowers and berries by the way for me as we went to school, and gave them all to me, saying, "I would not give them to Linda, Carry, nor anybody but *you;* for you are the prettiest girl in school, and my little wife, *aint* you?"

"Indeed I am, Paul; there's not a boy I like so well; and, when we are both older, — you twenty, and I eighteen, — you'll be a minister, and I the minister's wife. Won't that be fine?"

And then his blue eyes looked "unutterable things," as he replied, "I *will* be a minister, *if you wish* me to be."

He was more independent six years from that date, and became a staunch "Democrat" without my leave, although he knew *I* had been a "Whig" from the cradle; and, in revenge, I had my first flirtation, with Willie Ray, a pale, reflective youth, who studied Greek and *Cooper's Novels.*

Then I loved my cousin, Alexander Carey, who kissed me, *of course*, when he left for Yale, and said — well, no matter what. But he returned, the next vacation, to quarrel with me upon the subject of "woman's rights," and condemn "literary ladies" *en masse*, and asked me, as a "particular *favor to him*, not to write poetry," — ME, author of that "Tribute to the Memory of old Cesar!" And, after trying to annihilate *him* with a fortnight's pouting, I went, with my aunt Eunice to Saratoga; and there I met Captain Howard, an interesting gentleman of about sixty-five, who had golden attractions to a vast amount. He called me his "dear Miss Lee," and took many a pleasant stroll and ride with me, and told me I would be a celebrated author one day; and I *loved him* dearly.

"Don't you think you could like me for a husband," he said, (right before aunty,) "were it not for the disparity of years between us?"

I am sure I thought the "disparity" very immaterial, and I wished to tell him so; for I thought, if married to him, I should always be entertained with those "sea stories" which he told so admirably, having been a traveller for many years.

There — I may have *loved* many others; but, as my "chapter of loves" has grown somewhat lengthy, I will finish it in the *next book* I write.

I will tell you now about that most serious of my love affairs, whose consequences will overreach the grave.

Thus I should have written, if asked, a "Chapter upon the Loves of Ella Lee Lincoln."

Beloved of earlier years! I long to clasp even now your earnest hands, and weep — weep for the changes I have seen, the afflictions I have suffered, the hopes withered, the warm, gushing sympathies that have been met by "envy, malice, and all uncharitableness." And yet, friends of my youth, I cannot, even now, look back to your unselfish love as the only green oasis in a waste of withering cares. Here and there, like flowers scattered along a desolate path, I meet the "tried and true" of maturer years, though *few* — alas, *how few!*

CHAPTER VI.

> "I pray thee cease thy counsel,
> Which falls into mine ears as profitless
> As water in a sieve."

I WILL tell no "love stories," — they would spoil my book, — but, as a fact in my history, will merely say, that, after an uncounted number of blushes and monosyllables, Ella Lee was betrothed to Allen Lincoln.

My father opposed our union on account of his having been a speculator, hence the danger of reverses, while I was utterly ignorant of all kinds of business.

Said he, "Mr. Lincoln was born in the Green Mountains, and, although yet young, has 'pitched his tent' and '*settled*' in four different states. He is *here* to-day, to-morrow he may be in Alabama, next week in Mexico. 'A rolling stone gathers no moss,' and he cannot prosper."

"Do you think he is underwitted or unamiable, sir?"

"Neither."

"I am fond of travelling, and would like to see the world — *all of it.*"

"You would find it a different affair to travel about after marriage. You would find poverty a bitter thing to bear, also. And I tell you, Ella, finally, *poverty will be his lot.* Amiability is well enough, but is too often linked with indecision, and the liability to be misled by others. Your amiable man sells his coat for a song to the rogue who tells him it is 'a misfit,' or breaks up in the midst of a lucrative business, and starts for the ends of the earth, if some 'clever fellow' hails him with 'Come *this* way, you may make a fortune *here* directly.' But I shall not strongly oppose you in this matter. I am not *willing* to see you married to Mr. Lincoln; if you disregard my wishes, upon your own head will be the sad consequences."

My father sat upon the back piazza in an arm-chair, looking not so sternly as was his wont, but O, how sorrowful!

"Come hither, Ella. You have decided?"

"Yes, sir."

"Then all *I* can do for you will be to put your property into a situation that your husband cannot touch a dollar of it. If you consent, I will do this; not against your wishes."

My fingers played nervously with my auburn curls, and the hot blood rushed to my temples. I thought of the precipice upon which I stood; how all my happiness was about to be committed to the keeping of another; and, in case that other should prove a broken reed, how illy *I* was calculated to meet the bleak winds of adversity. I thought of all the lessons I had heard and read on "prudent marriages," and of some of the victims of matrimonial miscalculations within the circle of my own observation. I trembled, almost repenting of the position in which I stood. What if my father's fears *should* have foundation? What was *my* judgment, compared with his? For one brief moment,

I longed to throw my arms about his neck, and promise never to go contrary to his wishes, — never to wound him more.

But again the olden look of sternness had settled upon his countenance; he had crushed down the grief, and sat gazing into my face as if he took no farther interest in my reply.

The transitory feeling of distress which had swept over my heart-strings as a harsh discord, gave place again to confidence in the betrothed, and I calmly said: —

"My dear sir, I would prefer that the arrangement of property, of which you have spoken, should not be effected. I have been told that where women withhold their entire confidence from their husbands, it seldom ends well; and a life of unhappiness would weigh heavily in the balance against the safety of a few thousands."

"Very well, Ella."

A few years after that, a clause in "the last will and testament of Doctor Reuben Lee ran thus: —

"Whereas, Allen Lincoln, husband to my daughter Ella, has received *her* portion of my estate, etc., I do hereby will and decree that the said Allen Lincoln shall not receive any part or portion of said estate," etc.

"I tell you plainly, Miss Ella, that *I* don't approve of *this* at all," said Peggy, with more emphasis than was her wont. "It is a bad move, a bad move, going off with that are Green Mountain Vermonter, that's lived in Canada, New York, and, for all I know, all over the world. It's all nonsense, this *ere* gettin' married, when you have n't a thing to do, and have a good father's house, the best silk dresses of any girl within twenty miles, a good meetin' to go to, and old Peggy to see that you never want for anything reasonable.

"And then, to think of it; how you are a going away out West, among the wolves, and buffaloes, and Indians, and them *white* heathens that build big log houses and barns, and grow rich, never caring if the word of God is 'nt preached within ten miles of 'em. What *will* dear, good Mr. Kirk, the minister, say? and what would your sainted mother say if she could come back this minute and speak to you? Well, she instructed you in the right way while *she* lived; and I've done the best I could since she went home to heaven — my dear, blessed mistress! And there's master, too; I pity him after all *his* care in bringin' you up, and educatin' you, like a lady; and *this* is the end of our trouble!" and Peggy burst into tears.

"This is the dreadfulest trial I have had since *her* death! I shall never *git* over it — never!"

Never had I seen Peggy lose her self-command so completely; never had I felt so like a guilty creature in her presence.

I felt disposed to deny a few of her charges, as I stood there like a condemned culprit, her great, black, mournful eyes fixed steadily upon my face, the tears streaming over her ebon cheeks. Not a word *could* I utter, however, for I choked strangely in my throat, my limbs grew suddenly weak, and, thinking I *must* do something to extenuate my fault, I sank into a chair beside her, took her hand in mine, and wept with her in silence.

"Well, I'll *have* to forgive you, 'spose, poor child! for it's too late *now*, after you've promised him; and I'm sure he seems likely enough. There — don't cry another bit, child! I'll give you my blessin', and make all the weddin' cake *with my own hands.* And may the Lord convert your soul, and make you a good Christian, that you may be as a candle on a hill to them perishing heathen, that have'nt any churches nor means of grace."

"I have done penance for contemning *love.*"

"But now lead on,
In me is no delay; with thee to go,
Is to stay here; with thee here to stay
Is to go hence unwilling; thou to me
Art all things under heaven, all places thou."

Westward-ho! "Good-bye, dear father, brothers, sisters, servants, friends, one and all, good-bye, and God bless you." Down, weak heart! Away with fruitless tears — with tender recollections!

"Till death do us part." Now, Ella, thy childhood is indeed no more! Gird up thy strength, for the *true* "battle of life" with thee is commencing; *pray*, that amidst its coming toil and heat, you may not faint nor fly; *pray*, for the shield of paternal love is no longer overshadowing your young head; beware of worshipping a clay idol, and when the dark hours come, pour out your tale of sorrow into His ear, who will never mock you.

Ella is gone.

CHAPTER VII.

"Sudden they see from midst of all the main,
The surging waters like a mountain rise ;
And the great sea, puffed up with proud disdain,
To swell above the measure of his guise,
As threatening to devour all that his power despise."

ON a cool, foggy, disagreeable afternoon we took passage in the steamer "Michigan," and were borne away over the blue waters of Lake Erie.

Never was cabin so full to overflowing, never had deck a more varied representation of all the nations of the earth.

Ireland had sent forth, to seek their fortunes, a legion of her children; England was respectably represented; and broad tongued Scotchmen were conversing together on every side. A heterogeneous mass of all colors, sizes, and castes of women and children, climbed and descended the stairs, and surged over the deck.

In the cabin there was a discordant concert kept up by nurses and babies, and the whining tones of hopeless ill-nature mingled with the silvery treble of laughing sixteen.

The steamer glided on over the waste of waters, rocking but gently as wave after wave bowed its head beneath her prow; and the passengers were apparently as happy as any other promiscuous company whose only brotherhood is founded in a common sense of danger.

One by one the little eyelids of the children drooped and fell, and disrobed, they were laid away in the berths. One after another the wearied forms of the aged were stretched upon narrow, comfortless couches, and then the middle aged and the young gathered together in little knots upon the deck, to take a farewell view of the shore, which was still in sight far away to leeward, yet seen but dimly through the veil of mist.

Suddenly the wind arose and came sighing over the waters like the smothered tones of sorrow; the mists rolled away, condensing into clouds; the last rays of the setting sun trembled lovingly upon their fleecy borders, writing in rainbow tints a soft "good night!"

"A rough night; the boys will have some work before morning," said an old sailor, cap in hand, leisurely viewing the sky and sea, and then bending his glance keenly upon the boat, as if measuring her strength for the coming struggle.

"May I ask why you suppose we shall have a rough night, sir," I said, timidly laying my hand upon his arm to attract attention.

"Well, I'll tell you, sis; I *think it*, because I *know* it. You heard the wail of the wind, didn't you, as that confounded body of mist rolled up like a blanket, and took itself off in a jiffy? That was'nt *all* wind you heard. No; you can't deceive Old Jack! It was a warning from *the people below*. And didn't you see *them are* three white gulls that settled a minute on the mainmast, and then bore away to leeward; didn't you hear 'em screech, the imps; they didn't scream for nothin', I tell you! I'm use to 'em. They said just as plain as if they could talk, 'Blow! blow! blow!' And don't you feel a sort of short, quick jerk of the waves under the vessel now? There, that infernal moan agin! But never mind a gale — the boat is as tight a craft as swims; and what is to be will be."

"There, take her below, messmate," he said, addressing my husband; and, relighting a cigar which had died out during our conversation, he sat down, apparently as unconcerned as if he had uttered words more acceptable to timid ears.

"You had better try to sleep, Ella, the old sailor is no seer; and I see no foundation for his prophecy. It is a usually fair November night — these lakes are always somewhat rough."

Slam-bang, rattle and tear — screaming, crying, praying, hallooing, cursing — what is to pay?

Fifty old ladies poking their heads out of the berths nearest the floor; fifty middle aged women looking up their babies and husbands; fifty Catholic nurses crossing themselves and calling on the "virgin;" and a young girl sobbing in the corner, "Ah! Jon-a-than! dear Jon-a-than! you'll never see *me* again — never!"

The wind was blowing a gale; the boat rocking from side to side fearfully. We had struck a schooner, and the babel of noise we had just heard was the smashing in of the windows, the breaking of crockery and glass ware, the passengers springing from their berths upon the floor, the rushing of men to and fro upon deck, the shouts and curses of the men on both boat and schooner.

"There, we're afloat again," said the same old sailor; "hang the schooner! she came near to sending us all to Davie Jones's locker. Well, there's a harbor three miles along;—a good craft, aint she?"

And the "Michigan" *was* a strong boat. She rocked and rolled and plunged along through the boiling surges; not a timber broke, not a joint gave way; and, although somewhat shorn of her beauty, she cast anchor in the little harbor of "Siva," and there we found ourselves at daybreak safe, after a night of much confusion and terror.

We remained in the harbor many hours, on account of the roughness of the sea.

"Ho! ho! there lies the 'Flora' as helpless as a six weeks baby," exclaimed the same old tar at my elbow, of whom I have spoken before, as I stood upon deck watching the sun coming up from his ocean-bed, apparently rising out of the water.

There, truly she was a wreck, that beautiful steamer which left port only a few hours before us; her wheel and machinery twisted and broken, looking as if an evil demon had swept her deck. She lay over upon her side, all hands hard at work to prevent her sinking.

"Deuce take her!" said the captain; "she is heavily freighted with blood and bones, to say nothing about the luggage. But we'll take off the passengers. Heave to, boys!"

"I wish they had all gone to the bottom of the lake

together," growled the chambermaid, as they all came tumbling down the cabin stairs of the "Michigan;" old and young, married and single, gentle and simple, with a most formidable additional force of nurses and babies. "A pretty time I'll have of it," she continued, "stowing 'em away in the berths, when they're all full now; and such a crowding and jostling and squalling all day long. Goodness gracious! it's enough to drive the sense out of any living being! Well, *their* own chambermaid may do their chores, for *I* wont — that's flat."

There were but few state-rooms on the lake steamers at the date of my story; the price for them extravagant, hence ladies, many of them, preferred to sleep in the lower cabin.

The new comers were all weary or sick with the intense excitement of the last twenty-four hours; and as soon as they felt that the danger was past, they were all ready to lie down and *forget.*

The occupants of the berths below, startled by the unusual racket, occasioned by passing the living freight of one steamboat into another, had sprung to the floor, and were dressing with all despatch. There was a loud call for missing articles among the "younger fry;" and some of the old lady new-comers were petitioning impatiently for "a place to lie down." The chambermaid went about the cabin snapping like a steel-trap, and we all pitied without the power to help them.

Ella pitied just four of them *availably* — a young mother with a sick child, a poor consumptive lady, and a very aged one, by telling them if they would accept of the use of her stateroom she would show them the way

"They 'll steal your *things*, may-be," said the pert chambermaid, in a whisper. I tried to annihilate her with a look; but she was as callous as a turtle's back. After I had stowed them away in our berths, at the stateroom door I met Mr. Lincoln, with a gentleman and a very pretty young lady, waiting for me.

"Mrs. Lincoln, this is Mr. Trall, of Chicago, one of the passengers of the "Flora," and his niece, Miss Lisle, late of Baltimore. We have concluded, on account of the dangers and unpleasantness of the lakes at this season, that we will stop at Detroit and cross Michigan. Miss Lisle, like yourself, would be pleased to see the country. I have met Mr. Trall before, and we can comfort and protect each other."

"Won't it be delightful!" exclaimed the young lady, clasping my hand as warmly as if she had known me seven years; "just you and me with some seventeen gentlemen in a big stage wagon. We shall be taken such excellent care of in case our own gallants should not stand it through. We can link our destinies with those of some of those sturdy young farmers, help them break up the prairie, and live in cabins seven by nine, with wolves' eyes staring in through the cracks, and rattlesnakes sharing our pillows. Would n't that be romantic?"

"Why, Jeannie!" said Mr. Trall, half disposed to scold her for her volubility; "I say, Jeannie, have you so soon forgotten the sad scenes of the last thirty hours that you are jesting again?"

Oh! uncle, now that's all over and all safe, why refer to it? You should be more philosophic. If we always look backward to danger, and forward to death, where shall we look for happiness?"

I was pleased with my laughing companion for the long, tedious journey before me, and thought it indeed wonderful that a young lady of her buoyancy of spirits should also discourse so rationally. She was a jewel, indeed; and without her I should have been truly uncomfortable with such a little army of gentlemen as travelled with me across Michigan.

The roads were muddy, in some places frozen; and stage *coaches* had been abandoned as a matter of safety, except in some better sections for a few miles. We left Detroit in a coach, but were soon obliged to take our seats in a rude, farm wagon, or, more properly speaking, a stage wagon, built upon the same plan, but longer in proportion to the width. In our company were fifteen persons, including the driver.

Miss Lisle and myself were snugly disposed of in the middle of the vehicle, Mr. Trall and Mr. Lincoln at our side. I had noticed, as I climbed in, a small, square box, at the driver's feet, with hammer, pincers, and bolts, also a variety of nails in it, and a short chain or two.

"I say, Uncle, please, I'm *dying* to know, as people say when they don't know anything, for what purpose the driver carries along with him that great box of tools, chains, etc., which I tumbled over, to the great risk of breaking my neck, as I landed into this rolling scow?"

"What say you, Mrs. Lincoln: shall we torment her before the time?"

"O, no! If you think we shall meet a regiment of Mormons, or a clan of Ottawa Indians, and if those be the implements of war with which to defend ourselves, pray be silent; let us be happy till the first arrow whizzes along, grazing the bow of my bonnet. Uncle, may I sing? Do you sing, Mrs. Lincoln?"

"No, dear, but would be happy to hear you."

"I will be *very modest*, dear uncle, and the strangers will hardly hear me;" and Jeannie charmed us with a pleasant song. She was the light and life of the company, stealing like a sunbeam into all our hearts, cheating us of the tediousness of the way, and making us laugh, with our eyes yet moistened with the recollection of the friends left behind.

We had some very fine gentlemen in that company, with all of whom we became *intimately* acquainted, in the course of a few hours, as *western travellers do;* and Jeannie Lisle was parted from with deep regret by one and all at the end of the route. Any one of those gentlemen would have given his hopes of fame and fortune for her little, white hand—*I knew it.*

Almost a day had passed away without any remarkable occurrence. Our four strong horses were sometimes submerged in sloughs, and we rather swam than rode. Again we were almost upset by huge logs or stones in the way; and once even Miss Lisle and myself were obliged to get out, and, assisted by our friends, pick our way over a creek upon some stones, while the wagon was taken apart and lifted over.

We felt pretty well bruised and fatigued, and somewhat chilly; for night was approaching, and it had been a squally November day.

"We are over *the best* of the road now," said the driver, very calmly, and glancing mysteriously at *that box* under his feet. "The next twenty miles will be rough, and full of sloughs, and then we come to that quarter-of-a-mile log bridge over Black Creek; and then we have smoother prairie. If it doesn't freeze up to-night, and make an ugly crust, we'll get along better." And still he eyed *that box.*

"Ella, dear, let us wrap you in an extra shawl; and you too, Miss Lisle, will need more protection from the winds." And husband and Mr. Trall began to explore the travelling bags.

"Hold up, Mr. Driver!" said a tall, black-haired New-Englander; "the ladies wish to newly arrange their shawls, and, while they are about it, we may all as well wrap our blankets round us, and be ready for a bad night. We shall not reach the 'Buck-Horn Tavern' probably before ten o'clock, if we have no breakdown; and, from what I learned of this route before we started, it is more probable we may not get there until twelve or two." Then I observed that the gentlemen were almost all of them provided with "Mackinaw blankets."

"There, go ahead! all right!"

We went "ahead" for about fifteen minutes, when down went the four bays, up to their throats in a slough, and we after them, up to the wagon box. The leaders flounced and kicked, and the driver whipped, and hallooed, and cursed, till the prairies rang, all to no purpose. Poor beasts! they were weary, and fast in the mud; what could they do?

"Well, gentlemen, I shall be obliged to ask you to work your passage," said the driver, with a rueful countenance. "One of the leaders has hurt his shoulder; and the other is determined not to stir, if he dies there. You'll all have to get out, and carry *the women* over on your backs; then help me out with the horses and wagon."

"What say you, Mrs. Lincoln (allow me to call you Ella, please, as Mr. L. does) — what say you to being carried over the slough on the backs of a dozen gents? Didn't you notice the driver said, '*You must all carry the women*,' etc.?" whispered Jeannie, with whom I now made a bargain that we should call each other by our Christian names, "for short," as the school-boys say.

"How deep is it, driver?"

"O, I guess it isn't much over the tops of your boots, if they're long ones; and you mind and step on the bogs."

"Allow *me* to carry Miss Lisle?" said the tall gentleman with black hair to Mr. Trall, who was apparently sixty, and in delicate health.

"Thank you, thank you, my young friend; you will do me a favor if you will."

So they threw their blankets across Mr. Trall's shoulders; and the dark-haired gentleman and Mr. Lincoln carried us over on the bogs, without any very unfortunate missteps. Mr. Trall, Jeannie, and myself sat down upon an old stump, and covered ourselves with the blankets, while the young men returned to assist the driver. The ground was covered with dried leaves and partially frozen. The spot was wild, and a deep sense of loneliness stole over my spirit as my thoughts reverted to my absent friends — my pleasant father's house. A tear was rolling down my cheek, and I sighed heavily.

"Give me that cane of yours, please, uncle! I want to fish up a rattlesnake," said Jeannie, with a shy glance at my sorrowful face, yet not seeming to see it, and suiting the action to the words, she took the cane and began to overturn the leaves.

Old Nick is always near when talked about; and presently we heard a low, buzzing sound, like that of a nest of bumble-bees. In another moment up jumped a short, brown-spotted snake. Did n't *we* jump, too, and retreat behind that stump? even Jeannie sobered her countenance. Mr. Trall looked up a stick and despatched the rogue; and we looked sharply about us, lest he might have a mate. We did not sit down again, but stood there until the dew was falling and the darkness gathered round us.

By the aid of ropes and chains the company succeeded in getting out the horses and dragging the wagon over the slough. About an hour longer was consumed in putting that machinery all together, and then we moved forward. The horse that had hurt his shoulder when struggling in the slough was somewhat lame, and we progressed slowly; however, we *progressed*, and so did *our* appetites.

"Ella, dear," said Jeannie, somewhat sobered since

she "fished up" the rattlesnake, "I am growing hungry; are not you? Do n't you think there is any house *nearer* than that log tavern the driver talks about, where we might get a lunch? I think I heard uncle say we should get only pork, and potatoes with their jackets on; I never could bear pork, but now — why *now* — I could eat pork, rind and all — could n't you?"

"So *I could*, Jeannie, or the rind without the pork, if we ride much longer without stopping."

By this time there was a general interest in our conversation, and others began to wish for even *substantials*, delicacies out of the question. When lo! we attracted the attention of the driver.

"Who's hungry?"

"I!" — "I" "— "I" "—" "I—" was vociferated loudly from fourteen pairs of lips. "Why do you ask?"

"Oh, nothing; only I have a tin-pail-full of crackers and gingerbread rolled up in that old blanket under the seat, which I brought along in case we got belated and *all-fired* hungry; I never travel over this prairie without something. A penny a roll for the gingerbread, six crackers for a cent."

"Never mind the price — let us have them."

"Whoa! whoa!" Poor beasts, they did n't need the second word of command.

It was pitchy dark now, and he looked up our lunch by the light of a lantern.

"Hoot away, despair!" We were all as happy as kings and queens, out on that eight mile prairie at 9 P. M., munching crackers and gingerbread.

"I never travel without something," said the driver, as he cried "git ape" again; "and I never have any left when I get through, neither. Git ape!"

Upon the whole, we had a cozy time of it, crowded together into that big wagon, fourteen passengers from all quarters, like affectionate brothers and sisters.

I was so happy after that lunch of gingerbread that I leaned over upon Mr. Lincoln's lap and fell asleep. Jeannie's tongue was yet running when I crossed the threshold between reality and the land of dreams; and the driver was urging on his horses at *their* uttermost speed, which may have been over three feet of prairie to the hour; I cannot recollect, but know they were not *born race-horses.*

"Ella!"

"Sir."

"Wake up, Ella! here is that famous log bridge!"

"Hush, Allen! I'm sleepy. Never mind seeing sights!—What did you say, 'the Blue Ridge?' How can you see mountains this dark night? Please, Allen, be still; don't wake me again."

"But, my dear, you *must* waken! Every man must walk over it."

"Over that mountain?"

"Ella! gracious! What a sleepy child! Hear me! We — are — coming — to — the — quarter—of — a — mile — log — bridge — and — I — must — walk — over! You — must — sit — up!" he almost screamed.

"Yes, sir! I am awake now. Where's Jeannie?"

"Here I am! — have been asleep on uncle's lap. Oh dear, I am as sleepy as an owl at ten in the morning. Is the tavern on the bridge?" and Jeannie fell asleep again.

"I think, sir, *you* may better remain in the wagon," said Allen to Mr. Trall; "they are both so exhausted, and the bridge so rough, that they might be jarred out. We young men will see you three safely over."

"Yes, yes, let the elderly gentleman keep his seat," responded one and all, springing out as we bounced over the first log.

I opine, we waked up then! One — two — three — four — smash goes a ring-bolt; and here we are, delayed again! Now that mysterious box is lifted out, and the twelve men are dodging hither and thither, more in the way than all the good they do, nine-tenths of them! After some hammering and screwing and dodging the lantern under the wagon, the men tramp on; driver cries, "Git ape!" and the horses follow.

One — two — three — four — five — six — and here we are again — second bolt gone. The twelve men stop, and we witness the same manoeuvring, with box, hammer and lantern — and all move on again.

Now there was some hay in the bottom of the wagon, and I slid down from my seat and went to sleep resolutely. I could have ridden over the points of a hundred church steeples without waking.

"Ella, we are at our stopping place," said Allen, carrying me in, and seating me in the corner before a large, pleasant fire. "Here we are, at the tavern."

It was a large room, with a plentiful number of board-bottomed chairs and a pine table, now spread for supper. The floor was brown and bare, but clean; and against the two little four-pane windows hung short, white muslin curtains. In one corner was a smaller pine table, scoured as white as milk, upon which stood a water-pail with a tin-dipper suspended over it. Over that table hung also a mirror, a trifle larger than a sheet of note paper; and along the logs rows of male and female apparel. Upon a high shelf I noticed a gun, a hunter's pouch, and a pair of deer's antlers. Suspended to the beams overhead was a tin oven, a frying-pan, and various bunches of penny-royal and catnip, newly gathered and fragrant. On the hearth, stones supplied the place of andirons, and two large yellow dishes, covered with tin pans, stood between them.

This was "Ella Lincoln's" first opportunity of examining a log cabin; excuse her if she looked around it with more than ordinary interest, and eyes staring like the "man's in the moon."

Behind that room was a little shed where I peeped in and saw two little white-headed "cherubs," with dirty faces, asleep upon a trundle-bed, partly under another, which I supposed belonged to the heads of the family. All the while my eyes were roying about on an exploring expedition. I heard a tramping overhead, and a wonderful "spatting" of bolsters and pillows; and the light of a candle gleamed down through some twenty knot-holes in the rough planks.

"Here we are, Jeannie; did you manage to keep awake till we circumnavigated the remainder of those big logs, yclept the bridge?"

"Alive and running; for after you betook yourself to the hay, I just jumped out into your husband's arms, and thence upon a big log, and walked over with him. But the cracks were tremendous. Once I put my foot quite through one of them, and lo! the consequence!" and she held up one shoeless foot. "I had broken my gaiter-string early in the day, but had no other handy, and said nothing. So down it went into the dead sea below!"

"What *did* you do then?"

"When my foot first slipped, I gave Mr. Lincoln's arm such a jerk — I thought we were going quite through together. 'Why Miss Lisle, are you hurt?' said he, for I walked lame — those logs were terribly rough. 'No, thank you; are we almost there?' 'Within a few rods of the log-house.' And I walked on, for I didn't mean to stop right there and make an oration about *that* shoe, when it was too dark for the audience to see my gestures."

Now the landlady appeared and "steeped the tea," which I will do her the justice to say was pretty good; the gentlemen came in, and we gathered around the table.

It was a good substantial repast, of fried pork, potatoes, stewed crab-apples, and Indian bread. The hostess, a smart, black-eyed Yankee woman, seemed pleased to see us, and chatted like a mag-pie; the host dispensed pork and gravy like a gentleman. He had been a merchant in New York; his wife was educated and refined in her manners.

Here I might insert a paragraph about life's changes

and reverses; but it is half-past two o'clock; we have done eating. "Go to bed, sleepy heads."

The stairs is a ladder with slats, the width of my hand; and up we go — Ella and Jeannie piloted by the landlady.

Beds! beds! beds! seven of them, all in a row, and looking neatly. Away in the corner was one separated from the others by a quilt suspended to the roof.

"You two ladies will take that; the gentlemen who are with you the next." And Jeannie and Ella slept, like two tired children, in the same chamber with all their fellow travellers. Never were laid upon the same pillow two beings more tenderly nurtured, more utterly strangers to care and toil!

At six the next morning, with fresh horses and a fine day before us, we travelled on. In the meantime Mr. Trall and Mr. Lincoln had made themselves acquainted with the names of our fellow passengers, and we were introduced to them separately.

Two miles brought us to a narrow strip of woodland, on the other side of which the road turned, running along the margin, with a low, wet prairie on the right. Here and there a bush or stunted tree grew along the slope, at the bottom of which was a pond. The ground being hard, and our new driver having a "brick in his hat," he thought to improve the time, and struck the horses, reining them a trifle to the left, when snap went the bolt again, and the wagon turned a complete somerset, spilling us out, and rolling a part of us down the hill. I caught in a bush; Jeannie went past me like a flash; some of the gentlemen were buried under the wagon, the others away at the bottom of the slope; while the driver was holding the horses, and charging them — poor beasts! — with the whole catastrophe.

"I say, gentlemen," he remarked, coolly, as the more fortunate came to the rescue of their friends, "if these *ere* colts had a had Tim Moody there to break 'em when they were brought up, it wouldn't a happened. No man could a *driv* 'em better."

"All safe?" shouted Jeannie, from the bottom of the hill.

"All safe!" responded our friends at the wagon; and then Jeannie led the concert — and such a burst of bass and soprano never before rang through the woods of Michigan.

There, I will not trouble the reader with a description of the exact manner in which we gathered ourselves up, and went on again, but only say, that amidst snow-squalls and showers, cold winds and almost innumerable mishaps, we journeyed on, at last riding all night as well as all day; and when we finally hailed the "Garden City," Miss Lisle and myself had not been undressed in fifty hours. There we separated for our different places of destination, shaking hands heartily, and expressing good wishes.

"God bless *you*, my daughter!" said dear, good Mr. Trall, laying his hand affectionately upon my head; "life is all before you, and you seem hardly fitted, by nature or education, for the vicissitudes of Western society. But if sorrow *should* come, *you* will bend before the blast like a reed, and lift up your head when the storm is over; while Jeannie — my own laughing Jeannie — will lie uprooted by the first touch — killed by the first unkindness."

Years proved his word a true prophesy.

CHAPTER VIII.

"No splendid poverty, no smiling care,
No well-bred hate, or servile grandeur there."

MARIETTE, Ill., on the Plano River, was a small village, with two hotels, two churches, a saw, and flouring mill, and eight or ten stores. It was the county capital, with a forlorn court-house, and jail under it. It possessed a vast water-power, and every advantage for becoming finally a place of importance. It was the most available depot for the farmers throughout the county; and every Saturday its merchants heaped up their golden piles, the country women, for what reason I know not, preferring that as a day for the selection of new dresses.

"Allen Lincoln" was inscribed upon the front of the largest store in the village; and he was one of the most successful merchants in all prairie-land. He had also an interest in the mills, and owned a large tract of unimproved land in another county. He had been a resident of Mariette two years. I first met him at a mutual friend's in New York city.

"Ella, dear, this is our boarding-house," he said, as we were set down in front of a moderately large square hotel, quite imbedded in black mud, without fence, tree, or any agreeable object upon which to rest the eye. Inside, however, it was neat and well furnished for the times. We found the family pleasant, and the boarders gentlemanly. The landlady was one of the best of women.

I missed the elegances to which I had been accustomed; but I was not unhappy for the want of them. Allen studied my lightest wishes, and spent every hour at home, he could spare from business. We had brought with us a few books; and I employed much of the leisure during his absence in reading and scribbling rhyme.

I was cordially received by the ladies of Mariette; and invitations to tea came in frequently. I walked, and rode, and went out with the lady of the house, attended the little parties and "cotillon parties," hemmed frills, painted flowers, and *strung rhymes together;* but all in vain. Neither love nor duty, the pen nor pencil, the social party nor ball-room, proved preventives of home-sickness. I cried when Allen went out in the morning, when he came in at noon, at tea-time, *bed*-time, all night, all the week, for two months.

"Allen, let us keep house. I feel the want of occupation; something to make me forget. You are out so much of the time, that I dwell too much upon the past. My own room seems like a little prison; and, when neighbors call, they find me weeping. Even the old washerwoman, when she brought home the clothes to-day—poor, ignorant soul!—asked me very demurely 'if the masther had been afther batin me, shure?' I laughed then, for you are so kind; but, to confess all, I fear *I am getting* somewhat homesick."

"Ella, my poor child! it would be indeed strange if you were not. O, I have been very selfish!" and he blended his own tears with mine. Then, for the first time, I conquered myself.

"Forgive me, Allen! I will weep no more."

But the housekeeping? In just two weeks, we left the hotel, and, with what furniture we could get, commenced housekeeping over the store — I, that hardly knew a ladle from a gridiron, or flour from plaster, with a dumb German girl, who could not raise a loaf of bread, or turn a "flapjack." And a fine time we had of it! "The baker" was not there; there was no restaurant, at which to buy a ready-baked chicken. Betsy stared when I told her what I *would like* for dinner, and bawled out, "Yaw!" then did the thing exactly contrary, or asked *me* to "show" *her*, and I did not know myself.

Sometimes we had breakfast at eight; sometimes at ten; and on one occasion eleven, because we were trying to bake flapjacks, which were made wrong, and "stuck to the griddle." So, when Allen came up, and noticed *our progress*, he took a basket, and went away off, I never knew where, and bought bread. By the time he returned, I was in the middle of a good *cry*.

"Betsy," said I, "if *you* did not know how to cook, why did you come?"

"I came to learn," she replied.

Now, if Allen had even *looked* impatient, then Ella would have never learned; but he smiled, opened his basket, and said, "Poor Ella! I am sorry you are obliged to *fry yourself* over the stove. I will find you a more competent servant." Allen was a gentleman, and I appreciated his kindness. He *remembered* how

"Ella Lee" had been sheltered from the very shadow of care in her father's house, and knew that she was suffering now for *his sake.*

Next day, "Betsy" gave place to "Martha;" the next week, "Martha" to "Sarah;" "Sarah" to "Susan;" and so they came and went, until, at last, we succeeded in getting an excellent cook — an Irish woman, aged forty. She remained four days, and we liked her; but lo! when Sunday came, she went to "church," and returned as drunk as a loafer The next day I dismissed *her*

"Ella, shall we board again?"

"No, sir; I shall learn to cook. I will have a little girl to wash dishes, etc.; hire a woman to wash the clothes and clean, weekly; and I will never have another full-grown woman to annoy me, until capable of giving her orders."

"Well done, Ella! at least, well *said!* But remember, I am your servant whenever you shall desire to have a woman."

Six months from that date, I would not have "turned upon my heel" to give place to the head cook of Queen Victoria. But I had learned through much tribulation, experiments, and questioning my neighbors.

Allen Lincoln moved into a large, convenient house, with two servants; and *I* told them how to make puddings and pie-crust. *He* liked to invite friends to dinner; and *I* knew how to prepare the roast, and season the sauces. We both liked evening parties; and *I* was proud of my skill in the cakes and jellies.

Mariette improved rapidly, and so did the fortunes of Allen Lincoln. He builded a new and elegant store, improved the ground around his dwelling by trees and shrubbery, and seemed on the high road to independence. Population rolled in like a flood, bearing on its heterogeneous waves some jewels of intelligence and refinement. There was room for all; and the good and pure were like a band of brothers and sisters. We were very happy, freed from those cold forms which make eastern society a chain to the buoyant, trustful heart. Our only "aristocracy" was that of intellect.

Allen Lincoln was a kind, indulgent husband, a successful merchant and speculator, a highly respected citizen.

Allen Lincoln speculated in the town-lots of a mushroom western city. One of those "great cities" chalked out on the map by some lazy fellow, who means to reap what the honest and industrious are sowing.

Allen's step became less buoyant, his voice less cheerful; and friends looked at me and sighed: "So tenderly reared, nursed in affluence — God help her!"

CHAPTER IX.

"Whoe'er has travelled life's dull round,
Where'er his stages may have been,
Many sigh to think he still has found
The warmest welcome at an Inn."

We had thus far enjoyed a reasonable share of Dame Fortune's plum pudding; but at last she had seen fit to turn her back upon us, and we sat down, not like two babies to cry over her fickleness, but to consider our condition and decide upon a plan for the future.

My husband, whose education was mercantile, and who wielded an arm like a broomstick, could not think of wood-sawing or ditching, and my own pale face would hardly have recommended me to a lady who wanted a hard job of work done. But I was strong in resolution, and seeking an opportunity to turn my poor abilities to advantage in the way of house-wifery, I proposed and insisted upon "tavern keeping."

A single tear fell upon the hand he held in his, as he thought of the daughter of luxury, his own pet wife, foregoing tastes, and immuring herself within the walls of a country tavern; then he replied like a man:—

"What you are willing to endure, I should be ashamed to shrink from."

The winter set in in October. Snow fell, the frost

incrusted the windows, and such a winter commenced its rigorous reign as was never before witnessed in that section of country.

My husband had contracted for a tavern north of Chicago; and on the first of January we left our warm, comfortable home, and with our two babes, a young friend, and a little girl to assist in taking care of the children, we set out for the new residence. The children were delicate, and neither they nor their mother had been out since the first snow; hence a keen realization of the frosty air; but fie! were not we going to "keep tavern?" Why mind a trifling hardship!

At four o'clock on the second day we arrived at that log tenement, the largest I ever saw. An old sign, whose face had been washed so often by the rain that it reminded us of an over-neat little girl's wooden doll, whose face grows darker daily by frequent immersion, was swinging and creaking between two unseemly hickory posts. Although the first flush of its glory had passed away, it still bore the wretched picture of a farmer and his boy, binding each a sheaf of wheat — the wheat taller than the man — and "Traveller's Rest" was inscribed upon its forehead in letters of grayish black.

"Dear Ella, here is our home," said my husband, with a sigh, as one by one we stepped from the sleigh out into the shovelled path.

"Aha! I am satisfied," I replied for his sake, yet only half sincerely, for my heart beat like a frightened rabbit's as I contrasted the new home and new duties with the pleasant tenement I had left behind, and the cares which seemed light in comparison with those about to be assumed.

The landlord and landlady were elderly. They had built that house, and there remained until the hoary frosts of age hung heavily upon their temples. He welcomed us on the outside; and entering, we were introduced to all the married sons and daughters and their children, who had come to bid them and the good old home farewell!

One after another they left the paternal roof, and settled a few miles away—yet none of them so far distant that they could not visit their aged parents sometimes, and come to them in times of sickness or difficulty.

With tearful reverence, from the fathers and mothers of many children, to the "wee bit, toddling" babies, they kissed those wrinkled faces, and spoke a low "God bless you," and then the sleigh-bells jingled at the door, the buffalo robes were drawn up to their very noses, and away they went, the horses leaping like reindeer over the prairie.

Doubtless many a tear fell upon the wide stone hearths of their humble homes that night, and, "well the dear old home is gone out of the family," was uttered by many a sobbing voice—those voices which first lisped the name of "mother," while the wolves howled within the shadows of those tall, rude chimneys, and the traveller ventured not out after nightfall upon these pathless prairies. Oh, the changes of earth!

The ex-landlord and lady remained with us, as boarders, for a few months. They were quiet and good people, social and refined, in *their way*, and no doubt understood the philosophy of getting along smoothly in a country log tavern better than their unsophisticated successors.

When the old lady saw a fire kindled on every one of the six rude stone hearths, she said to me, with an equivocal smile, "Wood is cheap, but flesh and blood isn't; and, at the rate you are burning wood, it will take one hired man to haul it from the woods, another to cut it at the door." And, when she noticed the abundance with which we welcomed our travellers, she very kindly whispered in my ear a word about "economy."

We had yet the little girl we had brought with us from town, and we hired the *young lady* who had assisted our predecessors, to do the same for us. But her *ladyship* saw fit to be displeased with me, because, as she expressed it, I "was a town lady, had big notions, *stuck up* my nose at the old log house, held my baby more than there was any need of, and wasn't fit to keep tavern at all." The first morning that I came in from dream-land to congratulate myself that I was mistress of the "Traveller's Rest," my eyes opened upon a large hickory fire, which Mr. Lincoln had kindled in the room. There he stood, with carnation cheeks and a forehead wet with perspiration; for he had had "a time of it," setting that pyramid of wood and chips "agoing," with one pair of unaided lungs.

"Lie right there, Ella, for the babe is not well, and you yourself have a cold. I will see to the breakfast."

I looked my gratitude for his kindness, and then turned my face to the wall, to think how very strange it was that Ella Lincoln, whose first loaf of bread was made after marriage, should be really *there*, with great barrels, boxes, and sacks all around her, filled with flour, pork, lard, and molasses; and I could hardly realize that I was to convert them into other forms, and render them meet for the acceptance of our hungry customers, — when lo! I was startled in the midst of my morning's reverie about changes in general, and mine in particular, by a harsh voice in my room, saying, —

"Get up, *Miss* Lincoln; it's seven o'clock."

"That's my own business," I replied, somewhat sharply for me, the newly installed landlady of the "Traveller's Rest;" and out went madam, slamming the door, and saying she "never saw a landlady before too lazy to get up and help about the breakfast."

There were *two* babies in that bed then for about five minutes, till the *big* baby grew ashamed of herself.

The atmosphere of the room had yielded to the influence of the fire; and I stole softly away from the baby's side, dressed, and went to the dining-room. There I found some respectable travellers at breakfast; and husband was doing the honors of hot griddle-cakes, steak, and coffee, all gotten up under his superintendence; for he was the prince of landlords the very first day of his initiation. Of course, seeing all things as they should be, conciliated my temper; and, not knowing how to spare the sweet damsel just then, I leaned to the side of utility, and concluded not to send her away.

This resolution was not lasting. One of the neighbors, who lived a mile away, had a chance conversation with her about "hired girls being as good as anybody;" and her insolence increased until I could endure it no longer, and dismissed her

Then came the tug of war. I cooked, made beds, swept, and performed all manner of household work, washing excepted, with the aid of the little girl only, and the occasional kind offices of my husband.

Pies, puddings, and Johnny-cakes! how I rolled, stirred, kneaded and baked ye! It was a great school for pastry-making, that tavern kitchen — an excellent school for a young lady who had made her first batch of biscuit after marriage. I improved in my management, soon arriving at such perfection that I could persevere in getting up a dinner for *ten*, with Master Baby upon one arm, protesting against it loudly. At last, we procured a good-tempered, excellent woman, quick as a flash, and a host of herself.

In the mean time, our family had increased by the addition of two respectable bachelor farmers, two wood-choppers, and Jimmy, an Irishman, whose business was to haul and cut our wood, build the fires, and attend to all out-door work. He was tall and good-looking, with sandy hair, blue eyes, a smooth chin, and lips I cannot describe, because they were never still long enough to decide upon their exact expression.

Jimmy was skilled in roots and herbs, was a professed "cattle and horse doctor," and familiar with "charms," which were all-potent to cure the toothache, and expel "witches."

"Charley, the best horse, is dying!" said my husband one morning, with tears swimming in his eyes, and the sweat standing in drops upon his forehead.

"Charley? then are we ruined. He is worth more than anything we possess, outside our indomitable perseverance. Can nothing be done? What *shall* we do? Die! he *must* not die. O dear! have you a horse doctor?"

"Yes, and forty men or more. Every traveller has stopped to look at him for the last two hours. There he lies, stretched out and stiff, breathing only."

"Please, ma'am, have you a ball of twine?" said Jimmy, rushing into the house, and puffing like a high-pressure steamer. "You see, ma'am, it's an errand I've been doing about three miles over the prairie *afoot*, for I never take a horse when the distance is but a step or two; and little did I think to get back again, and find Charley in such a poor way. But it's only the worms that's a eaten up the insides of him intirely; and I know a spell — a charm like — that I learned in ould Ireland, that will cure him." And, taking the ball, he commenced unwinding it, and tying here and there a knot along the cord; as he did so, re-winding it upon a cob which he had brought in. Then he commenced repeating some gibberish, and started for the barn, tying knots and winding all the way.

Well, "truth *is* stranger than fiction." Jimmy was hailed with shouts of laughter, as he sat down against

Charley's head, and commenced unwinding that cord, and untying those knots, at the same time putting his mouth close to his ear, and whispering unintelligible words therein.

The laughter had subsided into respectful soberness, and the forty looked on in silence.

Death inspires solemnity and dread, even when we witness his relentless dealing with a poor, dumb creature; and, as the spasmodic breath upheaved the sleek sides of poor "Charley," and his wide nostrils seemed to gasp for air, other eyes than the afflicted owner's gazed upon him through the mists of sympathy.

But see! he starts! Those long limbs are gathered up in an effort to regain his feet; the glazed eyes light up with intelligence; he gives one loud, cheerful snort; and — "get out of his way, gentlemen!" — he is eating oats again. There is heard a loud, wild shout of "Long live Jimmy!" the clapping of fourscore hands; and the witnesses of that wonderful transformation from the image of death to life disperse, and go home to tell their families "how strange it was that the horse revived only under the treatment of Jimmy — strange that it *happened* so." So thought Ella Lincoln, taking first lessons in farriery; and I was as proud of Jimmy as Jimmy was of his success.

Reader, can you realize how happiness may nestle her bright head in the bosom of one who gazes from day to day upon the beams and plank floors of a prairie hotel, — with old-fashioned chimneys, and fireplaces so large that a little army might ensconce itself in the corners; with tiny seven-by-nine window-panes, and whitewashed doors with wooden latches? Can you imagine that such a dwelling is invulnerable to wind and storm; and, if the heart be in tune, the dweller therein may rise and rest, and sing, "Away, dull care!" as she performs life's varied duties, with as little *real* trouble as if those doors were made of ivory, beautifully wrought, and swung on golden hinges?

With poverty, give me a secluded home, where few know, none question me, with a reasonable amount of life's comforts, not luxuries, a good hickory fire, and health, not forgetting a few choice books, a bundle of quills, and an ink-bottle.

Our house, situated upon a bluff, fronted a wide, beautiful stream, bordered on the opposite side by a strip of woodland. I sat with my babe upon my knee, gazing away over that belt of prairie-land which skirted the river, and watching the travellers, in sleighs and on horseback, who moved along like floating specks upon a foamy sea. The little ones clapped their hands and shouted as they passed, hearing the sounds of the distant bells ringing melodiously upon the clear, keen atmosphere.

Yes, then I was comparatively happy. Poverty had come, but not in her harshest form. I had still *a home*, though a humble one; and the loved ones were there — all there!

William Miller had prophesied the speedy termination of all things; and, although not a "Millerite," I confess to having felt *shivery* at times; for the "signs" in the earth, air, and sky *were* portentous that winter.

We had "signs" in the house, too, which were somewhat alarming — some half a dozen *long faces*, and lips that preached "Millerism" from sunrise till midnight. The old lady-boarder, the ex-landlady, was very eloquent upon the subject, and made many proselytes in the neighborhood, if it may be called a neighborhood where the nearest neighbor is a mile away. That William Miller was a true philanthropist. Under the genial influence of his doctrine, *honesty* took root, and shot up, and "spread like a green bay tree," until that *fatal day* melted quietly away into the regions beyond sundown, when, alas! it withered in a night, like a crushed mushroom.

Wind, rain, hail, and snow! What a winter was that! In point of tediousness, was it ever equalled? No wonder we had "an unusual display of" — *long faces*.

An important comet was visible at that time; the aurora borealis was peculiarly changeful and brilliant; and the more observing saw "signs and wonders" above and below. But my own dull soul did not awake to any sights or sounds far beyond the andirons; and, being overwhelmed with the newness and variety of my duties, I left the "final consummation" to people of leisure. Nevertheless, she who holds this pen "owns up" to a medium-sized "bump of marvellousness," and a measure of superstition.

You smile; *you* are above being superstitious. Can you listen to a well told "ghost" story without feeling the slightest shiver run through your nerves? If you should be out in the night, and a tall, white figure should cross the darkness between yourself and some old ruin, famous for apparitions, would not a little moisture gather on *your* forehead, and *your* pulse beat faster? and if that "white thing" should turn and beckon, and come after you, would not you "cut stick," and around the corner like a love message by lightning? *Wouldn't you?* Then, since you *are* superstitious, *the very least bit* if you please, sit down patiently, and hear the story about our Jimmy, who was somewhat given to belief in the supernatural, as he was to the occasional taste of the contents of the bottle.

Our residence was eight miles from the city; and sometimes, when Jimmy returned from his errands there, he was intoxicated. He was always penitent next day, however; and being so useful, faithful to our interests, and quite harmless, even when in that unfortunate state, we had not the self-denial to bid him leave us.

"I've stopped drinkin', ma'am," said Jimmy, one day, as he threw a large armful of wood into the capacious fire-place.

"Well, Jimmy, I'm glad you *have* decided to reform. It is so dreadful for a young man to go down to a drunkard's grave! O, think of it, and never wet your lips with that poison again, and you may become one of the first citizens of the state. You may soon earn enough to buy a farm, fence and stock it, and then you may marry a good wife, and live happily all your days. It is so wicked, too, to get drunk!"

"Faith, and that isn't the thing at all, ma'am," said

he, turning square round, and presenting such a rueful countenance that I felt the muscles of my mouth giving way, and drew my hand over it as a screen.

"Well, Jimmy, what is it?"

"To speak the truth, ma'am, I'm neither a Catholic nor a Protestant; for my father was one, and my mother the other, and to have believed either one of them would have made the other a liar; so I thought, to treat them equally well, I'd just believe nothing at all.

"But the *end of the world* has begun already; and there's great signs in the clouds, and the sky, and the earth; and I have seen 'em. There's that great long-tailed comet, that comes out in the sky every night, and blazes and burns, and scares all the priests and *gastronemers*, and the common people — that's in the west.

"And away in the north is that *roarin'* borealis, that flashes and flares like a tallow candle; and then it turns into rollin' logs like, as if these hickory sticks was all up in the sky yonder, all of a coal; and the divil himself (savin' your presence) was there with his cloven foot, keeping 'em all agoing.

"And there's been a great earthquake, and swallowed up '*Divers Place*' (where that is I don't know, as I never studied geography); and the very divil's to pay all over the world, with shipwracks and *humors* of war (excepting ould Ireland, that hasn't been heard from); and a hin has laid an egg in one of them big barn-yards in the city of New York, and right on the shell of it is printed, in ligible writing, 'The world's to end."

"And there is one Mr. Miller, a reverend gentleman, a Protestant priest, who is learned in the Scriptures, and all sorts of *logics* and .rithmetics — he is preaching in tents and houses about the end of the world; and so, ma'am, I wouldn't like to be caught in a spree on the day of the *conflageration.* I will reform intirely, or it might be the worse for me."

Two months had fled. Seldom during all that time had we been able to see out without first scratching a hole in the frost on the pane. Men had frozen to death on the prairie; cattle died of starvation; and the new settlers had with difficulty obtained necessary provisions from the towns. Even those who were well supplied had sighed for spring, weary of solitude, storms, and snow-banks.

That comet had gone off demurely, without dropping a single spark from its fiery skirts; and the northern lights had kindled, rolled, and changed into all manner of shapes, without damage to the poor earth-worms below. That almost unremitted hurricane of wind, which had swept through the giant oaks around our dwelling, lifting miniature avalanches from our bluff, and scattering them over the prairie below, had subsided into more genial breezes; whilst those great, tall snow-banks yielded slowly to a more kindly atmosphere.

He who rules over the elements never forgets his children; and, though March was but a fourth edition of December, April came smiling in, with soft south winds and an unclouded sun. The green grass sprang up in patches, while the snow yet lingered in less protected spots. The little blue and yellow flowers peeped slyly up; the birds came with cheerful songs; and the brooks, released from long imprisonment, murmured low, pleasant music.

But where was ever a light without a shadow? Our Jimmy got drunk again.

"Why, Jimmy! have you forgotten your promise?"

"Faith, ma'am, I haven't, but I've broken it; and a fool I was when I made it.

"You see, ma'am, that star with a tail to it, that roarin' borealis, and the shipwracks and earthquakes, the egg with the printin' on it, and all the scare-crows, was just a trick of that are Protestant priest and the divil (savin' your presence); and, after all, the earth hasn't stirred a peg for 'em. The green grass is agrowin' again.

"And the cravin' afther the liquor has come on again, and it's eatin' me up intirely; and it's the son of my father I am, and the love of the liquor was bred in every bone of my body.

"But I've come in to bid you good bye, ma'am; for the masther is afther bein' out of patience with me for takin' up this 'vile habit' again, as he is pleased to call it, and says, if I *will drink*, I must find another place. So I must be going. God bless you! May you be young and handsome all your lifetime, and a hundred years afther! Good bye, ma'am!"

Poor Jimmy! with his honest heart, herculean frame, and every advantage for earning money and gaining respectability as a tiller of western soil, he may have already gone down to a drunkard's grave. O Rum! thou art as relentless as death — as unpitying as the grave!

Many amusing and some provoking incidents occurred during our experience in tavern-keeping. Sometimes the house was full to overflowing of natives of the "Emerald Isle," on their way to and from the city; and they would entertain us with merry songs by the wholesale, making the very logs of the house keep time to their music. Sleep before midnight was an absurdity. Sometimes families of beggars would turn in at nightfall, whom we could not refuse to shelter, although we pitied the sheets. Once, a family of *two* persons "put up" which became *three* before morning; and they all staid a fortnight — one of them a little fellow, who sometimes made "night hideous" with his eloquence; and the almost incessant call for "gruel" and "toast" was extremely troublesome to the "landlady," with but two "helps."

Once we were taken by storm by a family of "cooking movers." ("Cooking movers" are travellers who carry along with them raw meats and crude potatoes, and their own beds and bedding. At night, they pay for the use of a fire, and floors to spread their beds upon.) We were so crowded and mingled together that no one knew, hardly, which pair of feet was his own, for they counted fifteen children, besides scores of adults; and, when the hurry and din of their getting their suppers and washing their dishes had subsided, they stretched themselves over at least two thirds of the floor in the house. Then we said, in our hearts, "Peace be unto you! pleasant dreams, and an early exit in the morning!"

So they *did go* early; but, when we of the family got up, not a pound of tea, coffee, or loaf-sugar could be found in the house, some of those worthies having slept in the storeroom.

We held a family council about the utility of pursuing them, but concluded that, there being eight strong men among them, nothing short of a regiment could take them, and soldiers did not parade on that prairie; so we let the rascals go.

CHAPTER X.

"Go till the ground" — said God to man—
"Subdue the earth; it shall he thine;"
How grand, how glorious was the plan,
How wise the Law divine.

"ELLA, now that you have sufficiently proved your talents for playing 'the landlady,' how would it suit you now to be a farmer's wife? A gentleman at Hollyville, who is consumptive, is about to let his farm and go East, hoping thereby to prolong his life. It is one of the finest farms in Cook county, containing several hundred acres of land under cultivation; the rest is beautiful meadow. The house is large and convenient; and he will let it partly furnished. It is painted white, has green blinds, and a pretty yard in front. The garden is extra; there is a fine well at the door; and with the place he lets ten fine cows."

"I am content as I am; but if you can do as well farming, the frame house and all the other comforts will be just the thing. What of the neighborhood?"

"Oh, that will suit *you* — all Germans; not a word of English spoken there. You will have no disagreeable old women to watch over your housekeeping, no fears lest the rattlesnakes may creep in through the joints of the logs. What say you?"

"As you please; I long to be so situated that I can take time to read and write once more."

"But, my dear, that farm is also a hotel. However, your cares would not be increased, but diminished; for the establishment is so large that you cannot *begin* to be the housekeeper. I will keep as boarders yourself and the little ones."

"My other self, my counsel's consistory,
My oracle, my prophet! my dear cousin!
I, as a child, will go by thy direction

to Hollyville, Mexico, or Mecca." "How soon?"

"Next week."

I was pleased with the new place. We were fortunate in securing good servants; and, although the acknowledged mistress of the establishment, as Mr. Lincoln had promised, I had but little to attend to, except the care of the children. I found much time to cultivate my intellect, and indulged a natural propensity to write.

Such cream and butter, fresh eggs and poultry, vegetables of our own raising, and berries from our own garden as we had then, you never saw, city readers! We had also all fruits of the quicker growth, peaches, plums, and cherries. Apple and pear trees were there, but yet small, it being but a few years since the settlement of that prairie. The fine large flock of poultry had been left as an extra inducement for us to take good care of the property.

One of the German women was an excellent cook; the other managed the dairy very skilfully. We had also a German and his wife, who both worked in the field, neither of whom could speak a word of English. The little girl who accompanied us from town to the log house still remained, and a young man attended to gentlemen that called. Our company was respectable; profits satisfactory. I sometimes glanced at the table before the bell rang, to see that everything was in its proper place, and then I hid myself again in my room. Sometimes "the landlady" was inquired for by the social wives of farmers who had stopped for the night; but *she* never appeared, unless some sick person needed her especial care.

Ella Lincoln wished for no other society than that of her own family. She knew that her pale, thoughtful countenance and reserved air were not in keeping with her surroundings; and she dreaded lynx-eyed curiosity and the impertinent questions of unsympathizing coarseness.

So long as an absolute necessity for her being continually before the crowd remained, she shrank not from the post of duty; when that necessity was removed, she preferred to be unseen. The prejudices of her childhood clung to her in misfortune; she had not quite succeeded in conquering herself.

We had taken possession of "Hollyville House" on the first of April. The spring had been cold and backward, with copious showers of rain. But June came blushing in with mild breezes and warm sunshine, scattering her rich purple and golden blossoms over the prairie, and quickening vegetation in the fields and gardens. We had promise of an abundant harvest, and my husband toiled for it with unremitted energy. He arose early and retired late, attending to his varied duties like a man determined to conquer the difficulties which beset his onward march.

But what avails industry and carefulness when He in whose hands we are says, "No farther?"

On a warmer day than usual he came into my room, looking pale, and sank into a chair.

"Ella, I am sick. I was out in the field, and felt a strange dizziness coming over me, and so I lay down on the ground. When my consciousness returned, the men were carrying me home. They say that I was sun-struck. *I* do not think so. I have not been well for a fortnight, but did not wish to disturb you; hoped to be better soon, and said nothing. I think I am coming down of fever. My throat is dry and sore; my head aches, and my knees tremble as I walk. Ella, what will you do if I am sick long? What *can you* do if I should never get well?"

"Borrow no trouble about me, dear Allen. I have had a long rest since I have been 'boarding' with you at your farm hotel; it is time that I should work again. I can take your plac in the management of the house, and nurse you till you get well. So go to bed directly. The little girl must stop assisting the cook, and give her undivided time to the children. The farm must be entrusted to the Dutchman and his wife. There, all is right; go, try to sleep an hour, and perhaps you may feel better."

I knew that he would not be better in an hour, but that he was attacked with bilious fever in its worst form, and might need a good nurse and skilful physician for many weeks. The *nurse* was there, but where was the physician?

In the German village, half a mile from the house,

resided a German who was considered successful as a "Root Doctor," but there was not an educated physician within twenty miles.

After leaving him in a darkened room an hour, I found he had not slept, and was in a burning fever.

"Will you have a physician called, Allen?"

"A physician? Why, there's old Doctor Von Schneeder, of the settlement, would steam me into nonentity in half a day; and those city M. D's., with their calomel and mysticism, would charge without mercy — a dollar a minute for their time — and we cannot pay *them.* Well, if you say so, Ella, we will have the Dutchman *begin;* and if he does n't succeed, there will be time enough for the 'regulars' to come over and *see me off respectably.*"

"Oh, Allen, how can you trifle, when you are so very sick?"

Doctor Von Schneeder was no novice in the healing art. In three weeks the patient sat up in his room; the fourth, he was walking slowly about the grounds. The fact is, *the nurse* was as instrumental in his recovery as the doctor, and taking into consideration the duties she assumed in the landlord's stead, I claim for *her* two-thirds of the applause.

The healthsome glow had not yet returned to the cheek of the father, when little Harry, the older of the children, was seized with the same malady.

"I am sick, mamma; so sick," he said, pitifully, laying his little head in my lap; "please to put the baby down and hold *me,* just a little while."

I took the sweet sufferer in my arms, and laid his

velvet cheek against my own; it was hot with fever. I put my hand over his little heart — it beat like a frightened bird's. While I yet pressed his dear form to my bosom, thinking what to do, he started, almost springing out of my arms; his eyelids rose and fell spasmodically, his teeth closed like a vice, and I screamed for help. It was ten, A. M.

At twelve o'clock, P. M., he lay before us exhausted, and white as the pillow which supported his head. Until that hour he had incessant convulsions.

With tender nursing, and the attentions of good Doctor Von Schneeder, he too was soon upon his feet again.

Mr. Lincoln was now able to take charge of his own duties in the house, and Ella *took time to cry.* I was weary and worn, and somewhat discouraged about the unhealthfulness of the place; and all of life's sweet poetry seemed merging into a long dull chapter of unwritten prose.

My turn came also; and then the cook and chambermaid's, and the laborers in the fields — and before October, every *living soul* whose home was at Hollyville House, "baby" excepted, had become experimentally convinced of the skill of Doctor Von Schneeder.

But, "long wet, long dry;" and so of troubles in Western fevers. In the vicinities of marshes, or as they are called there "sloughs," they come and go yearly, leaving behind them sallow faces and obstructed livers.

The Western towns which are located upon dry

prairies are healthsome and pleasant, and *vice versa.* Let the traveller in search of a home select high, clean prairie land; then plant out a grove of trees to shelter his house, dig a well at the door, and lay out a beautiful garden, and he has a little "Eden" of his own, barring the *rattlesnakes*, which are truly pestiferous upon all fenced lands.

Outside the farms, thousands of them fall victims to the hogs, that shovel them up with their long under-jaws, like so many precious morsels. Think of this, O ye pork eaters! What a delightful association of ideas —*pork and snakes!*

I never learned whether or not their pigships devour snakes of lower castes — striped or green, for instance, but presume they do.

Snakes, although they never injured me, have always been to me objects of disgust and dread. I never could look upon the very smallest of the loathsome creatures without a thrill of horror running through my veins. What then was my utter consternation when, looking out of my chamber window, I saw my own blessed "baby" playing with "pussy" and a moderately large striped snake. Pussey had caught it, and while she yet held it in her mouth, "Baby" had lifted both together, and put them into a chip-basket — so I inferred when I saw him tipping the basket this way and that, and shouting as pussy played with her prize. I did not wait for pussy to decapitate that crawling imp; I did not speak to her civilly again in a fortnight, and I have never *kissed a cat* since.

"Indeed, Mrs. Lincoln, I'm very sorry! I only left

him there, playing with the basket, while I went to see the new calf," said the little repentant nurse, wiping her eyes with her apron.

On another occasion I was returning from the garden, and lo! there lay a large black snake upon the door-sill. It was twilight, and I could not see exactly whether he was spotted; so I did not wait for him to introduce himself, and tell to what family he belonged, but made all haste for the front door; and I passed through to the kitchen, telling the cook, who stole a march upon him with a tea-kettle full of hot water, and, *I opine*, if he had been asked the next day to what particular family of snakes he belonged, he would have been puzzled to frame a reply.

I might tell you many snake stories, friends, but I fear you would think them all "fish stories." Were I sure you would believe me, I should state that early one Sabbath morning we found one in the dining-room under the table, the same week another in the parlor, both harmless, however, and they seemed to have a subterranean city near the barn.

The time of wild beasts had nearly passed by before it was our lot to reside upon the prairies. We sometimes heard of panthers, never of bears; we saw a few wolves. Some unfeeling boys captured a wolf in our cornfield, and, after wounding it, muzzled its nose, then dragged it into the road, and spent several hours in tormenting it. Its piteous cries disturbed us all, and frightened the little ones. They were German boys, who did not understand our language, hence I could not expostulate with them upon their unfeeling conduct, but sent one of the German girls with a handful of cakes to tell them they might have them if they would take the poor wolf away out of sight and kill it immediately; and we heard no more of them.

During the twenty-six months that we spent upon that prairie we heard but one sermon. At Hollyville there was a German Lutheran Church, where the preaching was in that language. We had become somewhat acquainted with the minister, and requested him to preach once in English. He did so, and that sermon would have graced any pulpit in the commonwealth. The congregation smiled, as he played so harmoniously with those syllables which to them conveyed no meaning; and we felt conscience striken in thus monopolizing all of that eloquent discourse. That such a man should be the pastor of a people illiterate, even in their own language, was a mystery.

The profits of the farm were satisfactory. Hans and his wife Margaret had been faithful, and indeed all persons employed upon the place merited our warmest gratitude for their industry and fidelity to our interests. We had not a stereotyped "harvest home," as our German neighbors, but gathered in all the rich gifts of our Heavenly Father in quiet thankfulness, sufficiently strong-handed of ourselves. Any unusual commotion in the family would have injured the interests of the "hotel."

By the way, I will stop a moment to say, that after *I* was called to "face the music" in my husband's stead in welcoming men women and children to the hospitalities of "Hollyville House," it never again seemed exactly convenient for me to decline a certain portion of the responsibilities I had assumed. As soon as harvest was over, the Dutchman and his wife were dismissed, leaving more out-door employment for "John," the man-of-all-work; and "Mr. Lincoln" being sometimes obliged to do the lighter parts of John's work, "Mrs. Lincoln" in turn assumed the lighter duties of her "liege lord."

Then there was a call for an industrious hand at the needle, as the autumn approached, and the little ones were in need of warm flannels and hose. Shirts were needed, too, in place of those now waxing thin; and when the fall sewing was really at an end, winter was far advanced. At the "log house" I had assisted so much in the pastry, etc., that I had not felt it my duty to offer my services as seamstress generally, but now I had leisure, for economy's sake I felt it right that it should be turned to a good account.

I was not a genius in the way of cutting, snaping, and putting seams together, but I had in all other departments found that "where there was the will, there was a way," and I meant in this to find the "way."

Such a "way!" One day Mr. Lincoln returned from the city with a pair of heavy cassimeres, cut by a fashionable tailor, and said to the little girl: "Annie, will you run over to the settlement with this bundle, and ask Mrs. Ross, the tailoress, to do the work as soon as she can?"

"What is it, Allen?"

"A pair of pantaloons."

"Let *me* make them — please do!"

"You, Ella!" And you should have heard him laugh.

"Yes, me, Ella; I insist upon it. Why not *I?* I've seen others sew upon cloth, and *I* know *I can.*"

"Well, take your own way. You wont spoil them, will you?"

Better might I have undertaken to build a ship or reduce a fortress. Wherever there was a notch, there was no corresponding corner; and the corners came opposite strait edges, and they were *twistified* and mystified, and wrong side up and rear side foremost; and the more I tried, the worse they grew.

At last, coming to the pockets, the most difficult of all, and finding them extremely obstinate about "going in," I took the liberty to trim them off, to fit them to the "pigeon hole" I had left for them, stitching them resolutely in. To be sure they would scarce admit my own little fist; they must be right — did n't a fashionable tailor cut them? And the seams gathered here and there; but that was the tailor's fault; *he* cut them too long on one side. At any rate they were *strong* — no *rip* to those seams!

"Well, Allen, they are done; not quite so handsomely finished as if Mrs. Ross had made them, but you know *I've saved the money.*"

"Thank you, Ella, I am pleased with your work."

And he *was* "pleased;" so well "pleased" that *he* laughed till *I cried*, and ended his uncivil behavior by saying, he "wished it had happened before he had the fever, there would have been less need of Doctor Von Schneeder."

I never saw those cassimeres afterwards. "Our paths were thenceforth separate."

CHAPTER XI.

"Not in vain the distance beckons;
Forward, forward, let us range."

THE second year at Hollyville was in all respects more fortunate than the first, the crops being heavier, the summer less sickly, and the travelling custom much increased.

Allen was inclined to return to Mariette; and I was glad to hear him say, "We will go home. There I will have a small store, do a cash business, and we can live comfortably, though not extravagantly. Friends will rally around me for the sake of 'auld lang syne;' and you, Ella, will be restored to congenial society."

Mariette had grown astonishingly during our absence. A new sign, with an unknown name, in gilt letters, had taken the place of "Allen Lincoln's;" and new faces looked out of the windows as I passed our once pleasant home. The trees that Allen had planted had grown taller, and the vines that I had trained were still there, heavy with foliage. But I dashed away the intruding tear, for friends were calling my name from the windows, all along the street, and coming to meet me, and give me such a welcome as only true-hearted western women know how to give. We took possession of a small, neat cottage; and life seemed fair again. Not a friend had deserted us, and Allen's old customers came flocking to the smaller store.

A year rolled on, and a competence rolled in.

A church had been erected during our absence — My mother's church! and again I remembered old Peggy's 'Saturday' warning — "Well, Miss Ella, to-morrow'll be Sunday, *if you and I lives to see it*" — and her concluding words — "forever and forever."

My sainted mother's church! Not the old stone church, with the small square windows, the old-fashioned sounding-board over the pulpit, but a place where I heard the same teachings which fell from her lips in the long ago.

> "How often has the thought
> Of my mourned mother brought
> Peace to my troubled spirit, and new power
> The tempter to repel."

However, from conviction, our religious views may change as years roll on, the true-hearted child still holds in solemn reverence his mother's faith.

"How do you like my partner, Ella?" asked Allen, with flushed cheek and brow, the same morning he drew up an article of copartnership with Ralph Burt, late of Boston, Mass.

"He looks well, is gentlemanly and intelligent; of course, I cannot judge of his business capacities."

"I'll tell you, Ella; I have been doing well, but wish to do better. Mr. Burt is rich, and seems honest. His property consists principally of land, of which he holds a vast amount; and he wishes to dispose of it all, and go into the mercantile business. He promises to put a thousand into the concern immediately, the rest after the land-sales. I shall go on *swimmingly* with him."

"There is an old saying, Allen, 'Let well enough alone.'"

"And another, Ella, 'Nothing venture, nothing have.'"

A fortnight later, he said, "My dear, Mr. Burt goes to New York for goods in my stead."

"Has he put his share into the firm?"

"No, but he will, soon. I have thought it better for him to take what I have on hand, and purchase a pretty variety of goods now; and one of us will go on again in midsummer. He is acquainted with some of the best houses in the city, and can purchase at as good advantage as myself."

Ralph Burt *went — to Texas.* Allen *went*, after him, to New York, and, not finding him, compromised with his creditors, returned, gave up the store, and hired as clerk to the gentleman that became its master. He had no one to whom to look for help, having received and used my patrimony before his first failure. I leave comments to those who love his memory less.

Poor Allen! The villanies of that man unnerved him. He went about his duties with a heavy heart, discouraged.

I too was heart-weary, but did not utterly despond. There were the little ones, and for their sakes we *must* still struggle on. My first thought was, how I should curtail expenses. We were living comfortably, not extravagantly. I was willing to suffer inconvenience, and proposed that we should take a cheaper house, for rents had risen at Mariette.

"A cheaper house? This is small, Ella."

"Never mind that; it is neat and pretty, hence commands a high rent. We will take an old one, in a less pleasant situation — any kind of tenement that will shelter us from the storm. I wish to save a portion of your salary. There I will in a measure withdraw myself from society, and do my own work with the aid of a little girl. We must learn *to tack* amidst these flaws of fortune. Never while we have heads to plan, or hearts to work, let us drift helplessly into the gulf of despair."

"God bless you, Ella! I will try to be *a man*, let what may come, for your sake. But, when I think of the luxuries which surrounded you in the home of your childhood, that there you had no wish not gratified, and again of what you have suffered for my sake, I am almost mad. Worse than all, I have wasted your property with mine! O, why did your father 'answer a fool according to his folly'?"

"Hush, Allen! you do not know all!"

It was a small, red house, with a single door and two windows in front, which had been slightly built at first, and greatly abused by its successive tenants. Below was one room and kitchen; the roof over the kitchen leaked sadly. Up stairs was a small, walled chamber in one corner; the rest, a garret. There was a yard and vegetable garden. An old oak shaded the house in front, and a wild hop-vine hung luxuriantly over the kitchen window. Along the garden fence grew sunflowers, catnip, and thistles. It was a cool, pleasant home while the summer lasted. The little ones were as happy as before; even happier, for no one cautioned them now "not to crush *the flowers*."

Winter had come. The bleak winds stole in through the shrunken doors, shaking the quilts which hung over them as a protection from the cold; and rags were stuffed into many a yawning crack.

The kitchen was not tenantable; hence the cooking-stove was removed into the *one* room which was carpeted and comfortably furnished. The fumes of the cooking, the steam of boiling water, almost suffocated a pale sufferer on the bed — that sufferer Ella Lincoln, the daughter of luxury. Neither sin nor idleness of her own or others had placed her there, but the common miscalculations of youth, the mischances of business, and the villany of one whose outward seeming was that of honesty and truth.

No one was to blame. The house I had selected against my husband's wishes, because the rent was cheap, thinking only of our pecuniary circumstances, not liability to sickness there.

Allen Lincoln, yet young, had become a weary, careworn man. He bent over the pillow of his beloved wife with an agony like unto death's. The wondering little ones looked at him, at the grave physician, at their pale, pale mother, whose quick, short breathings were interrupted with prayers for "life," mingled with the continual cry of "That stove — it suffocates me!"

"I was wild, calling upon my distant "father!" my buried "mother!" — crying, "Life! life! O God! not for its own sake, but the sake of these dear babes!"

It was a long agony, a lingering fever. Another burden was laid upon the shoulders of the poor; another soul was given to our earthly keeping.

Sweet babe! he has long since gone home to heaven; and, though his birthplace was lowly, it far exceeded that in which the blessed Saviour lay. We were enabled to shelter *him* through his brief life from earth's ruder storms — two winters, two summers, and his days were all counted.

With strict economy, we were enabled to save a third of Mr. Lincoln's salary; and I did not regret in the end that I had submitted to the inconveniences of the old red house. The next fall we hired a better, and the ensuing spring purchased a little *bird-cage* of a tenement in a pleasant location.

Property advancing rapidly in value, that little homestead soon became an anchor, to which we might cling in times of sickness and adversity; for so long as there is land, there is credit. I began to look forward once more to better days, such as we had formerly seen, when "Allen Lincoln" would be "himself again," wearing the olden smile.

CHAPTER XII.

"Delusive gold, a smiling fiend thou art,
Severing the hands that death alone should part."

Compared with the mass of emigrants to California, few die there. He "without whose notice not a sparrow falls to the ground," watches over the poor wanderers by land and sea, removing the obstacles in their overland path, or levelling the waves that foam and dash before them, threatening to ingulf their ships.

As the heart of the earthly parent yearns over the wayward and undutiful child, still mindful of his future happiness, so the heavenly Father commissions his angels to watch over his erring children, wandering in forbidden paths, worshipping Mammon, the forbidden god.

True, some leave their pleasant homes and the dust of their kindred for rude graves and unlettered stones in the far-off pathway of the stranger. Some reach the goal of their dearest hopes to gaze upon the glittering dust with fading eyes; and some return to cast the fruit of their toil into the laps of their families, and then lie down to rest forever.

But these are the exceptions. The mass return, with improved health and amended fortunes.

Persons who have never earned their bread by the sweat of their brow are generally poor economists, when they first find themselves in the sober-hued path of poverty. The first year of comparative destitution is spent in useless complaining or childish indecision. Then comes reaction, the will to do and dare even to desperation. Such are the men who go to California, return, and induce their neighbors to risk the same stake for wealth.

"Ella, Ernest Wood has returned from California with fifty thousand dollars."

"Very well; I am pleased to hear it."

"But he advises *me* to go, Ella."

"You, Allen? Impossible!"

A strange expression of sadness, almost sternness, was upon his countenance; and I noticed for the first time that premature wrinkles had intruded upon the rounded lineaments of thirty-three.

Ella Lincoln, is thy strength sufficient for this hour?

Yes, more than equal! Long hast thou met the exigencies of a checkered destiny with unflinching fortitude; and the deep under-current coursing on beneath the surface-waves has been seen by only One.

"Ella, are you willing I shall ge? Will you go with me?"

"I will consent to your going, Allen, if you wish it earnestly. I will not consent to go with you. The babe is but a few months old; the others, scarcely more than babes. The journey would kill our children, perhaps me; for you know my health has long been delicate. But I have watched with solicitude your broken spirits; and, if you can leave *us* comfortably situated for the present, and if *you* are equal to the separation, go! and God protect you and us!"

Often, and thoughtlessly, it is said of him who goes to California, and her who remains at home, "if the attachment were strong they would not separate." Little knows the careless observer how year after year of reiterated disappointments at last engenders the one strong desire of change, which urges us forward to the attainment of some imagined good over bleeding affections, even though death may be within the range of easy probabilities before us.

More solicitous about leaving a support for his family than his own personal comfort, my husband concluded to make the journey overland, with a party of friends, who were to set out on the first of April.

There was a running to and fro, "striped shirts" were being made here and there, and wood being hauled for those families which were to continue housekeeping.

"Ella, I am having sufficient wood sawed and stacked in the barn for your use one year. My cousin, Mr. Banks, owes me two hundred dollars. He will pay over that sum to you in the course of a fortnight, or in smaller sums, as may suit your convenience. Mr. Banks, you owe me this sum, and will pay it to Mrs. Lincoln after I am gone!" And Mr. Banks, whom he had brought in for that purpose, said:—

"I most certainly will."

"Ella, you have confidence in him; if you have not, I will yet make another arrangement."

Mr. Banks made a speech about the propriety of his

taking care of his "cousin's" family during his absence, etc., and said, looking me in the face, "You will trust to my honesty and kindness, Mrs. Lincoln?"

Now I *had* never questioned the honesty or goodness of Jabez Banks till that moment, for his reputation was fair, his piety undoubted. But that set speech, his smile, every motion of his hand and wink of his eye I noted with a new feeling of distrust, and from that hour I disliked him.

But the company designed starting next day; to express a doubt of his friend would both wound and inconvenience my husband. And why yield to what might prove an ungenerous suspicion. I replied: "I will trust you, sir." And so I *did, and am "trusting" him yet.* Others trust him too; and his word and his check is respected in more than one city; but *there is a bank away up yonder* where *his* note will be "protested and dishonored," for, with all his long-faced hypocrisy, he has no treasure there.

The arrangements were completed. Every one of those adventurers had left a *small* amount of money and a *large* promise of an early remittance. The "striped shirts" were stowed away, the "parched corn" put into sacks, as the last remedy in case of starvation, and the long row of wagons, with white tops, mules, and tar buckets, stood there, surrounded by the friends of the gold seekers.

I wrestled mightily with myself, but the torrent came; one wild, gushing tide of unmitigated agony — then I conquered. The two little boys looked on with tearful eyes, sympathizing in the sorrow they could not fully understand; the sweet babe smiled through tears; even he in a measure comprehending that all was not well.

Shaking like an aspen leaf, *he* clasped us one after another in a passionate embrace, then broke resolutely away, and was gone.

I watched him from the window, as he passed through the gate, then turned to my little family with a strange calmness of spirit, silently commending him to His care, who only could protect him.

I heard from my husband by the way, occasionally receiving a hastily penned letter; sometimes through communications of others. Often strange rumors reached me of "murder," "starvation," and "cholera," — the possibility of their truth driving me for a moment almost to madness — then I resolutely resolved to believe no stories not well authenticated.

Unwilling to add to my solicitude through all those long months of weariness, facing death in a thousand forms, he never wrote the worst, but intimated that he was progressing on his journey as pleasantly as he ought to expect, hoped soon to be there, and spoke of the happiness in store for us after he should return with the golden pile. Willing to suffer, for the future good of the loved ones at home, he forded rivers, crossed morasses, climbed perpendicular heights, scorched by a burning sun, thirsty when no spring was near, hungry when but a crust remained, weary when came his turn to watch.

Worn out at last, so utterly exhausted that it seemed as if outraged nature could not have endured another day, he set his feet upon the golden sands of California.

He was there! Cares seemed but feathers now. Gay visions of luxury and leisure, such as I had enjoyed in early youth, floated upon the surface of a buoyant imagination. There were a few, a dastardly few, who had "passed by on the other side" since the shadows lay heavily upon our fortunes, and, forgetting the Divine injunction, I said in my heart, "the time is coming when I will make them *feel* that I am their superior."

We are all human! Mis-name it as we may, the principle of retaliation exists in a greater or less degree in the breast of every living soul. It is a part of the life of every creature. There is no beast so dumb, no worm so senseless, that it will not turn to strike the hand which is raised to do it harm. God help us! We may "clothe and feed" our enemy, *trying* to "love him as ourselves," but death only wipes out the recollection of our wrongs.

Remember, ye who wound a human heart, that reverses come suddenly, and to-morrow *you may feel* the neglect you are "putting out at interest" to-day. God only fully renders "good for evil."

CHAPTER XIII.

He was a man
Who stole the livery of the court of heaven
To serve the devil in."

When my husband left home for California, he left in my purse five dollars. To even that I objected, "for," said I, "your cousin, Mr. Banks, will bring the 'two hundred' in a few days, and we have provisions sufficient for the present." Mr. Banks did not come; and weeks rolled on. I had practised economy to the utmost extent of my ability; and, after I had spent the contents of my purse, I had traded with friendly merchants upon credit.

Autumn was advancing, and the little ones and myself needed warmer clothing. Friends were kind, and offered me "credit,"—still "credit;" but unwilling to be in debt, I hesitated, and hoped on. A strange presentiment of evil swept over my heart-strings—the olden suspicion of Allen's cousin deepened into almost certainty. I had sent him messages through friends, had written note after note, stating my need of *that money*, but there came no reply, I heard of him here and there, but he did not call at our house, hence I knew that he avoided me.

"*This* will not do!" I said, a long, hysterical sigh closing a fit of weeping; "*this* will not do; tears will not turn into bread. To-morrow I will sell the parlor carpet to Mrs. Riggs, who is about purchasing, and the large mirror to Mrs. Stanley, who has broken hers. I will sell all the furniture, and then *let* the parlor and the rooms up stairs. May I perish if ever I stoop so low as to ask aid of others while I can raise a dollar." And the next day I put those determinations into execution.

I was annoyed by the noise up stairs, and the coarse familiarity of the family in the room below, and those six dirty children playing in the yard, sometimes using profane language, and words not to be named, mortified and grieved me. There they were, from morn till night, tramping over the grass, crushing the flowers, and initiating my little ones into their disgusting vocabulary. But there was no remedy; I needed the rent for those rooms — beggars must not mind trifles.

"Five months, since I have heard from Allen. Can he be dead? Is he pining upon a bed of sickness, unattended, uncared for? Has misfortune followed him to that distant land? Oh! Allen, my husband, what *have we done* that the chastisement of our Father still rests so heavily upon us?"

"Good evening, Mrs. Lincoln!"

"Good evening, Mrs. Curdy."

"I stepped in to ask you if you would like to take in sewing? Mrs. Hatch has more than she can do, cleverly; and she says she guesses *you* might suit her, as she sees Harry and Tommy's clothes are made pretty well."

Ella Lincoln's CRY was over. The indignant blood

rushed to her temples as she replied: "Thank you; when I want sewing to do, I will ask for it."

Now, Ella *had learned* to make shirts for Allen, and was somewhat skilful in *stitching pantaloons* — did n't she prove this at Hollyville? She had learned, also, to fit loose sacks and trousers to Harry and Tommy; she had been the mistress of two prairie hotels, and since she returned to the village, had met all her "ups and downs" unflinchingly.

But now, when a *coarse* woman, in a *coarse* manner, offered her the privilege of fitting *coarse* garments to *coarse* boyhood, her heart rebelled: proud Ella Lincoln!

I should not have felt thus, I thought upon reflection; for many in better circumstances had done the same, and probably no insult was intended by either Mrs. Curdy or Mrs. Hatch — their abruptness was the result of ignorance, my suffering of extreme sensitiveness and imperfect early training. They had seen the articles of furniture which I had sold removed, and concluded that I must be very destitute. *So I was;* but I preferred to suggest my own remedies. I was willing to say to the whole world, "*I am poor*," but not to be reminded of my poverty by those who had not the will or power to assist me. There is a great deal of sham sympathy in this money-loving world.

Some are "sorry" — *a few words*, some *crocodile tears;* others insult the unfortunate. A few — a blessed few — see, without seeming to see, the festering wound, and apply the only balm in secresy and silence.

"Poor and proud," has grown into an "old saying."

Where there is poverty without pride, God help *the worm!* — the poor grovelling worm!

I had commenced dealing with myself severely, for answering Mrs. Curdy as summarily as I did, only to *add* to the misdemeanor by flinging missiles at poor humanity in general, as I rattled the dishes preparing the table for our evening meal.

"Mrs. Lincoln?"

"Yes, sir."

"Mr. Sutphen, of Ten Mile Prairie."

"Mr. Sutphen, I am pleased to see you; I think Mr. Lincoln sometimes mentioned your name. Has the fever subsided on your prairie, sir?"

"Well, yes, we're all tolerably now, thank you; cold weather is coming on fast, and scares up the ager."

"But it sometimes continues through the winter, I think."

"Yes, hangs on sometimes like a starved blood-sucker, and breaks a fellow right down into liver complaint, *rheumatiz*, or quick consumption. But my plan is to dose it with quinine and whiskey — ten grains in a gill of whiskey, four times a day, will rout the worst *ager* that ever snapped. Why don't you come over some time? Mrs. Sutphen would like right well to have you — and fetch the children; plenty of *fodder* for man and beast out there. I don't like your little, nasty, stuck-up towns, not bigger than my farm, that pattern after city fashions, with their dancing and playing cards, and carousing nights. I tell you there's no good in 'em.

There's Hiram Steele, the lawyer, that come out here along o' me six years ago; he's fallen into the snares of them are blacklegs, and got to drinkin', and he isn't worth the dirt it 'll take to cover him *bim-by.* And there's Sam Carr; well, Sam was a good fellow, and owned a good farm down East. He tried to court my wife; but she wasn't the lark to be ketched by an owl! The fact is, *he* is a good fellow, or *was*, but lacking in the upper story. He drinks like a fish, now, and sets up till three o'clock many a night, fooling over them infernal cards.

"I could call the roll from this till dooms-day of men that have been tee-totally ruined by gambling and drinkin'. There's something else not to be mentioned "to ears polite" — that's your poetry stuff, you know more 'n I do about *that* — that's the shame and disgrace of Mariette, and every other Western settlement. *You* know it; so do I! I don't pretend to any sort of learning — my mother had thirteen of us, and it was all my father could do to scratch round and get our bread and butter. But I know right from wrong, and a good, honest man from a scoundrel. When did you hear from your man?"

"It is many months since."

"He's gone up into the mountains, likely. They say there's the best gold pickin' up there; but there's no mail away up there, and I 'spose that's the reason you don't hear. That puts me in mind of my errand. Do you know Tim Schenk, that lives out at Seven Mile Grove?"

"I have seen him."

"Well—I hate to tell you most *allfi'adly;* but that's what I come for, and I might as well out with it. Tim holds a note against your man and that cousin of his, Jabez Banks—a good-for-nothing stick up, and rascal to boot!—and 'Allen Lincoln's' name is first on that note, and you'll have to pay it. Banks will slick himself of it somehow—the little, slippery, pettifogger of a lawyer. Well, there's no use a contending with a lawyer—they're the devil's own. I don't say this to hurt your feelings, but to put you on your guard."

"What *shall* I do?" Please, sir, what was the note given for, and when, and what is the amount?"

"Three hundred dollars is the amount. It was given four weeks before your husband started, for value rec'd' in mules for the journey."

"This overwhelms me! Why *did* Allen deceive me thus? Why leave me so completely in the power of others. It was cruel—Oh, *how cruel!*"

"Hush! a word once gone out of your mouth never comes back. It goes floating about all over the world, and gets into one mouth and another, and gathers some dirt in every one of them as it goes along, and at last it is so altered that *you* don't know it yourself, and the very folks that helped it at the start are ashamed of it. It's a ticklish thing for a woman to be left alone in this great, foul-mouthed world, without any natural protector, more especially if she's good-looking and smart; and the very folks that fight like cats and dogs at home are the ones to make trouble betwixt man and wife.

"*I say* 'Allen Lincoln' was a fool and a madman to leave you in this fix; but *you* mus'nt say it, no how."

"Excuse me, Mr. Sutphen; but I have had so many trials and vexations before, this new trouble unnerves me."

"I'm sorry for you, poor thing; I don't believe in saying *sorry* ten times over — for words don't cost anything — but this I *will say*, if you get into any tight place that you can't get out of, just come to my house and stay till the worst of the muss is over. I know Mrs. Sutphen will be glad to see you, for she is terribly pleased with them poetry pieces you put in the paper, and always looks 'em up first thing. Her learning is better than mine. But I must be going. The fact is, I heard Jabez Banks and Tim Schenk talking about that note, and saying it must be got out of the house, somehow; and I was bent on giving you a friendly warning."

And Farmer Sutphen passed out of the house, not even listening to my reiterated thanks. He left his honest countenance and russet coat daguerreotyped indellibly upon the tablet of my heart, until death shall wipe out the impression.

"Ella Lincoln" had new strength vouchsafed her, even for this hour. She proceeded to give the little ones their suppers, undressed and put them to bed, and then she sat down and thus communed with herself: —

"Almost a year has expired since that note was given, and soon it *must*-be paid. I have borrowed of my friend, Mr. Templeton, fifty dollars; I owe for store goods, etc., fifty more. My winter's expenses *will* amount to one-fifty or two hundred—for I cannot economize as I have done; my health being not so good, I must hire a servant. I will sell the house. True, it is rising in value, and would sell at a hundred per cent. more another year; but such an imperative *now*, pressing upon me, I must sell it at once.

"Oh, Allen, if *you knew* all this, you would fly to the rescue! No doubt you were deluded into the idea that Jabez Banks would meet that note. Yes, there has been a private understanding between you to that effect. *I* was left in blessed ignorance, lest I might be uneasy. It is well I have a 'power of attorney;' to-morrow I will look for a purchaser."

"I think, Mr. Kenedy, the house *is worth* a thousand dollars, and will be worth twelve hundred in the spring."

"That's nothing to do with it. 'Tis a bad time o' year selling out. I'll buy it to *obleege* you, and give eight hundred, cash down, one half; a note, payable in nine months, for the rest. You see, we business men don't buy things according to what they *may be* worth another year, but for the least we can get them at now—that's the way! You women are smart enough in *your way;* but, when it comes to making bargains, we have the start of you."

"It is true. You may have the house upon your own terms."

The tide of fall emigration had poured into Mariette

until there was a pressing demand for rooms — I cannot say "houses," for but few of all those adventurers felt able or willing to occupy a whole house. Some had but sufficient to "buy farms with" in the spring; some but a limited sum to invest in business; and some who came with pockets full of cash had the wisdom to practise self-denial and forego "appearances," knowing that, while they had that *yellow dust* in their pockets, they could *buy* a "position" in society when it suited their convenience.

After walking many hours, I found a room in an old yellow tenement, half a mile from the village, already occupied by two families. My entrance was in the rear, through a crazy old gate, between two wood-piles; through a shed, filled with cut wood, wash-tubs, soap-casks, pork and molasses barrels; then up a flight of stairs, so narrow and rough that I sometimes "got hung" to the splinters projecting therefrom; then I turned to the right, passing through a narrow passage between two dilapidated rooms; then through a low, whitewashed door, that would have decapitated a six-footer; and then — *I was there.*

There I found two small windows, a wall patched until it was *more patch* than foundation, sloping from the centre to the eaves, the floor warped and cracks in it full half an inch wide; but it was a *room*, and a *roomy* room.

After pasting strips of cloth over the cracks, and covering the floor with a layer of straw, then a carpet, we moved in.

Six chairs, two beds, two tables, a bureau, stand, clock, mirror, cupboard, kettles, pails, pans, dishes, tubs, wardrobes for three, and still plenty of "sea-room."

Here we are — Harry, and Tommy, and I! Not a shadow of doubt concerning our welcome, and a positive certainty that any one who takes the trouble to find us there, climbs up to our domicile for affection's (or curiosity's) sake. Put on the tea-kettle!

The boys are as happy as two kittens — blessed children! Smile on, Ella!

Let not the shadow of *thy* darkened lot
Cross their young life-paths: 'twere a selfish thought.

CHAPTER XIV.

How can I give thee up? — my own,
My pure and undefiled,
Thou whitest lamb of all my flock —
My youngest, darling child!

"Restore him to us, O Father! let not the time be distant when his arms will again encircle us, when we shall *all* be happy," I repeated, placing the last of my three rose-buds upon the pillow, and seated myself by the bed-side to watch their gentle breathing, in memory retreading the paths of my own childhood, watched over by my own gentle mother, protected and fed by a kind father. I thought of my own little sisters and brothers, of the playmates of my youth who met me on the hill-side.

The beautiful picture of the past glowed and danced before me. There was the old family wreath unbroken, not a flower plucked away by death. And then a change came over it; the full-blown rose was gone, and the dew of sorrow lay heavily upon the buds, and weighed down the foliage of the tree that overshadowed them. And again time brought the light of happiness, whose golden beams stole in among the shadows, and with their genial warmth exhaled the dew of sorrow.

Then thought reverted home again to the rose and the buds from which the tree-shadow had been removed, that I might see more clearly the hand of the Infinite Protector.

"Mamma! drink! drink!"

"Jesse, darling, what ails my baby?"

"Sick! O, sick!"

He clenched the cup, emptied it, and asked for "more! more!"

I lifted him up; he was very hot with fever. I placed a pillow under his head upon my lap, and there I sat, all night, *alone.* What else *could I do?* The physician was half a mile away; the servant had been dismissed a week; it was dark outside! O, how bitterly I felt now my worse than widowhood!

"Drink! drink!" All night he tossed his little arms and moaned in his sleep, or, waking, asked for "drink!"

All night — that night, O God! how long it seemed, with those little flushed cheeks and parched lips before me — none there to whom I could say, "How sick he is!" and receive in return a few blessed words of sympathy! But morning broke at last; and then I dressed little Harry, and sent him with a message to a friend.

Day and night I hung over that little prostrate form, soothing him to patience and rest, and attending to the prescription of the physician; and still I asked the question, "Is he better?" to be answered, "Not yet."

Slowly my heart admitted the possibility of his death, and nerved itself for the worst. We are slow to believe what we are not willing should occur; and when, at last, that announcement. "No hope," comes reluctantly from the lips of the medical adviser, it falls on startled ears.

My own sweet Jesse, the babe of two summers, with the pure white brow, the sweet blue eyes, and tresses as soft and beautiful as ever swept the temples of a seraph, went up to heaven. I bent over his cradle to feel his last dear breath upon my cheek; a ray of intelligence lit up his fading eyes; he strove to return my kiss; and, as if noting the tears that fell upon his face, said, as he had been wont to do in health, "Poor, poor mamma!" and all was over. But the smile of the angel that sealed his lips was still reflected there; and when friends repeated, in the low undertone of sympathy, "Be comforted, it is well with the child," his own glad spirit answered from the realms of glory, "It is well."

"*Alone* in my misery!"

"No, not alone yet," responded the minister of God; "you have two living children. Provoke not Him who has chastised you, by a rebellious heart. You will live to realize that behind this cloud there is great mercy."

In many an after-hour, *alone*, destitute, with broken health, and two helpless children looking *to me* for care and happiness, I have said, "It is well that the babe was taken home to heaven. He at least has escaped the unkindly dealings of a cold, cold world."

Not *quite all* "*cold*." There is a sunny, as well as shady side to human character. He who denies this, underrates the image of his Maker, and is himself the least of all His creatures.

Not all "cold." They have buried my dead; they have wept for the sorrows they could not mitigate; they have saved me from starvation and despair. All are imperfect; but MAN has left in him yet something good.

CHAPTER XV.

> One has a soul,
> Shrunken, and narrow as a needle's point;
> The other, wide as the world.

LIFE is the sum of many trifles. Benevolence is not always a mighty river, rushing, roaring, sweeping on. It is the morning exhalations of the dew of kindness; here a drop and there a drop; a *trifle* to the giver, precious to the receiver.

The presentation of a flower, or a single word of sympathy, awakens gladness and gratitude in the bosom of the sick man. Brush back the damp locks from his forehead, adjust the pillow more comfortably, bathe his aching limbs, and he suddenly discovers that he is "better." What drug is so life-giving as earnest sympathy?

Cast a red apple from your window to that little child, and see how gleefully he bounds away under his burden of rags and dirt, poverty and grief alike forgotten.

Present some trifle to the lone widow, just as the tears are gathering, when memory is busy with the past, — and she smiles again like April through the raindrops; again she sings cheerfully over her stitching.

Praise the poor student, wearing out flesh and brain in the thorny path of literature; he wipes away the perspiration of debility, thinks better of this cold world, and struggles on.

Lay your hand softly upon the head of the poor Christian, commending him to the Father of all, blending your tears with his; he forgets for a season the buffetings of the unrighteous, and lifts up his head again, setting his face more firmly Zionward.

A few kind words, "a cup of cold water" in God's name, are registered in the archives of heaven.

On the contrary, the churl, who never speaks a kindly word but to secure a customer, the mouth of whose purse never opens but to swallow, is guilty of a twofold sin, withholding words and deeds.

In every community of noble-hearted men, we find some dwarfish souls, wrapped in their own selfishness, deaf to the calls of helplessness and virtue — men who would not risk a dollar to save a fellow-creature from want or degradation; who would stand bantering for the last half-cent if the trumpet of the archangel were already sounding, and reply to the imperative call to judgment, "*Wait till I get my change!*" Such a man is Ebin Fip.

Every ill treated woman becomes *a pet*, finally, if there are "gentlemen about;" and Ella Lincoln, away up in the garret, over wood-piles, pork-barrels, etc., had *friends — available friends.* Lawyers advised her gratuitously; farmers filled her corner of the cellar with potatoes; merchants told her to come and get all she needed, upon credit; ladies, the loveliest, best, most talented, clung to her resolutely as she breasted the adverse tide. Ella Lincoln, amid all her trials, was yet hopeful, happy, and proud.

The little people were looking straight into the fire with more of thoughtfulness on their smooth brows than was wont to rest there so soon after a repast of honey and hot biscuit.

"Well, my little philosophers!" I said, laying a hand on each tiny head, and bending over my treasures. "Master Harry, what are you thinking about? Tommy, what new mischief may your restless brain be contriving?"

"I was thinking about our butter. It was so *puckerish* and *salty*, it made me almost cry. I couldn't taste the biscuit through it. Did you like it, Tommy?"

"O, no; I *thinked* of codfish, onions, and hoarhound candy, without any candy in it. What did you think, mamma?"

"I thought butter was scarce, and it was difficult to get that which is very good; yet we should be thankful for what we have. But, Harry, dear, come hither. Here is your cap; now your mittens and tippet; and here is the little tin pail. Run down to Mr. Fip's grocery, and ask him if he has good, sweet butter; and, if he has, get two pounds, and say I will settle for it soon." And away he went to the nearest grocery.

"Have you any fresh butter?"

"Yes, very good. How much do you want?

"I want two pounds. Mamma says I can't carry any more."

"Don't talk! I don't like children."

"Why, you ain't bad. are you. Mamma says good people love children."

"Stop your noise! John, weigh out two pounds, and put it into that pail. Quick! he'll talk me to death, the saucebox."

Harry waited until the butter was deposited in the little pail; then said, as he had been instructed

"Mamma will settle for it soon."

"What! didn't you bring the money? John, empty that pail again; and you, boy, tell your mother we don't trust here."

"I'll tell mamma that you're as cross as can be — I will!" answered Harry, indignantly, and beginning to sing a tune familiar to the ears of all mothers.

"What *is* the matter? what *is* the matter?" I almost screamed, running to meet the little darling, who came rattling the empty pail, and crying with all his might.

"O mamma! mamma! there *was* butter there, but he — he — he — he wouldn't let *me* have — have it — mamma — he said — said — "

"Never mind what he said. Cheer up, little man; we'll try again. I have thought of another place.—We will leave Tommy with Mrs. Coe down stairs, and go to the village. Mr. Baxter has butter, generally."

"Any butter, Mr. Baxter?" I said, half afraid of another rebuff.

"Butter? yes, ma'am, a fresh supply of nice, fresh butter, from the hands of one of the best butter-makers in the county. Please look at it, Mrs. Lincoln. Isn't it beautiful? Won't you take it *all?* Allow me to send it over.

"It is long since I have had the pleasure of seeing you, Mrs. Lincoln. When have you heard from your husband? What else can we sell you?"

"But, my dear sir, I came empty-handed; cannot pay to-night —"

"Not a word! Let us open an account with you. We have sweet potatoes, winter squashes, an assortment of fowls, honey, and dried fruit. What else shall we put up?"

I *did* venture to run in debt for a few nice things, and went home — *to cry;* not because Mr. Fip had been so niggardly, but Mr. Baxter had been so kind. Kindness melts, rudeness hardens, the heart.

"Ebin Fip, Grocer," may yet be seen in front of a low building in the suburbs of Mariette; but the proprietor has not grown rich, and Ella Lincoln is not very sorry. No woman has been silly enough to marry him, probably from the dread of starvation, or seeing her children murdered. There he lives, fat, sour, and unhonored; while Mr. Baxter has become an extensive capitalist, has a sweet wife, lovely children, and the lifelong gratitude and good wishes, not only of Ella Lincoln and her boys, but of all his townsmen and the surrounding villagers.

CHAPTER XVI.

Hope, smiling cheat, still lures us on,
And ever whispers — TRY.

"He comes! dread Brama shakes the sunless sky."

"*His* daily prayer, far better understood
In acts than words, was simply DOING GOOD."

I HAD always, since the absence of my husband, corresponded with different Journals and received compensation. I had written for the great "New York Jupiter," under the nom-de-plume of "Prairie Bird;" for the "Philadelphia Balloon," under that of "Aunt Esther;" for the Cincinnati "Western Light," under that of "Blue Bell;" for the Mariette Journals, under "E. L." But meagre indeed was the remuneration. The city editors had "such a press of matter — so many *under pay* who had been contributors for a number of years, and so many gratuitous contributors, that, really, although they were pleased with my articles, and were willing to give a trifling remuneration for them, — it was out of their power to do as much for 'me,' as their deep sympathy for one so peculiarly situated would lead them to do under any other circumstances."

Ahem! *May be* Ella Lincoln did not know that "The New York Jupiter" patronized "Mrs. Bumblebee," the author of a book, so dull that Ella *herself* could have written it with her eyes shut; that her newspaper articles were all moonshine, their most attractive feature the "sign" at the head — "By Mrs. Matilda Atherton Bumblebee, author of the 'Delights of Imagination,'" — and *perhaps* Ella *did n't* know that *she* was hired at ten dollars a column, the same week that "Prairie Bird" was offered "two."

Perhaps Ella did not know that the Cincinnati "Western Light" reduced her salary from two, to one and a half, the same week they hired "Miss Ethelwena McPherson," author of "Fragments of Song," — in the proportion of two songs to one idea throughout, — and gave *her seven* dollars per column. *Perhaps* "Blue Bell" believed, that "The Western Light" had "one regular rate of remuneration." *Perhaps* Ella knew that "Aunt Esther" did n't wield as ready a pen as "Aunt Tabitha;" that that *was* the reason why Tabitha received more "puffs" and more pay. Of course "Aunt Tabitha," *being a rich broker's wife, needed money.*

Ella knew two country editors who were very kind, — country editors have souls — almost all of them They are like "Prairie Birds," not *known* all over the commonwealth. Ella owes *one* of them something more than thanks — and there is some danger that she *always will.* She likes editors as a class — of this, more anon.

One day I took up "The Mariette Times," and my eye fell upon a flashy announcement, running thus: —

"John Ralph, daguerrean artist, who has been a resident of Mariette for two years, being about to remove to the *far west*, offers, for a small compensation, to thoroughly instruct any person in this elegant art who will obligate himself to buy *his* apparatus and take his room immediately."

Now, said I, in my heart, "writing is unprofitable. Editors care less *how* a person writes, than *who she is.* Presumptious mediocrity, with a few thousands, drives talent to starvation, — *I flatter myself I am talented, because I live in a garret.* Away with the pen! here I go to John Ralph's daguerrean rooms to learn the art, buy the apparatus, and supersede 'John' in '*taking faces.*'"

In just ten minutes I had concluded a bargain with Mrs. Fox, in one of the rooms below, to keep the children a certain part of every day, while their "mamma" learned the way to make a fortune.

"John Ralph, daguerrean artist, up stairs," was on the street door.

> Before you leave your earthly places,
> Come and let me take your faces,

on the inside of door "No. 3," up stairs. No one could have doubted that all those "faces" scattered about the table and hanging against the wall, had been taken by the same genius that manufactured the *poetry.*

"Seventy-five dollars for the camera obscura, and sixty per year for the rent of the room," — and Ella sighed.

"I would like to learn, sir, if the business be as profitable as you have led me to imagine by your remarks."

"You can see for yourself. I came here a poor boy,

two years ago, and now, if I live to get to 'Buffalo Prairie,' I shall buy a farm there," and John looked as innocent of deception as a rag baby.

I felt extremely anxious to buy him out, and whilst I pondered the matter, a friend entered.

"Good morning, Mrs. Lincoln. Out so early? Sitting for your picture?"

"Good morning, Captain George. I am not here for that purpose. I came" — and the Captain being an old friend, I told him the whole truth.

"I'll see what I can do for you," he said.

"John! John Ralph! you don't want seventy-five dollars for that old rattle-trap you 'take faces' with; it was *old* when you bought it. Say sixty, and I'll talk with you about buying it for my friend Mrs. Lincoln."

"I might *a-most* as well *give* it away."

"Look here, John; I know more about *you*, probably, than you do yourself. It is not worth *sixty*, but I'll give that, to oblige *her*, — not a cent over."

"It's a bargain."

"And you engage to make her mistress of the art in three weeks?"

"Yes, sir."

"Very well. Mrs. Lincoln, if before that time expires you should have other views, I will settle with him for his trouble; if you conclude to take the room, I will loan you what money you need. Good morning."

My residence was three fourths of a mile from the artist's room. I arose every morning at six prepared breakfast for the family, finished the necessary work, and at eight went to my lessons. I returned to get dinner, and went back in the afternoon. The ground was frozen in the morning, muddy in the afternoon; the wind blew fresh and cold from the lake. I contracted a cold, from which I have never ceased to suffer, at times. The tenth day I was so hoarse I could not speak aloud; and my throat and lungs were exceedingly sore. I was attacked with lung fever, which left me with a cough, and at the end of two months, instead of daguerreotyping other people's "faces," I was startled at the picture of my own. Since then, my strength has ever been as a spider's web — I have been slowly, slowly dying.

That long illness increased my expenses, and saddened my spirits. I feared that I should not prove equal to the struggle with such complicated difficulties, and sink into the grave.

Young as they were, my children in a measure realized the danger of separation, and clung to me from early morn till late in the evening, with the shadow of a great sorrow resting upon their unwritten foreheads, performing every little act of kindness with their own tiny hands, which they thought might soothe or comfort me.

Mothers of little children, living in palatial homes, were you ever sick, almost unto death? Your children would have missed *your* love and tenderness had you been called away — *little more*. *Mine* would have lost their all — *they knew it*. Often at night, when the flickering fire-light played over my pallid features, they would awake from their troubled dreams, and satisfying themselves that the weary nurse was asleep, creep up from their low trundle-bed to my pillow, and say, "Mamma, are you better? you will not die, will you? Nobody would care for us if you were gone."

Oh, with what kisses of mingled love and agony I clasped them to my bosom then. "Not yet, my God! not yet! Grant me a few more years for their dear sakes! I am willing to suffer, but not *to die*, — not yet, not yet!"

Down, memory! I weep as I write.

It is sorrowful, it is pleasant to remember. God was merciful. Friends were there, — the aged physician, the affectionate pastor, the kind nurse; the rich, poor, talented, honest, and good; the aged father, the stripling youth, the beautiful girl, the little child, — all came to the humble home of Ella Lincoln, all climbed those narrow stairs, all gazed down into her pale, thin face, with tones and looks of sympathy; all went away to reflect upon the mutability of human destinies.

Rosy May had come. I sat up a part of the time, my strength was slowly returning. I was thinking of the nice bits I had received during my illness from the hands of farmer Sutphen, my friend of the "note" memory, when lo! I heard a heavy step upon the stairs, and in another moment *he* was before me.

"How are you to-day, Mrs. Lincoln? I have brought along a couple of as nice prairie chickens as ever you saw, — my son Billy shot them, — and my wife has sent along a roll of fresh butter, and a few fresh eggs."

"Many thanks, my dear friend. How can I repay you for your kindness?"

"Well, when I give away a thing I don't expect *pay*, generally; if you like them, I am satisfied. No, no, I can't sit down possibly. But I'll do my errand standing. You see my wife and I have been talking over the matter about your sickness, and how weak you are yet, and all that, and how them little boys has been shut right up in this store-room all winter, and we've concluded to ask you to get ready and come out and spend a while with *us*, at the farm. My daughter Polly says she'll put a cot in *our* room, for herself to sleep on, and you may have her bed. You know our house is log, with one frame room and bed-room, — the bed-room's Polly's. And there the children can have milk that *is milk*, and grow fat on it. Your town cows, that run on the prairie, don't give as good milk as ours, that run in clover; and we can feed you up on chickens and young turkeys, and get you well again. I've always *liked you*, because you don't give up and cry about every little thing, but tough it out, let what will come. You shall be just as welcome as my own children; and — to-day is Tuesday — next week Saturday, you'll be stronger; and do you be ready, and I'll come, if it doesn't rain, without fail."

He hurried out, his heavy boots tramping along the passage and down stairs.

A *little rain* fell upon my lap, as I looked at the presents, and told the *little men* of the nice ride in prospect, and that pleasant visit; and I was glad he didn't stay for an answer, lest he might have concluded that I *did* "*cry*" about some "little things."

At the appointed time, he came, with a span of fat ponies, in a large farm-wagon. In it was a rocking-chair for me to sit in, and a common quilt upon some straw in the bottom.

"You just sit right down there on that quilt, you little shavers, for these colts travel like all *forty*, and you might tumble out; and you sit in that chair, Mrs. Lincoln, and, if I drive too fast for *you*, sing out."

There were no stones in our path; for I can hardly say it was a road, the grass being but a little shorter there than on either side. The flowers had sprung up, golden, purple, and white, making the prairie as a waving sea of flowers; the birds, butterflies, and bees flitted about among the lilies and wild roses; and the two little freed prisoners in the wagon clapped their hands, and shouted as we rolled smoothly on.

Here we are! A rail fence encircles the garden; a board fence the door-yard. The house is, as our friend described it, "log except one room." There come the whole family to welcome us, not stopping till they are outside the gate — Mrs. Sutphen, with her smooth, pleasant countenance, dressed in clean gingham; Miss Polly, with her sweet, rosy face and blue eyes; and the boys, whose ages range from six to eighteen.

I had seen Mrs. Sutphen before, during my illness.

The oldest son helped me to alight; and, as I passed in, I saw Harry and Tommy riding off upon the shoulders of two stout urchins of twelve and fourteen.

That was the last I saw of them for an hour. They were off among the colts and calves. Before they had been there a week, they "owned," nominally, half of all the stock upon the farm. "My black colt," "my bay one," "my white turkey," "my gosling." Poor children! they were somewhat richer than their mother.

Farmer Sutphen's was a well regulated family, of which he was "prophet, priest, and king;" and, whether I saw him with a child upon his knee, or, on bended knee, bowing his own will submissively to his God's, I equally admired and loved him. Mrs. Sutphen was affectionate, sweet-tempered, industrious, and pious, and, except that she was moving in a different sphere of life, reminded me of my own long-lost mother. They had no servant. Herself and daughter, a lovely girl of sixteen, performed all the household labor cheerfully and well.

Such a table! Upon it all the luxuries of the town and country were combined. My health improved; the children grew fat and rosy. A pattern family was Farmer Sutphen's; the longer I staid, the better I liked them all.

"What will you give me for what I hold in my hand?" said Mr. Sutphen, one day, returning from the village, and holding up his broad hand with a mischievous look, as I peeped round to discover what was in it.

"Come along to the barn, boys, all of you. I never like to see a lot of lads in the house, when it's all blue sky up yonder." And as he went out, the boys following, he flung a letter into my hand.

"Mrs. Ella Lincoln, Mariette, Cook Co., Ill." (Postmarked "Placerville, Cal.") Hold on, Ella! don't let that letter fall! There goes the envelope! Take care! you will have it all torn to bits! What! dizzy? suffocating? blind? "Water! she has fainted!"

On my own bed, Mrs. Sutphen and Polly beside me, the crushed epistle in my hand. It reads thus:

"My dear Ella, — You must have been disappointed, not hearing from me for so many long months; but I trust to your kindness for pardon. Having had but moderate success at Placerville, earning barely enough there to pay the enormous price for board, soon after writing the first letter, I concluded to go up into the mountains. Of my mountain life, I might write a volume, but will only say, that, after difficulties and dangers of which the uninitiated can have no conception, I have succeeded in earning a few hundreds.

"Enclosed you will find a draft on 'Gregory & Co.' for eight hundred dollars, which I hope may be in time to save you from any uneasiness lest you might be out of funds.

"When I arrived at this place, I found one letter from you," (I had written a dozen,) "that written long ago.

"Then our sweet Jesse is dead! Ella, I had a strange presentiment that something had occurred to that child. Often, when I lay down upon the ground wrapped in my blanket, with no roof but the heavens over my head, the image of that beautiful babe, as I last saw him, passed before my mental vision; and, when the breath of the mountain touched my cheek, I seemed to feel the brush of his silken hair; *his* tiny fingers lifted the locks from my temples. I raised my arms impulsively to catch the bright image that floated between me and the stars; and it was gone. Jesse was there, with me, Ella; he was far away, with you. It was *his* nightly task to watch over us all; he was the sweet messenger of love between our faithful hearts. I knew that an angel watched over me, and I slept sweetly in that mountain fastness, far from the loved ones I could have died to shield from harm."

"A little, thin slip of paper to be worth eight hundred dollars!" Happy Ella, "debts" will be all paid now, and that garret-room left "alone in its glory." I will pay Mr. Sutphen for board till fall; then, all in health and happy, we will return to the village; and, for want of better business, *one of us* scribble for the newspapers.

"Yes, certainly, Mrs. Lincoln, if you can put up with our accommodations; and, since you say you won't stay without, I'll take a dollar a head all round, not counting the youngest, that lives on pudding and milk mostly. That'll be just two dollars a week; and, if ever you get hard up again, I'll give it back to you — that's the bargain."

"But, my dear sir —"

"Hush! When I make a bargain with a woman, I

never let *her* talk and spoil it. Where's the use?" and he went out.

"Sure enough, Mrs. Lincoln, from the day that we were married till this, he has always slyly taken his own way; but that way has been for the best good of all he dealt with. Where a man *has* common sense, he ought to control his own house; where he hasn't, let *petticoats* rule — that's my idea. James Sutphen has never caused *me* to shed one tear by unkindness. It is my pride and pleasure to obey him, asking no questions." She was a happy wife.

It was harvest time. Mrs. Sutphen and her daughter were unusually busy for a week, "seeding raisins," "looking over coffee," and making nice, large cakes. Then came the harvesters — healthy, sprightly, intelligent young men, with coarse, clean shirts, open at the throat, and cotton trowsers. Call them "backwoodsmen," you pert, spindle-shanked, powdered, and scented city dandies! Men with hearts and souls, not ashamed to "earn their bread by the sweat of their brows." Any one of those dozen brown right hands could brush you into nonentity in a moment. "Sitting down to eat without coats!" Better *without* than coats that properly belong to the merchant and the tailor. It was a beautiful sight to peep in from that log kitchen, and see them at the table, happier than the kings of the earth, to hear their pleasant jokes, and witness that keen relish for food which is the result of honest toil.

After they went out, the cloth was relaid, and Mrs.

Sutphen, her children, and Ella and hers, sat down. Of all the luxuries in the wide, wide world, give me those of the liberal farmer's table.

True, there are families upon the western prairies who live upon pork, potatoes, and sour bread, selling their eggs, butter, poultry, and green peas, drinking "corn coffee," "sage tea," and buttermilk; but such instances are rare.

Western farmers generally live well — better than the cooped up, half-starved city people that slander them. It takes all kinds of humanity to make a world; but let no man slander the "western farmers," or Ella will write "a book of revelations" of what she has seen not a thousand miles away from this inkstand.

The "reaper" had swept over the fields; the "threshing machine" had accomplished its office; and the grain was sifted and in sacks ready for the market. There it was, every sack marked "J. S.," stowed away snugly in the barn.

"You just keep away from all them sacks in the corner, you little fellows; I won't have 'em rolled down no how."

"We won't touch 'em, father."

A cloud rose in the west. At first, it appeared light and feathery, and scarce larger than a pigeon's wing; and then it darkened and spread, and came up rapidly, hiding the sun, and stretching away over the prairie till its heavy folds sank into the long prairie grass.

The wind sighed mournfully under the eaves; then gathered up its mighty wings, and rushed roaring, piping, thundering over the plain. The grass and the flowers bowed low as it passed, and the young trees were twisted into shreds. The cattle ran bellowing away like a herd of frightened buffaloes; and the birds were lifted and whirled along like withered leaves.

Then came the lightning, the thunder, the pattering rain, the pelting hail; and then the cheerful light broke through, and the cloud rolled back and away, spanned by the rainbow, its few lingering drops sparkling like jewels in the sunbeams.

It was just five o'clock, and we had gathered in the "sitting-room" for tea, when that tempest startled us with its suddenness and power; and, as soon as the room grew light again, we seated ourselves at the table.

"Pretty considerable of a shower!" remarked Mr. Sutphen, as he helped us to broiled ham, cucumbers, and raspberries. "I saw my wheat straw go flying over the prairie when it begun; and them prairie chickens and birds — I pitied 'em. But it isn't anything to what I *have seen* in my day. There was a gale two years ago, that lifted up my big wagon, carried it several feet, and sot it right down into the middle of a slough; and my oldest, Billy, who happened to be out, was landed right down *onto* the old red cow's back. It tore my hay-stacks all to pieces, and played ball with my fences, and everybody else's within five miles.

"See here, Harry and Tommy; after tea, you'll have a nice time, gathering up them big hail-stones that ain't melted yet, won't you? I always like children, when they *are children*, and let big folks talk at the table, and do their own hallooing out-doors."

"Father, the barn's on fire!"

"Why, Billy! is it possible? has the lightning struck it? Where's my hat? Sure enough, it burns like a candle! Come on, Billy, and all the rest of you! let's get out them bags! Thomas, you blindfold them horses, and lead 'em out! Fred, you untie that calf, and start it! No fuss nor noise — just keep your wits about you; but hurry! that mow will be down in five minutes! There, we've saved the most of 'em; never mind the rest! There comes roof and upper floor; glad there wasn't any more hay in it! Get out of the way! Now come and help bring boards from behind the house to cover up the wheat, and be thankful things isn't no worse."

The barn had burned down like a flash, filled as it was with hay and straw, and roofed with pine.

The next day, a temporary shelter was erected; and, in a few weeks, a new barn took its place.

It was autumn. We bade our kind friends "Good bye," and returned to the village, where I had engaged a comfortable house.

Another remittance of five hundred dollars had arrived from California. Allen was well, and my heart beat as lightly as a bird's. Surely the tide had turned; prosperity was at hand; *he would* return, and my cares be over.

CHAPTER XVII.

"When sorry for others, remember
You have a few rights of your own."

THAT excellent girl and housekeeper who had nursed me through the long winter, had "found a home of her own," as she told me on Saturday before she was married to Peter McMahon on Sunday.

In her place, I had secured an inferior girl, that "wasn't *obleeged* to work out, but came to help for accommodation," and wash dishes in white undersleeves, at the moderate price of $2 per week, and "all of Sunday to be her own." She took sly opportunities to teaze little Harry; and I actually stole a march upon her, one day, just as she pushed Tommy over into a tub of warm, dirty suds.

"What do you mean by that, Rachel?"

"I mean that I aint *obleeged* to work out, for my father's well off, and I've a home to go to; and I didn't come here to be bothered with anybody's young uns; and I'm a going home to-morrow — that I am — now see if I don't!"

"Very well; go to-day, if you wish; I am ready to settle with you."

"I'll stay if you'll take care of your own young uns."

"I shall not do that. With your wages, you ought to do my little house-work, and assist about the children. You can go home *now* — to-day."

"Good bye, ma'am," said Rachel, hurrying tnrough the room with an enormous bundle, and slamming the door unmercifully.

The next time I opened my bureau drawers, they were minus all those articles of dress which are not the less useful for not being conspicuous; and I was obliged to borrow "a change" of my next-door neighbor. Whence Rachel came, or whither she went, no one knew. All that I could do, after the excitement of sending her off, was to get our own suppers, and put the children to bed; and, when I discovered my loss, it was too late to trace her.

In those days, "help" was easily obtained, but not generally good. "Hired girls" were either ignorant foreigners, or farmers' daughters who "had homes of their own;" and if, with an eastern education, any one of us happened to call "a hired girl" a "servant," it was well if there was a "baking aforehand," and the clothes were newly washed and ironed, for *madam* was off like a streak. Girls came and went, unknown, unrecommended, doing what and as much as pleased them. Every delicate woman at the head of a house was doomed to suffer from their indolence and insolence; every master of a house had a rich experience in "girl hunting." I will not tell the story in full about the miserses of keeping servants in newly settled towns. I will merely assert that those "helps" were considered prizes who never got drunk, pinched the babies, nor stole things of more importance than a few eggs, a lump of butter, or a bar of hard soap.

"Well, here I am again," said I, throwing myself

upon the settee, weary in every limb. "No help! Jane was the only decent girl I ever hired, and *she* must be married! She is 'Mrs. Peter McMahon' now, to be sure! What did *he* want of a wife? I'm sure *he* was extremely selfish in taking her away." And there I lay an hour, thinking and contriving, and trying to be angry with poor Peter, when lo! there was a tap at the door, and I welcomed the pleasant face of my next-door neighbor, Mrs. Pry, to whom I revealed my troubles.

"If you wish my advice, my dear Mrs. Lincoln, it is this: give up housekeeping, and take a room in the 'New York House.' The building is old, but respectable, and somewhat retired. Mr. and Mrs. Snapp, the new occupants, are reported as excellent persons. They have no children, and but few boarders. They have been unfortunate; and *your* going there would advance the interests of the house."

"Unfortunate! poor!"—that was enough. My *heart* was always where my head ought to be. Poor—Mr. and Mrs. Snapp!" Ella Lincoln had herself known poverty; and, at the sound of that magic word, she was ready, unquestioned, to take a viper to her bosom, and warm it into life.

"I will ask my pastor if he thinks there would be any impropriety in such a step," I said to Mrs. Pry, who had come in to assist me to dispose of the furniture in case I should move to the hotel; and I put on my sun-bonnet, and ran over the way.

"Certainly not, my dear Mrs. Lincoln. All western boarding-houses are small hotels. Your respectability would, at all hazards, be a guaranty against remarks. You need to be free from the perplexities of house-keeping. You could not do better, with your health."

"What a good, fatherly minister Mr. Brown is!" thought Ella, taking two steps at a time, as she ran back to tell Mrs. Pry.

Ah, Mr. Brown, you knew more about the "Psalms" and the "Book of Esther" than about the propriety of an unprotected woman going out to board. You, in your own honest goodness, never thought that a lady, boarding, is, in a measure, in the power of the host and hostess under whose roof she is; that, upon the first pique, they may lead strangers to underrate her character; that by them she may be fed or starved, warmed or frozen, made happy or persecuted, until she suffers any inconvenience of person or purse to be freed again from their hateful presence You did not know *that*, Mr. Brown. You would as soon have expected snow in August, or pirates upon dry land, as harm to Ella Lincoln at the "New York House."

The large upper room which I had contracted for was in a state of dilapidation; and Mr. Snapp asked me to occupy another until he could have it repaired. "Of course." Poor Mr. Snapp — anything to oblige him. I was given a back room in its stead, from the windows of which I had a fine view of the stables, a dirty yard, etc. But, not minding a temporary annoyance, I said in my heart, "My own room will at best be ready in a few weeks, and then all will be pleasant." I saw some large yellow patches on the wall, which indicated a leaky roof; but fie! it wouldn't rain again until my own room would be done. The table was strangely like an "outline map," the coffee muddy and tea flat, pie-crust like India rubber, and the cake — Tommy and Harry whispered, "Mamma, isn't there soap in it?" — the cake *was* green with saleratus. But — poor Mr. and Mrs. Snapp! They were just commencing in the new business, and could not afford many eggs. I was determined to be satisfied with the table.

I tried to like the personal appearance of the host and hostess. Mr. Snapp was a trim, short, active person, with a little black eye and smoothly shaven face, always smiling. Mrs. Snapp was tall and straight as an Indian, with a creamy-white complexion, and hair not much darker, low brow, little head, and skim-milk eyes with just the least perceptible shade of blue in them. Her nose — may it never be measured; her mouth — never be explored.

But, God made her; *she* was not responsible for her personal appearance. I resolutely *began* to like her. I could have succeeded better if her dress had not been so *outré;* but she wore the Bloomer costume — *exceedingly Bloomerish.* She had a right to her own taste.

She was bold and loud-toned, and her tramp was like that of an elephant. Even all these things I forgave her, determined not to judge of the jewel by the roughness of the casket.

The summer advanced, cold and stormy. The little ones fretted at the chilliness of the room — that back room, for my own was not yet finished. I ventured to remind Mr. Snapp that he had promised me the front room; and then he complained of poverty. He "was very sorry, but really he did not know where to get the money." I, Ella Lincoln, loaned it to him, leaping like a prisoner from a wall in the dark, risking his neck, with the bare possibility of bettering his condition. I was so weary of that dark, cold back room, and of being turned out of bed by the rain, that I was glad of any alternative. But I tried to blame no one in particular. Clouds would come, and rain would fall; and, whenever it did rain, I bounded out of bed instanter. One night I awoke in a fright, thinking I had an alarming palpitation of the heart, to which I had long been subject. Yes, I could *hear it!* It was like a Methodist minister of seventy years since, impressing his congregation by constantly pounding on the pulpit cushion; like the dropping of water from a broken bucket upon the ground; like the everlasting tongue of a scold, *yet more endurable.*

There I lay, not daring to stir hand or foot, lest *that* might hasten the dissolution of nature, and mentally praying to the Father in heaven that he would be very merciful to one whose life had been so erring, and watch over my unprotected babes. It is an awfully solemn moment when we wait for the last beat of the heart.— Whew! what's that? A drop of water pattering in my face. Up go hands, and down they fall upon my chest, splash into a puddle of water which has collected upon the coverlet. Ella is alive again, and up in a hurry.

"It is a long lane that hath no turning." I had

been at the "New York House" three months, when the landlord politely informed me that the room for which I had contracted was duly plastered and papered, and I moved in, saying, "Now we shall be happy. Harry and Tommy will have more room, and from those front windows we shall see the world again." "Man never is, but always to be, blest."

Court week was approaching; all the landlords in ecstasies; their harvest at hand. Away they went, scouring the country after pigs, turkeys, and green peas. There was bustle in the bed-rooms, bustle in the bar-room, confusion and racket among kettles and tin ovens.

O, what a nice thing I thought it was to be snugly out of the way in my room, where, with my children, I could remain unmolested.

Not willing to be in the crowd, I requested the landlord to allow me to sit with my children at the second table. I would have preferred that my meals should be sent up, but had heard the white-eyed landlady descant upon "false delicacy," and feared to prefer even so reasonable a request.

Mr. Snapp had advertised to take boarders at seventy-five cents per day, and of course Mr. Snapp was favored with a crowd — and such a crowd! Often, after the first tableful had risen, a second would rush in, and it fell to my lot to eat at the third, when, alas! only the spirit of emptiness remained. Meat, vegetables, and sauces were not there. Sometimes I found a few crums of the dressing of fowls, and no potatoes; sometimes potatoes, no crums of the dressing. That white-eyed Mrs. Snapp was a "close calculator." The children cried. After dinner, to pacify them, I went out and bought them cakes and candy — poor boys!

"Court *week*" lasted at least twenty days; but its duration was not my worst form of grievance, for the host and hostess seemed determined that I should share in all its troubles. There was a case of prosecution for stealing; and the defendant, and all the witnesses on the defence, boarded at that house. Among these were some of the most arrant, troublesome women I ever saw. They walked into my room uninvited, at all hours, if the door happened to be unlocked. The weather was warm; I had neither shutters nor shade trees on the sunny side; hence the only alternative, from the *women*, was suffocation. Two of them actually came in with pipes in their mouths, when, abhorring tobacco, I took the liberty to say that I disliked smoke, and they — "went out?" Not they; they just walked forward, and, each seating herself in a front window, puffed away. "There, now it will blow out the window," said one; and "La sakes! 'most everybody likes it," chimed in the other. Then followed a succession of questions about my past and future, such as the ignorant delight to ask, and the refined dislike to answer. All these annoyances I bore, rather than be at open war with Mr. Snapp, whose friends they were; and I feared to offend Mr. Snapp, in whose power were the few comforts we possessed, because I had foolishly obliged him by paying our board in advance.

Court week was over. We rejoiced in the possession of our own room, and the present seemed more endurable by contrasting it with the past; but O, how many difficulties and vexations I yet endured! When the children were sick, I watched over them alone; and, when I was sick, none cared for me — *none under that roof.* I had friends, many friends, to whom I might have gone for counsel and sympathy; but I did not feel willing to let them know how foolishly I had entrapped myself by paying in advance. As soon as our accounts balance, I said to myself, I will escape from this unpleasant situation.

I had received company in my own room, supposing it to be more proper than to go down alone to the public parlor. There was no "ladies' parlor" (it was a village hotel of many years ago.) The friends of my absent husband had called at any and all times, I *supposed* unquestioned. But this did not suit the white-eyed landlady.

One day, a lawyer called upon business, having a paper for my signature; and afterwards he advised me as a friend concerning the future. He remained an hour, little Harry and Tommy playing the mischief all that time with "Gleason's Pictorial," which I had given them to keep them quiet.

Soon after he went out, "*Short-Skirts*" came up stairs like a whirlwind. I heard her portentous tread, and softly turned the key.

"Mrs. Lincoln! Mrs. Lincoln!" she vociferated, with a short, spiteful rap, that sounded in my ear like the collapsing of a steel trap. After a moment's hesitation,

I opened the door. Her eyes were dilated to what seemed to me the size of two full moons; her short, dowdy figure was drawn up to its extreme height; her vinegar lips quivered.

"What will you have, Mrs. Snapp?"

"What will I have, indeed? I *would* have the ladies who board here receive gentlemen's calls in the public parlor. *My* reputation is at stake; and let me tell you, even you are not above suspicion."

"Very well, madam; now that your errand is accomplished, I hope to have the privilege of my own room."

Utterly foiled by my composure, she made a speedy exit; and I turned the key behind her, realizing — O, how bitterly! — that I was in the power of an envious, unfeeling woman, who might deteriorate my character as a lady. But for confidence in the faithfulness of those who had known me long and well, I should have been driven to madness. I wept long and bitterly; and then a strong hand uplifted my spirit out of the darkness, and a "still small voice" whispered, "All is well."

That night, I had pleasant dreams under the roof of a friend, except that once I was startled by the apparition of a gigantic bird of bantum species, that crowed most threateningly over my pillow; and, as I raised my hand to scare him away, he gazed back saucily in my face with the veritable head and eyes of the white-eyed landlady.

About that time, I conceived a decided aversion to boarding in general, (which feeling lasted about a week,) and I jotted down my opinion in simple rhyme.

Whatsoever ills befall you, —
  Fain would I advise you once, —
Let no boarding-house inthrall you:
  List to a repentant dunce.

If your home be neat and spacious,
  Warm, and filled with comforts rare,
Thanking Him who is so gracious,
  Never mind your meed of care.

If your home be rude and scanty,
  And but scantily supplied,
But a straw-thatched, leaky shanty,
  Strive to smile with naught beside.

Wooden be both plate and platter,
  Sip your coffee from a gourd,
Gather crums the nabobs scatter,
  But — I warn you — never board.

The next week found the dear little fellows and myself so pleasantly situated in a first-class boarding-house, that the muses, who are fond of melancholy, actually soared away in disgust.

CHAPTER XVIII.

"How many 'angels unawares' have crossed thy casual way!"

Mr. Alton, the proprietor of the "Boston House" was a gentleman. Mrs. Alton made no unnecessary noise, assumed no unwarrantable guardianship over her boarders, but kept a general superintendence of the house without seeming to be there. She was a person of uncommon intellect without egotism; had seen enough of the world, through suffering, to constitute her a judge of its ways and wickedness; was a lady in the parlor, a mistress in the kitchen, an ornament in general society.

The boarders were courteous and respectful — genuine gentlemen and ladies, who knew the way to their own rooms, and *when* it was time to go there; and they made it a religious duty to "mind their own business."

The servants of the "Boston House" were as superior to those of the "New York House" as the master and mistress of the latter to those of the former. Genteel hotels command genteel servants.

My rooms were peculiarly pleasant, being on the first floor, with a front and back entrance. I furnished them comfortably from the remains of the furniture of the house, and much enjoyed having a room and bedroom once more. When "Court week" came, I feared no intruding women who would sit in the front windows and smoke long pipes. I apprehended no feminine "court-martial" after friends had called upon business, neglect in sickness, nor scanty fare. I drew one long, comfortable breath, after the last article of furniture was adjusted to my taste, and said, in the fulness of contentment, "HOME!"

"When the little ones are hungry, this is the place to come," said Mrs. Alton, flinging open a cupboard in the dining-room, and displaying the long rows of pies and cakes, that might have tempted an epicurean millionaire; "and here are the knives" — opening a drawer — "just bring them out, and help them to what they ask for."

Dear, kind Mrs. Alton! Since then, it has sometimes been my lot to board where the face of the mistress *turned wrong side out*, if I asked with *solemn reverence* for "a piece of bread and butter for Tommy;" and my thoughts have reverted to that whole-souled woman, who, loving *her own* offspring, remembered that other mothers' bosoms were made of the same flesh, subject to the same painful emotions over a grieved child. Some women actually become cross-eyed from keeping one eye constantly upon the pantry while the other attends to the world in general.

O money, money! none but those who have known poverty to the very dregs can fully appreciate thy worth. I bought "*a dress or two*," once more, without the fear that I should atone for the waste by the lack of bread. I went into society without the harrowing fear that the "poor-house" waited in the distance. I did not carry a face there as long as a penitential friar's; I was happy to be there, pleased with all I saw. I had *new clothes*, *new* rooms, *new* hopes, *new* treatment, and wore a *new* countenance.

But my health was yet delicate; and after the winter set in cold and windy, I remained generally at home.

I had a poet-friend, whom I shall call "Florence Day," who came sometimes to see me, and then we were *so* happy. Sweet Florence Day! I had loved her long before we met. There was a mournful cadence in her verse; a breaking heart breathed its inspirations through every line; and all the holiest sympathies of my poetic nature rose up in reverence to meet her fair ideal. I longed to tell her how I appreciated her worth; to clasp her to my heart of hearts, unawed by her superiority. We met as sister meets sister, and communed together as they only can whose hopes alike overreach the grave.

She was a frail creature, with a sweet blue eye, and a world of thought upon her forehead; pious, but not bigoted; conversable, but not *talkative;* with proper self-respect, yet setting no factitious value upon her own attainments. She was the genuine old-fashioned lady — no surface politeness. Where she gave her hand, her heart accompanied it. You might have given her the keys of your soul's hiding-place, assured she would not betray you.

At home she was domestic and plain, the pattern mother, pattern housekeeper. She was yet in the early noon of life, if her age had been counted in years; but if by lines of care, by clouds of grief, in early evening.

A few snow-flakes blended with the bright-brown locks upon her temples; her figure was skeleton-like, her hands almost transparent, the blue veins interlacing each other like net-work, upon the surface. I watched her often, long and sorrowfully, thinking of the wealth of affection she had lavished upon a thankless world, and remembered those beautiful lines which came up from the over-tried heart of a sweet songstress;

> "Her lot is on you; silent tears to weep,
> And patient smiles to wear through suffering's hour;
> And sumless riches, from affection's deep,
> To pour on broken reeds a wasted shower;
> To make you idols, and to find them *clay;*
> And to bewail that worship — therefore pray."

I pondered upon the strange mystery, that others, less gifted, less deserving, were sitting in "high places," while to her were not awarded those laurels which were her due; nor competence which ought to have resulted from such talent and industry.

A mother toiling for her children, wearing out flesh and brain in the thankless profession of a writer, — not cursed with vain ambition, — with no unhallowed thirst for empty applause, — turning her faltering footsteps to the thorny path of literature, as the only avenue through which she might find her daily bread, — *why* was she still *so poor?*

For the want of *one available friend,* one with the heart and ability to risk a few hundreds in her behalf, to take her, as a brother, by the hand, publish her valuable works, and demand *for her* the immediate attention of a hurrying, thoughtless world. She had written long and well, her talents had been moderately appreciated by the public, but *she* could not write gratuitously, to be paid in "puffs," — she had no millionaire friend to *insert favorable notices at advertisement prices.*

She, whom poverty obliges to eat the bread of carefulness, and mend her own clothes, if she wield the pen of the author, will reap her reward in disappointment, mortification, and an early death. The literary *man* may go forth alone to wrestle for his rights with those meaner souls, who, through accident, money, or friends, have gained the long coveted goal; *but woman,* self-doubting, shrinking woman, in this, as in everything, needs encouragement. Protect her, and she goes forward; without protection she falls back, appalled at the difficulties that surround her. I speak of *what I know.* These words may reach the bleeding heart of many a "Florence Day," weary and worn till the life-lamp burns feebly, flickering in the socket. A "Florence Day," who in her great struggle turns her beseeching eyes to even her successful sisters, to be met with cold, scornful looks; clenched hands, — "Florence Day," — tracing with feeble fingers her last lines to some heartless employer, beseeching him for the stinted remuneration "due for her last story."

She is gone! Her blue eye waxed strangely brilliant; her pale cheek glowed with a bright crimson spot; her step dragged heavily over the floor, and she lay down to die. The destroyer was slow in his work, that the teachings of her pure spirit might be heard, and remembered long by those who loved her. Earth has seemed more lonely and desolate to Ella since *she* went *home!*

"Died of consumption." *I know,*—the loved ones who watched over her to the last *know,*—that reiterated disappointments, a keen realization of the unkindly dealings of those who might, *and ought* to have advanced her literary interests, preyed upon her sensitive nature, and hurried her prematurely into the grave. Sweet Florence Day!

"There's not a look, a word of thine,
My soul hath e'er forgot;
Thou ne'er hast bid a ringlet shine,
Nor given thy locks one graceful twine,
That I remember not."

CHAPTER XIX.

"So much to gain, so much to lose,
No wonder that I fear to choose."

"Where is the strength that spurned decay;
The step that rolled so light away;
The heart's blithe tone?——"

"My dear Mrs. Lincoln, how would it suit you to be associated with me in 'The Republican.' Would not daily occupation beguile you of your present loneliness; and the kind of employment I should offer you be a profitable discipline for your intellect? I know you have editorial talent of a high order; and, at some future time, the little experience gained at Mariette might be useful to you in a more widely circulated Journal."

"But, my dear Sir, to become a dabbler in grave editorials, has never suggested itself to my fancy in my wildest moods. Recollect, if I should disgrace myself, I should disgrace you.

"I have no fears."

"My health would not admit of exposure."

"You can stay in your own room. I will call upon you here as often as necessary. What shall I say to our readers next week?"

"Tell them I'll *try*,"—and Mr. Ward was gone. What next, Ella?

"Our new Volume. We have introduced improvements which cannot fail of gratifying our friends. Mrs.

Ella Lincoln, whose graceful pen has often contributed to our columns, will now be associated with us in the editorial management.

In consideration of our efforts to keep pace with the improvements around us, we confidently appeal to a generous public for a more extensive patronage.

Especially do we invoke the smiles of the ladies, realizing that what they encourage must succeed.

In behalf of *our associates*, we promise them that no pains shall be spared, to render our paper a fitting companion for the boudoir or the parlor." — *Mariette Republican.*

" Mrs. Lincoln, a talented writer of both prose and poetry, has become associated with Mr. Ward, in the Mariette Republican. We most cordially welcome her to the editorial chair, and congratulate our friend on such an accession to his strength."—*Mariettte Jacksonian.*

" Mrs. Lincoln wields the pen of a ready writer; and her editorial talents are not surpassed by any lady's in the West."—*Putnamville Spy.*

" We have long known Mrs. Lincoln, as a writer, and a woman, and have full confidence in her ability and success."—*Chicago Aurora.*

" She is caustic and keen. We shall have good things from her pen. She is extensively known in the West as a poetess."—*Milwaukee Star.*

There, puffing myself like a quack doctor. Those are *specimens.* I'll read you the rest when we've finished " The Story."

I believe Mr. Ward was satisfied with my success, and I wrote homilies, obituaries, puffs, and notices of strolling singers, *almost* as well as he did.

Friends were pleased to commend me, for the faithfulness with which I battled for truth and justice; though the young gentlemen thought me hard upon "dancing," because I insisted upon it, that if they danced five nights in the week, they ought to take the sixth for rest and repentance.

Western people "go in for" amusements; generally look at the bright side of a thunder storm; and never cry "fire" till a roof caves in. *They* don't *groan* a half a day over every hand-bill that announces something *new;* or "wonder *who* will be there;" but *go right along;* taking for granted the *spectators* make the show respectable,—not that the show can un-make the witnesses.

They are not yet cursed with as many "castes" as the Brahmins. Industry, honesty and intelligence are not pushed aside by ignorant coxcombry, backed by the "almighty dollar." When a lady of respectable appearance is seen in a western town, her sister ladies do not wait to inform themselves if she be "a Governor's daughter," or sister to "Senator Buster," before they extend to her the courtesies due to all lonely strangers. "Old aristocratic family," is a phrase unknown there. If some millionaire's wife *should* so far forget her true interest, as to put on airs, and claim supremacy, from the fact of her having been one of the "first settlers," it would be lucky indeed for her, if, in that same company, there were none who could remember, to have seen *her* rinsing clothes in the creek with the water up to ——— where her gaiters would have come, if she had had them on, and they had been as long as gentlemen's boots.

"First settlers;" and some who settled after them, would do well to look wise and say nothing about "classes."

Probably, some of the "first settlers" of Mariette will teach their children, privately, that money is the *chief good;* and the surface of the third generation will be plentifully sprinkled with FOOLS talking of the "old families," etc.,—for such is the fashion of the world. He who moved his family to the "far west" in a coarse wagon; camping out at night; who lived the first summer in a wretched cabin, without glass in the windows; with a coverlet hanging in the place of a door; whose meals were prepared by a fire outside, the kettle resting on two stones, becomes rich; occupies a tall, brick mansion; rides in a carriage; gives oyster suppers;—He says to his little son, "Look there! do you see those white wagon covers away off upon the prairie? Those are the wagons of the cooking movers; plain, honest people, who are moving out farther West."

"Oh, yes. May be they'll stop here always; if they do, will you and mamma call and see them?"

"Of course not; my little unsophisticated pussy! *they* cannot move in our circle."

The village grows into a town, the town becomes a city; the once "Far West is the interior; the white man still treads in the track of the Indian, the Indian marches onward towards the setting sun.

> " God guides us through perpetual change,
> Yet does not change his plan."

I was called to tea; as usual; before the rush of the boarders, at the ringing of the bell.

Opposite sat an elderly gentleman whom I immediately recognized as Mr. Trall, of Chicago, the uncle of Jeannie Lisle. Mr. Trall and Jeannie were the companions of our journey Westward through Michigan, of whom mention was made in a former chapter.

His hair had become snowy white; otherwise he was not much changed in personal appearance; but I thought, as he answered some questions of the attendant, that his voice was sadder; even mournful in its tone.

The past, that rough, yet not unpleasant journey — with all its little incidents; its vexatious accidents; its overturnings and detentions; rushed over my memory. The companions of that weary ride; as varied in character as features; the dark haired Bostonian, that carried sweet Jeannie Lisle over the slough; the smiling young farmers, the merchants; the professional men; — all came back before me in that momentary review, with almost a bewildering power.

" Mamma, does your head ache?" asked Tommy, noticing that I passed my hand over my brow as if in pain.

" No, dear, I am quite well."

" Mrs. Lincoln; is it possible!" said Mr. Trall, starting to his feet and coming round to our side of the table. "Our acquaintance was brief; and it is long since we parted; yet you seem as an old friend. I am happy, very happy to meet you again. You are changed; the rose has given place to the lily; and yet the expression remains — these are your little ones?"

"They are; — What of Miss Lisle — of Jeannie?"

"My dear, after tea — this evening I will call at your room, and there we will talk of Jeannie."

After tea in my room.

Sweet Jeannie. You remember her vividly, I know. She was one whom no one could *see*, and forget. So womanly, and yet so child-like; so affectionate, unsuspicious; trustful, to her own hurt. She never forgot *you* for even one week — called you 'Ella, dear Ella Lincoln.'

You remember the dark haired Bostonian who travelled with us; who carried Jeannie in my stead, over the slough? He was a tall, handsome youth, with an eagle eye, a high, intellectual brow, but somewhat reserved, among us. Bernard McIntosh

After we parted from you, he told me that he was about to settle in Chicago, and practise law there. He presented credentials of character, signed by some of the most respectable citizens of Boston, and the president of Yale College; also Hugh Bancroft of New York, an old college mate of my own; and then, he asked the favor of considering me a friend, and making a permanent acquaintance with Miss Lisle.

I was proud to take so promising a youth to my heart, and make him welcome at all times to my home. It was both a privilege and duty. He came and went, his reserve wore slowly away, and his conversational powers proved brilliant. He was a prominent member of the bar, for one so young, very conspicuous as a speaker. He delivered a fourth of July oration, — one of the most thrillingly eloquent addresses I ever heard, — he lectured upon "poetry and the arts," enchanting the audience with the variety of his knowledge and the beauty of his style. He was welcomed into every circle, loved wherever he went. When he asked for Jeannie's hand in marriage, I hesitated. How *could* I give her up? She was my only sister's child, all that remained to remind me of her, and so like her. Just so beautiful, frank, and childlike was my own Annette, who only lived to smile upon her babe, and died. Then her noble husband fell a victim to consumption, and bequeathed me Jeannie, to be my own, with his last breath. I took the wee bit creature to my bosom, as a precious gift; and, having need of nothing, was enabled to shield her through infancy and childhood from the rude buffetings of a cold, hard world.

When you saw Jeannie, she was returning with me from the Institute at Baltimore, where she had finished her education. I took her from there, to be the idol of my wife, who had no children. Alas, we all made her "a household god!" Of society she was an ornament and *pet*. But I will not dwell upon those three years she spent with us.

Jeannie loved Bernard McIntosh, — it was her destiny.

"I will run in and kiss you every day, dear uncle and and aunt," she said, half playfully, half tearfully, as she crossed the threshold, leaning upon *his* arm, a beautiful bride; and then we felt that the light of the house was gone out, and another had gathered the flower which we had tended with unwearying care.

One year Jeannie was happy. Her laugh rang out as clearly, wildly as before; she came in every day to "kiss" us, as she had promised, and, although we were lonely, without her, when she was gone, we said, it is right, for where, in all the world, could she have found a more perfect companion than Bernard McIntosh?

But a time came when Jeannie entered the door with a less elastic step; when the smile that dimpled her cheek was mocked by a tearful eye. We knew that a cloud was settling upon her life-path, that the worm of sorrow was already eating into her heart-strings.

Then it was whispered among friends, that Bernard had fallen a victim to the arts of the fiends of the gambling saloons; that he had been seen intoxicated, — that he was lost.

Jeannie came to me one night, and said: —

"He is gone again! he is there. Of late he seldom comes home until *three*, in the morning, and then — then ——"

"What is it, my child? speak, — what then?"

"O, how *can* I say! how *can* I tell, even you?" and it seemed as if those great, heavy sobs would burst her bosom. "How can I? O, that I could die!"

She flung herself heavily upon the sofa, and, in her great agony, flinging up her arm, her white, drapery sleeve fell back to the shoulder, and revealed a black, frightful bruise.

For a moment I held my breath, with grief and rage. I felt as if I should go out and shoot the villain, — shoot him in the *hell* where he was defiling himself, — dishonoring the image of God, breaking the heart of the loveliest of her sex. No, no, upon second thought, I would not hurry the poor besotted maniac into the presence of his God. "Vengeance is *mine*," saith the Eternal.

"Jeannie, my own dear child; you have come *home* to remain. Never, with my consent, shall you go forth again. When Bernard sees you it shall be here, in my presence, or that of your aunt."

"O, how *I have loved* him! how I love him yet! But I am sick, dear uncle, aunt; have me carried to a chamber ——"

Bernard was sent for in the morning, at her request. He looked upon the wreck that he had made, and wept. He beat his great, broad breast, and called on God to curse him.

"Jeannie! O, my wife! live, and I will be your slave. I will forsake those evil companions, will turn again to my long forsaken God. *Not yet!* Oh, Thou who upholdest all life, not yet! Spare, O, spare her!"

"Turn my head toward you, Bernard," she said, with a sweet smile; "the fiat has gone forth, I cannot live. Repent, pray; not for my life, but *your* guilt-stained soul. *He* is merciful! Kiss me, dearest, — I forgive you."

The day wore on, — the physician still answered,

"no hope." Bernard, driven from her presence, raved and wept; while Jeannie slept, occasionally murmuring in her dreams, "Poor Bernard! forgive him, for my sake."

At midnight there was a low, feeble cry, — and then the spirits of Jeannie and her new-born babe went up to heaven together.

The old man bowed himself upon the table, and wept.

"And Bernard McIntosh?"

"He repented for a season, as the fiends 'of hell' repent, then returned to the cup and the cards, and NOW lives, the most degraded of men."

CHAPTER XX.

Death paused beside each household pet,
And raised his hand to slay.

Ella was sick for a few weeks, and Harry had a very serious turn of illness. For a few days it seemed as if his short life was almost ended; and I watched over him with inexpressible solicitude and sorrow. He had been a delicate child, from the cradle, and this was the second attack of lung fever within a few months. But the physician, who was very skilful, watched over him day and night, and, although at one time I called the landlord, and other members of the family, as I supposed, to *see him die*, his little, fragile form rose up again, as the reed which has been bent by the wind.

During his illness, and my own, and several periods of sickness of later date, we received the kindest, most considerate attentions from the family and boarders at the Boston House. All knew our history, all felt for our unprotected loneliness. Kind neighbors came daily to offer their services as nurses, and speak soothing words; and, indeed, if it be not an anomaly to say "a pleasant illness," I should say we had more happiness than misery, even then, it was *so* pleasant to have *such friends*.

In the main, I am confident that I acquitted myself

as an editor, with satisfaction to Mr. Ward, the proprietor, and my numerous friends, and also secured the friendship of many of the readers of "The Republican," before unknown. Gentlemen, of whose approbation I was truly *proud*, were pleased to praise me for the faithfulness with which I discharged my duties.

Naturally impulsive and plain spoken, I may not always have modified the truth sufficiently to suit all the crabs and snap-turtles living in those western sloughs; but I know I was favorably received, as a writer, by the better class, and that includes ninety-nine hundredths of the whole population.

In the west, few women give their attention to literature. Here and there, a lady of wealth and leisure, not particularly fond of society, or one who is poor, and has no children to occupy her attention, writes for the newspapers, or a magazine, generally gratuitously; but western ladies, as a community, are much occupied with domestic cares, more especially in the earlier portion of the day; and they are fond of visiting and evening amusements. They are intelligent, but not *literary*, readers but not writers. Hence a woman who spends the greater portion of her time in literary employment, is a more marked character in a western town, than in one of our eastern cities, where every tenth pair of *bonnet* strings rhymes together, or writes "love" and "murder" stories for the wonder-loving public.

In the west, the lady who writes for the newspaper is petted and respected, whether her home be in a mansion or a garret; in the east, she whose life is summed up in "chapters" and "paragraphs," must expect competition and envy at her elbow; and to be obliged to *demand* the place, which, though merited, will be slowly conceded. You remember the old saying, "*two* of a trade cannot agree;" how then can *hundreds* "of a trade agree?"

The ladies of Mariette,—God bless them! I have been a weary time away; but as often as some new wave of sorrow passes over me; when the whole heart is weary and the head sick, I think of *them*—their unselfish principles; their unassuming intelligence; their frank, open-hearted manners.

I have heart-sisters—heart-brothers—away in the prairie land, whose pictures are daguerreotyped upon the walls of memory;—time cannot dim their beauty, nor sorrow wash it out.

I was gazing out over the broad strip of prairie between the town and the Plano River, when my attention was attracted by a crowd of persons standing upon the bank.

My children had been out of my room, perhaps half an hour; I supposed they were in the garden, or at the barn, where they were fond of going to play; and, having always forbidden them to go towards the water, I had no uneasiness about them.

But that crowd, all along the river—what meant that? Some horse had been drowned, probably, in attempting to ford the stream; or possibly, some little, neglected child had fallen in. Presently a tiny figure separated from the crowd, and as it approached, I discovered that it was hatless — a little nearer — it was my own Harry.

"Mamma, Tommy is drowned!"

For a moment my very heart stopped beating. I was stunned — suffocated — speechless with horror.

Mechanically I started for the river, without shawl or bonnet.

"Here is your bonnet," said the little fellow, following; and I took it into my hand, but did not put it on. I walked slowly; my limbs were hardly subject to my bewildered will. As I drew nearer, I saw a man holding him up by his heels; and coming very near, I discovered that he was black in the face, and, apparently, dead. Friends spoke to me, but I did not reply. I breathed with difficulty, my head felt enlarged and strangely; I was very chilly.

The water ran down from his mouth in a stream at first, then less freely, then only dropped.

"That will do," said a bystander; "now put him down on the grass."

And then they stripped away the thin frock from his little bosom, and commened rubbing and rolling him, — a man putting his lips to his, and breathing into his mouth.

There was a bubbling sound in his chest; — simultaneously he threw up his little hands and sobbed — sobbed.

"There, he breathes!"

"Yes, he's safe; another moment in the water would have told the story!"

"Yes, it *is* a miracle; — now he breathes pretty well — let's put him in a wagon and take him home."

' Yes, and drive fast," said the doctor, jumping into a wagon whose owner had stopped there to see what was the matter.

"Get in, Mrs. Lincoln," said a friend.

I gazed at the wagon with its inmates; the doctor; the man who held the child, and others; but my feet refused to climb — I shook my head. They drove away.

A friend took me by the hand and led me slowly home. When we arrived, he was lying on the bed, crying. They were removing his wet clothes; combing his hair. I watched them, but said nothing. The room was crowded with friends for about an hour, talking and doing little deeds of kindness; and then all left but one; and the doctor said, "let him sleep."

I answered all questions in monosyllables during the afternoon. My head was still full and felt strangely; my chest felt as if being crushed in by a heavy weight. Harry came and laid his head upon my lap; but I asked him no questions.

"I am sorry — so sorry," he said, "that I took him there; but a big boy coaxed me to go and see him swim; and he took me into the water to teach *me* to swim; and while I was in there, Tommy fell in; and I did not know it. But a man saw his hat on the top of the water; and he said, 'there is a boy drowned,' and he dove in for him, and got him out,— so I heard him say to the other men. Excuse me this once, mamma, and I'll never swim again — never;" and Harry wept.

At three o'clock, P. M., Tommy was brought home — at twelve o'clock, *I wept.* I wept all night at intervals; and was relieved. The great weight left my brain and bosom — tears — blessed tears! — never before had I realized their value!

"I'll tell you, mamma," said Tommy, who now was worth to me forty times his "weight in gold"—*aye in diamonds* — "I'll tell you how I felt. Well, I knew I was in the water; and a great many people was there; and I was sorry for *you*;— and mad at Tim, for coaxing bubby to go and swim; and I was afraid nobody'd find me; and then I forgot."

CHAPTER XXI.

"Wherefore dost thou doubt? if present good 's round thee?"

"Not writing, as usual; and *such* an expression — such a care-worn, troubled brow? Why, my dear friend, what *has* occurred to disturb 'the even tenor of your way?' Any bad news from husband?"

"Oh, Mr. Brown! I cannot write, read, sew, or talk any more. I am so miserable. It has been many, many months since I have heard from my husband! I am beginning to indulge in all manner of fancies. I fear he may have died of starvation; or by the hand of violence; or that he has started for home and been lost at sea. I fear everything, without any definite fear; — I am wild — wild!"

"Wild! indeed; you seem exceedingly sane. And really I think are doing *well*, alone. At a good boarding house; with plenty of means, or for *this week*, at least; surrounded by the best of friends; in good health, *for you;* and the children *well.* Besides all these blessings," he continued, eyeing me archly, from beneath those great, black brows, a little mixed with gray; "you ought to have one consolation, *he can't* treat you unkindly *now*,— no harsh words, no blows."

"Mr. Brown! Sir! What do you mean! Allen Lincoln was never unkind to me! True, he was unfortunate — a speculator; a gloomy, miserable man before he left me, but he was kind — oh, how kind! Pray Sir, *who* has belied him? And how can you repeat that falsehood to *me*. I had thought better things of *you!*" And did n't I look as savagely as a bearded Turk?

"Ha! ha! ha! ha! — I like a spirited woman;" shouted Mr. Brown at the top of his lungs, "I only meant to change your mood, that's all; better a fit of anger than despondency;" and he laughed on, till I joined in the chorus.

"He will do well; no doubt of it. Letters have miscarried — he is up in the mountains; picking up an ounce to the second — anything but *dead;* ha! ha! ha! Let us see — what time is it? Seven? Yes, there is time, I must tell you a story about my cousin in Pompeii, Illinois. Mrs. Etta Carlisle Clark; the wife of a wealthy lawyer there. I wish to prove to you, that you have been happy through all your misfortunes, in having married *a man*, not a donkey.

Just imagine 'Etta Carlisle, A Prairie Sketch,' by Revd. Mr. Brown, over the first column in the "Republican;" and come right along with me. We commence our Story in Philadelphia.

"But you are not serious, Etta; you do not expect Hubert Carr to visit *you* as an accepted lover? You are aware of your different positions in society; you cannot recognize in him an *equal?*" And the mother bent over the beautiful girl with a look both earnest and sorrowful.

"I am not jesting, mother," replied the young girl, raising her fan to hide the emotions now writing a forbidden language in crimson hues on neck, cheek and brow.

"Remember, Etta! Hubert Carr was the only child of a poor widow, whom, for charity's sake we received into our family as seamstress; and after a year's residence with us, she died. We did not cast out her child upon the world; but kept him still, dressed him, sent him to school with yourself and brother, hoping to elevate him above the class in which he was born.

Strange to tell; at fifteen, he ceased to learn; was slovenly in dress and habits; unmannerly at home, disobedient to teachers. Your father placed him in a store; he was soon dismissed and on our hands again; with no other ostensible business but playing the agreeable to a little lady eight years his junior.

Large and ungraceful, he was not admired as a parlor ornament; and we began to ponder in our hearts, how to rid ourselves of the incumbrance, with honor to ourselves and advantage to himself.

Your father gave him means to buy western land, and, after much trouble, prevailed upon him to depart; hoping that in some way he might prove useful to his race.

We did not hear from him for the first two years; but for three years pas the has been writing letters of friendship and gratitude to your father; who sometimes laughs, wondering 'what prairie school-master helps him to surpass himself.' I cannot believe *he* composes those epistles — they are above his capacity. And now he writes *you* also; I say plainly, he *hires his love-making*."

"Mother, you are unjust. I cannot hear such language! I have loved Hubert Carr from infancy. I have promised to be his wife."

"Never, with my consent!"

"Nor with mine," added Mr. Carlisle, entering; and striding about that elegant apartment like a tramping war-horse.

Hubert Carr went to Philadelphia; to be ejected from the house of his former benefactor. But he lingered clandestinely about the city, and in an evil hour met Etta Carlisle, and persuaded her to elope with him.

With crushed hearts the parents read a letter, written during the journey westward; in which she already repented of her great sin.

It was too late to save her, and they said: "we will not remember *her* unkindly — vengeance is not ours — God pity her!"

"Why Hubert, where are we stopping? please *don't* go in here — I am afraid of Indians. Why did not you tell me they yet lingered in the vicinity of your farm?" said the fair traveller, after a six miles ride over a beautifully rolling prairie.

Tired of steamboats, railroads, and the bustle of travelling generally, she had experienced a childish delight in this more primitive mode of conquering distance; and, as her unbounded vision roamed over that sea of grass and flowers, she expected every moment to see that "white cottage home, with the tall picket fence, half hidden among the wild roses," which Hubert had so often described to her in his letters. Yes, poor child! she every moment expected to see it emerge from behind some swell of the prairie, and bless her with the waking realization of her most romantic dreams.

The horses stood at the bars of the rude door-yard fenced with rails; and with something like a flush of shame deepening the ruddiness of his cheeks, he answered her late question, "Where are we?" with, "this is our home."

Petrified with astonishment, that *he* should have been guilty of falsehood, she neither wept nor smiled, as he lighted her from the carriage to the ground. There she stood, as if bound by an enchanter's spell, gazing at four log buildings, not unlike in outward aspect, except that a smoke issued from the chimney of one. The largest was a barn, the second a house, the third a pig-stye, the fourth a chicken-coop.

There was a well with a water-trough, a few bright red and yellow flowers, and here and there a pale wild rose scattered along the path between the *bars* and the door of the cabin.

Kindly nature gives us, here and there, a few sweet wild flowers, lifting their angel brows amidst life's sterner realities, to whisper of the *better home*, where weariness and care are forgotten.

The baggage being removed, the sound of the carriage again rolling over the prairie on its return to the depot at Pompeii, aroused her from that stupor of amazement, and she followed her husband into the house.

"Please ma'am, take off your things," said Bridget, the maid-of-all-work.

She declined removing her bonnet immediately, and pulled it over her face, to hide the tears now gathering upon her eyelashes. Was *that* her home, *hers*, the child of luxury and refinement?

The dinner was steaming upon a huge cooking-stove, the bread tray, covered with a brown napkin, was behind it, and Mrs. "Pussy," with her five kittens, lay lazily dreaming on a corner of that napkin, — *over the bread*, — a tender mother, to find that nice place for the five little ones.

The floor, brightly swept, was rough and black. A great woollen coverlet, suspended from two nails in the beams overhead, indicated the presence of a bed.

There were two pine tables in good condition, except a few patches of lamp oil, which had sturdily resisted the efforts of the scouring-brush; a mirror, the size of a schoolboy's slate, hung over table No. 1; under it, suspended by a string, was a comb and brush, for heads in general. A gun and broom leaned lovingly together, in a corner; a pail, and dipper for all mouths, were perched upon table No. 2. A pine shelf held a set of blue crockery; kettles and tin pans were reversed under it, upon the floor.

Etta looked in vain for the door of another room; her eye resting only upon the rude stair leading to the garret above.

"Make yourself at home, Etta; you will find it comfortable here, though not citified, like your old home," said the fat, rosy lover.

"An surely I've done my best to get ready for the like of her; cleaning the house, hangin' up the kiverlit by the bed, and all. I hope she may be plaised indade," said Bridget. "But it's a weary way that she's afther comin', sure, and her heart is sore for the father and mother behind her, — God bless her! for it's but a baby she is, sure." Moved by Bridget's rude sympathy, her tears gushed forth like an April shower.

Against the logs of that cabin hung the silver colored satin dress, the rich velvet mantilla, the big lash whip, the hired man's green flannel jacket. At the same table dined Etta Carlisle, in the fashionable dress, Hans Vandoozer, in the dirty, blue frock, Bridget Mahoney, in the greasy checked apron, Anthony Phelps, a respectable young farmer, hired for the summer, Herbert Carr, the fat, lazy, stony-hearted master of them all.

Etta received the only courtesies due to her sex and position from Anthony Phelps, who was educated, and naturally a gentleman. He had come West to teach, but, thinking to improve his health thereby, hired as "farmer" for one summer.

The lord of the cabin sat with his boots on a level

with his nose, smoking a puffing duet with Hans Vandoozer. Etta, with her black silk dress, lace cape, and beautifully arranged hair, looked strangely out of place If a stranger had been asked to select " Mrs. Carr," he would have pointed to Bridget Mahoney.

" Ah, Anthony, I am glad you have come in at last," and she smiled such a smile as the innocent babe wakes up with, on its mother's bosom.

The viper, jealousy, hissed in her husband's bosom.

" Mrs. Carr, that dress and cape became you better in your *city home.* Next month I expect the harvesters, and I wouldn't have *them tell* that *my wife* was dressed up in silk and curls, like a doll baby, — it wouldn't sound well."

The hot blood rushed from heart to brain, — she felt as if ready to die with grief and indignation. Was *that* Hubert Carr, the idol of her childhood, the man for whose sake she had broken God's holy law, and stolen away from her parents, as a guilty thing, unblessed and unforgiven?

The curse which follows disobedience was settling upon her, as a cloud which no rainbow spanned. O, if in this hour of utter desolation she could have laid her head upon a tender mother's bosom, there to weep away the first keen edge of suffering, how comparatively happy would have been her lot. God help her who barters a mother's love and counsel, for *his*, whose love is but a selfish thought, a blaze which opposition kindles, fruition turns to ashes!

Pride hurried to the rescue, and she answered, in a scornful tone, " Very well, sir."

Jealousy is never born till love is dead. Anthony pitied her, but, like a wise man, said nothing.

In a few days, Etta arrayed herself in blue calico, and twisted her long chestnut tresses into a graceless knot behind, — still beautiful, though sorrow had cast a twilight mellowness over those faultless features.

She was a slave, a married chattel, of less account in her owner's estimation than his favorite horse. She knew it; but sometimes she *forgot*, and was happy. Then, for an hour, with her white sun-bonnet on her head, she would fly like a bird over the prairie, or hide her slight figure among the rushes beside some tiny pond.

Who does not love the western prairie? Vast, green, and flower-decked; dotted with herds of cattle, calm and glimmering as an ocean at rest!

"How beautiful!" An echo answered, — she ran timidly back to the cabin, — "wished some one would walk with her sometimes. Pshaw! where's the use of going?"

Harvest had come.

"Meat pies, fruit pies, puddings, sauces, for twenty; only two hands to make them all with, and a mistress just in the way," said Bridget to herself, just before she modestly suggested to *her*, the propriety of having "another woman" to assist her.

Now Etta would have been more perplexed to adjust the different pieces of fowls, and season properly the interior of a great "chicken pie," than to have translated into her mother tongue the ugliest sentence in the most crooked language that has come down from the tower of Babel. So she thought to parry her responsibility by merely repeating to her husband Bridget's request.

"*Why*, can't *you* do any thing? If you are *above work*, you should not have married a farmer."

Etta wished in her heart she *had not*. With a face like condensed vinegar he set down the second "help" upon that cabin floor.

"Mrs. Carr is very beautiful," said a handsome young farmer, seeing her for the first time.

"She looks well enough."

"Will you not build a house soon, Hubert?" said Etta.

"House is good enough."

"But if father and mother should come?"

"What's good enough for *me*, is good enough for them."

"Please drive to the village, to church, next Sabbath?"

"Pshaw! I don't like meetings."

"Wild Rose, — who can she be?" said Mr. Stokes, the editor, to his wife.

"I have heard it is the young wife of Hubert Carr."

"I'll be bound it is. I saw her a few weeks since in a store, where she was buying blue calico. Such large, dreamy eyes, — pure white forehead! she has the grace of a high-born lady. Sweet child! she is wasting her life among thorns; her coarse husband cannot appreciate her worth."

Next day, meeting Mr. Carr, he said: —

"May I ask if 'Wild Rose,' my new contributor, is Mrs. Carr?"

" I *bleve my wife does* write verses, — the more's the pity. It isn't women's business; but I'd as lief she'd write for you as anybody."

" Thank you! and please tell her that I am grateful for her contributions. She writes very sweetly. Probably she is an orphan, sir. That low, thrilling pathos in her lines, seems like the voice of sorrow. Good morning, sir."

" Ah, yes," he continued mentally, " her heart is breaking; her poetry is the music swept from its failing cord."

" Etta, you needn't write any more for Mr. Stokes, editor of the ' Pompeii Herald,' you'd better be a making *my shirts*."

" Very well, sir." She had ceased to contradict him, and always said " very well, sir," mildly.

Etta was no longer the " wild rose," but the white lily, growing close by the water's edge, nourished by the spring of tears. Her cheek was like chiselled marble; a smile lingered mournfully sweet about her beautiful mouth, which told that some rainbow of promise had risen upon the darkness of her lot.

" A cherub had from heaven strayed,
  And deigned with us to dwell;
And we had called him ours, and loved
  The little stranger well;
But God reclaimed the boon he'd given,
  And called the wanderer home;
Why should we wish him back from heaven,
  To share our earthly doom?"

"Now that the baby is dead, you can get along without the nurse, can't you? She has been here four weeks, — keeping *two* women is expensive."

"Just as you please," she replied, feebly; then turned to the wall and wept.

"You are not so well to-day," said Doctor Clark, taking her hand and gazing earnestly into her face. "A mental fever hangs its flushed flag outside. Tell me, my child, as your friend, your father, what sorrow greater than the loss of the babe is preying upon you continually, nullifying those remedies which in like cases I have never administered in vain?"

She motioned him to bow his head to the pillow, and whispered in his ear, — "A discontented heart," and wept.

"Be calm, my daughter; the evil which God only can remove, man may palliate. I will prepare a *new* medicine now. Come, tell me about your native city. In what street does your father reside?"

She told him, and that night a letter left Pompeii superscribed "Hon. Hugh Carlisle, etc., Philadelphia."

"I hope you are better this morning. You can bear *good news*, can't you?" said the doctor, as Etta looked up with a smile. "I have heard that your parents are coming, — perhaps next week, or sooner, — may come to-day."

A bounding pulse, a shower of tears, a look of gratitude, and a pressure of the doctor's hand, saying, "The new medicine, — when will I see my dear father and mother?" The doctor stepped back, — the parents were reunited to their child.

"We understand each other, Mr. Carr; our daughter will remain with us in Philadelphia, until such a time as you shall have erected a comfortable home."

"I spose so."

Hubert was glad they *were* going, wife and all. Hadn't they kept the house in confusion, with their city ways; and hadn't he felt like a convicted felon every time they looked at him? He drew a long breath of relief, as the carriage rolled away, saying, "So much for marrying for money, — yes, *money!* When the old fool dies, I'll turn over a new leaf in my own house, I will."

Rich curtains fell gracefully over the windows of their city home, the glow of the gas lights fell softly upon the costly furniture. Seated at the table were Mr. and Mrs. Carlisle, Etta, and her brother. Etta had been domesticated in the old house for six weeks, and no one would have recognized in her the fashionable young lady, *Etta, of the blue calico and log cabin.*

"Your friend, Mr. Stokes, of the Pompeii Herald, remembers you weekly, Etta," said her father, tossing her a paper. Do you know as often as I went from the farm to Pompeii, he never forgot to inquire after your health, and speak of your talents as a poetess?"

"*Why, Etta, did you write poetry?* What ever set you to stringing rhymes together?" said the brother.

"Sorrow inspired me, dear brother. You know I was far away from you all, and ——"

Just then her eye was riveted to a paragraph running thus: —

"Killed by lightning. — On Sunday last, during one of the most terrific storms which ever passed over this village, Hubert Carr, residing on a farm six miles from Pompeii. The destructive fluid passed down the chimney, killing him instantly.

"Two servants, Hans Vandoozer, a German, and Bridget Mahoney, an Irish woman, who were sitting near him at the time, remained unhurt. His wife is absent, on a visit in Philadelphia; but on account of the heat of the weather it is thought proper to inter him, not waiting for her return. He will be buried to-morrow at 2 P. M."

"Etta, sister! what ails you?" exclaimed the frightened brother, as she fell heavily upon his shoulder. She had fainted.

"Your will is law," said the beautiful woman, yet; turning her eyes to each of her parents, as if life depended on that decision; "have you even the shadow of a doubt?"

"None, my daughter. Edward Clark is worthy of you. Not the least of his recommendations, that he is the son of my old friend, the doctor, whose timely interference saved you from an early grave."

Seven years from the date of the first marriage she was again a bride.

Etta Clarke is my *own cousin*, and I learned her story from her own lips. Her husband is a prominent lawyer, and one of the best of men. In happy womanhood she sometimes relates the story of her married childhood.

I, her "reverend" cousin, Mr. Brown, and your pastor and humble servant, have thought it my duty to preach one sermon yearly, upon the folly, sin, and certain punishment of disobedience to parents, ever since I learned her history. Good night!

CHAPTER XXII.

> "We must not stint
> Our necessary actions in the fear
> To cope malicious censurers ;————"

Mehitabel Screggs "belonged to *our church.*" She sat opposite our slip every Sunday, with her old, yellow, straw bonnet, which poked out a foot over her nose, the crown towering up like a steeple; and a stiff bow of faded purple ribbon half way up the steeple.

Her nose was wonderfully long and tapering; her forehead and chin receding; her skin sallow; her two little blue eyes stuck out like bell buttons; and two long curls of brown, sprinkled with gray, fell like pipestems over her temples.

But Mehitabel could not help her looks; neither could I help looking at her. My attention was divided between her and the minister, the larger portion to Mehitabel. She looked so long, narrow, puritanical and pharisaical; she drew down the corners of her mouth so devoutly whenever she opened the hymn book and stretched the lids over her eyes so piously whenever the minister prayed; that, "for the life of me," I could not feel the solemnity of the place as I ought, and lost the spirit of my own devotions in watching Mehitabel, while she *went through with hers.*

I sometimes thought, that while she looked so intently at Mr. Brown, she cast a stray glance at me, occasionally; and did her the injustice to suppose that she was admiring my new buff muslin, and white silk bonnet. I had met her sometimes at the "sewing circle," and found her somewhat talkative, and an intolerable questioner.

Very pious was Mehitabel; and for that I tolerated as well as I could, her oddities and infirmities.

I was just commencing an article for "the Republican," which must necessarily be finished before night, and it was 2 P. M.

I had plunged my pen to the bottom of the inkstand, and turned my eyes upward to catch a little inspiration, when lo! a knock; and *who* should come in but Mehitabel?

"How do you do, Mrs. Lincoln?"

"Ah! Miss Screggs — I am happy to see you." (Not a word of truth in that.)

"Well, I thought, as I had never called round at your room, and it was a pleasant day; I'd just put on my things and come — just as I was."

"It *is* a fine day for walking."—(thought I would'nt tell another "fib," about being *glad* to see her.)

"I've wanted to talk with you for a good while; and the more I thought on't, the more I thought I ought to — but may be I interrupted your writing?"

"No."— (there went another story.)

"I guess I'll take off my bonnet; it's kinder warm in this room."

"Of course — I did n't think to"— (hush, Ella, not

another *lie.*) And I took that long canal boat of a bonnet, and put in the back room with a sigh, for I knew the office-boy would come for my article at sunset — and taking off that bonnet looked so portentous.

" Heard from your man lately ? "

" Not for a long time."

" Don't see how you ever *could* consent to let him go, in the first place."

" He was his own master; *I* did not *send him away.*"

" But, *they say*, there never was a man *more fonder* of a woman, than he was of you. You *could* have coaxed him to stay, could n't you ? "

" I did not try."

" So I thought you did n't: but I hope you coax him to come back, don't you ? "

" Not much. When he is ready I shall be happy to see him."

" Well, I hope it is n't meddling with what is none of my business; but, I come just to speak with you about another thing; the way you dress. You know it's such an observing, talking world." (*Ella thought so.*) " That new buff muslin dress of yours, is made up so light and trifling like, for a woman whose husband is n't to home; and that white silk bonnet, with the pink roses in the inside — well, they disturb me considerably Sundays; to think how you lay yourself liable to be talked about."

" The bonnet cost three dollars, the dress two-fifty. Am I extravagant ? "

"No,—*not that* but you look so sort o' gay in 'em like — that's all.'

"What would you have me wear?"

"Well, a dark purple or drab bonnet, and a sort of a brown muslin I think would become you better; considering all the circumstances. It's a pretty ticklish thing, I can tell you, for a woman to be living along without her husband, all alone, and boarding at a tavern; and them are folks from the printing office coming in every day. Not that *I* think there is any harm in it; but the world is so evil spoken."

"Why; have you *heard* anything?"

"No, but I've spoken to some seven or eight of the church members about it; and they *was* all very mealy-mouthed about saying anything against you. They say you'r one of the properest women in your manners there is among us. But there is the world's people — *they* might talk."

"Very well, Miss Screggs; I'll consider upon what you have said; but, really, I must beg you to excuse me *now*, as I have an article to write before sunset, and cannot delay another moment."

"'Spose, then I may as well be going — hope you'll take it all in good part — I only meant it as a friendly warning."

"Oh! all right."

"Good day; — I'll call over again some time when you ain't so busy."

"Gracious goodness! I hope not," thought Ella — "long live her *pious* soul."

"She'll ring my name the length and breadth of

Mariette 'ere to-morrow; as having said that I did n't try to hinder Allen from going."

The next Sunday, the buff muslin and pink buds sat in the same place, and Mehitabel stared again, in perfect horror of the same.

CHAPTER XXIII.

> "The world's a hive
> From whence thou canst derive
> No good but what thy soul's vexation brings."

"THE Ladies' Sewing Circle will meet on Wednesday afternoon at the house of Mrs. Small," read Mr. Brown, on Sunday, among his other announcements for the week.

"I say, my dear Mrs. Lincoln; how did *you* get up a tea for the 'Sewing Circle' whilst you kept house, and when it came your turn?"

"Oh,— biscuit, gingerbread, dried fruit, etc., with tea and coffee."

"Was n't it a great deal of trouble?"

"Yes, so much, that *I* gave up the whole affair long ago."

"And my name will be *great*, instead of "Small," before I ever undertake to get them up another supper. But I have excused myself as long as I can with decency; and now I am bound to get up that supper. It is n't the work I care for, nor the expense, particularly; but I hate the whole thing.

In the first place, I don't know *how*; in the second, I don't wish to know such a heterogeneus tribe of women, of all ages, sizes, shapes and complexions; with their characters and tastes as unlike as their faces; all packed in together in my little parlor — it's ridiculous to think of it.

There will be the minister's wife, Mrs. Brown, as tall and stately as a queen; Mrs. Tuttle, the doctor's wife, as precise and fidgety, as if her whole future destiny hung upon every word she utters; Mrs. Condit, the butcher's wife, forever telling how to "try out lard," and "make soft soap;" Mrs. Pinch, the grocer's wife, telling for the fortheth time, "how *poor*" Mr. Pinch was when he started in life, and how "well to do in the world" he is now; Mehitabel Screggs, descanting upon dress and folly in general, "—— and their name is legion." *You* must come, Mrs. Lincoln, and see me safely through, and I will never ask your company again, upon a like occasion — never — good bye — be sure to come."

I dropped in occasionally through the week, to see how her preparations sped, and when Wednesday came, *remembered* to go.

The day was pleasant, and such a company in that little parlor! It reminded me of a flock of sheep in a pen, — of flies around a molasses hogshead.

The work was a quilt. Some of the "sisters" had kindly been in and put it into the frame in the morning, that no time might be lost. But time sped, and at six o'clock, Mrs. Small whispered in my ear, "come out and see my table." The refreshments stood upon a table, looking nicely; and I said, "all is right — they are to stand?"

" Yes, there would not be room for chairs.—Oh, dear, I am so tired — but I will ring the bell now, for the ladies have concluded to remain and quilt till nine o'clock." And she rung.

The Minister and a Theological student had come in, kindly, to assist in dispensing the tea, and, except that some one tipped a full cup of coffee over and spoiled Miss Singleton's new, pea green silk dress, no more serious accidents happened, than a general treading upon toes. All were in high spirits, and "had a good time."

" It's going off nicely," said Mrs. Small, as the last pair of slippers tripped back to the parlor — " but bless me! I'd forgotten the lamp." And so she put the lard to melt, while I went for the lamp.

" There, it is ready."

After a rest of half an hour, the ladies drew near the quilt again.

" The lamp ? "

" Here it is." And the lamp was set upon a large plate in the centre of the quilt.

" That is too heavy — it sinks too — won't do at all."

" I'll arrange it for you, ladies," said the student, taking up a stand from the corner and placing it under the quilt, while some one held the lamp, now lighted.

" Oh, this is too low," and seeing some books, he placed two of them upon the stand.

" That 's it exactly," said a lady setting down the lamp upon the quilt, over the books —" now all hands to work."

Swiftly moved those fair hands over the patch work; and, all things going on so pleasantly, I began to repent that I had condemned 'Sewing Circles' en masse — and resolved upon doing better in future; when lo! those morocco-bound intelligences under the lamp, and beneath the quilt, concluded to "strike for liberty;" and, sliding away over the stand, fell upon the floor, overturning that great solar "luminary," spilling the lard which was yet as soft as oil, and spreading darkness and consternation where all was peace before.

The quilt was spoiled; the vile stream dripping through, ruined the carpet below; and those treacherous books atoned for their trick by having their covers disgraced forevermore.

"That Carpet,— so new and good — *that* I set more value upon it than any article in the house;" whispered Mrs. Small to me, as she proceeded to take up the lard with a spoon.

Then followed a string of "receipts for removing grease;" and offers of assistance, not accepted; and then the "circle" dispersed. It met in sunshine, dispersed under a cloud.

"Please, Madam, I have taken the liberty to call and ask you if you know of any lady who wants plain sewing done," said a pale widow the next week, leading a little child of about two years old, and sinking wearily upon the seat I offered her. "I used to get all the work I wanted, before my husband died — he was long sick. But now the 'sewing circles,' that they have in all the churches, take in all the work, such as I could do, and I have hard work to get along, with this baby and the two boys."

It was long since Ella had heard from Allen, and she was not flush of money, but she said in her heart; as I do unto this poor widow, may God put it into the hearts of others to do unto me and mine, if ever I stand in like need; and she gave her a dollar, and promised to remember her to others.

CHAPTER XXIV.

"Slowly folding, how she lingered
O'er the words his hands had traced."

"You may have wondered, my dear Ella, that I have not remitted you any money of late; but *I know* you will be satisfied with my explanation.

"Know then, that the picking at Placerville had become not quite so good, on account of the great crowd assembled there; and the last time I was there (when I sent you the $500,) I entered into an arrangement with a company to go to this place, 'Little Fork Creek,' and turn the river from its bed, by digging a canal around it, that we may secure the gold which is hidden at the bottom. It is a pretty formidable piece of work, and will require a great amount of capital, so that I felt justifiable in not remitting you any money, just now, as I think you have still enough for present wants.

"Our little canal is progressing finely, and I hope we shall, ere many weeks, have the pleasure of seeing 'Little Fork Creek' step out of his bed, leaving us the the golden feathers.

"A friend has forwarded from Placerville some half dozen letters from you. I presume you have received several from me, — although you do not mention them.

"Then Banks has wronged you. As soon would I have expected to see an angel with black wings, as to find a rogue in my most pious, honorable cousin. But, never mind it, Ella; *you* shall never want for money whilst I live; and, as for Banks, if I ever see his face again, *I'll take care of him.* I will remit to you in about a month. I think the canal will be done as soon."

Six weeks later: —

"MY DEAR ELLA, — I am grieved, mortified, confounded with a new misfortune. That creek was not worth its length and breadth in thistle blossoms. There were twenty men in our company; and, after enduring all manner of hardships for many, many weeks, — wading in the water almost to our throats; going to our cabin every night as muddy as so many swine, — when at last we got the whole thing accomplished, and 'Little Fork Creek' walked out at our command, into that little neat ditch, which we had paid a hundred men for digging, there was not as much gold there as would have filled my boots.

"But these things *will occur* in California; we must all venture, all lose sometimes. If I had not a dear family to provide for, I should not feel so very badly about *this;* but, as it is, I am unhappy, for their sakes.

"You will not be discouraged, Ella? To-day, I am here without a dollar; but next week I may be doing well again. Think as well of me as you can. Kiss the little ones for me. God bless you.

ALLEN."

Three months later: —

"MY DEAR ELLA,— I am building a quartz mill, in company with eight of the old Little Fork Creek boys. We went back to Placerville, picked up a little dust, and here we are on Yellow Brook.

"I think our prospects for making fortunes better than before; the quartz being very near, on the mountain, and the water-power couldn't be beaten.

"You have still some means in your hands; and I will defer sending a remittance till our mill starts. I know you have had debts to pay, and of course your expenses are somewhat heavy, you are so feeble and the children so often sick. It was a burning shame that you were obliged to sell our home — curse that villain! But 'there is a good time coming,' dear wife. I am determined to succeed or die. Borrow no trouble; do not lose confidence in

ALLEN."

Four months later: —

"I remit only *fifty*, my dear Ella, just to show my good will. One month from now look out for *a pile.*

"Our mill has just started. There is not a prettier piece of machinery on Yellow Brook; it goes like a whirlwind. I look up at the tall mountain over our heads, and fancy we shall grind a goodly portion of it to powder, 'ere long.

"At the end of one year I will sell out my share, and come home with "a pocket full of rocks," etc.

Later: —

"Our machinery proved too light. We are having heavier wheels cast, in the city; this delays us some weeks. As soon as we get started again, that "pile," I promised you will be forthcoming," etc.

Later: —

"I send another fifty, for a mere introduction to that "pile." Our expenses, for repairs, have been heavy. But now that she is going again, there is n't as noble a mill on Yellow Brook. One month from this day I intend to send you a remittance worth counting. May you be as happy in spending, as I am in earning it. Good bye; and most faithfully yours,

ALLEN LINCOLN.

Later: —

"My wife, my dear Ella! How can I write you? Oh, I am wild, — crazed! *Again a beggar!*

Scarcely had I written you last, when it commenced storming. First rain, then snow, then rain and snow alternately. It seemed as if there had come another deluge to destroy the earth. When it rained, it poured; when it snowed, it fell in avalanches. After the storm had lasted three days there was a short cessation, — the wind rose, the clouds rolled back against the mountain, the sun appeared, and the snow melted, pouring down in streams.

Yellow Brook rushed and roared like an angry sea. Great timbers floated on its surface, and grass and roots, and canoes, which had been swept from their mooring, and barrels and boxes which had been emptied of their contents and left outside the cabin, along the stream.

We had intended to connect a rude stone house with our mill, and the lumber was already drawn there, and lying outside; so we employed our time, after the brook commenced rising, in propping our mill with it, as well as we could; and it *did* seem stout enough to have resisted a very deluge.

But scarcely had we rejoiced in a streak of sunshine, when the clouds gathered again; and, if any difference, the storm was more severe than before. Our cabin floor, which consisted of a few loose planks, began to show symptoms of moving, provided the logs would get out of the way; so we took our blankets, clothes, and what provisions we could, and our cow from her stable on one side the cabin, our mules from the other, (we kept them so near, and locked up, to prevent their being stolen,) and then started for the mountain. There was an old, deserted wigwam a few rods up, and towards that we directed our steps.

A more forlorn set of men than we, never trod the soil of California. We were wet, muddy, and worn with our late exertions to save our property; and we all had the stamp on our foreheads of those whose loved ones were afar, looking to us for the bread about to be swept away. However, we "hoped against hope." Kindling a fire in the wigwam, from whence we could look down upon our mill, we set some one at the door to watch, and then commenced drying our clothes.

"There she goes!" said the man on the look-out, and we rushed outside. She swam off like a duck; followed by the cabin, lumber — everything. Not a stick remained that we could call our own. We watched the mill until it parted and fell, and was swept on with the general mass of wrecks, toward the Pacific; and then — then, Ella, we crowded into that hut again, — to weep. Yes, to weep. There we had garnered up our hopes, — there some of us had invested our all. Life looked all dreary and dark before us, — how could we try again?

Ella, I loved every one of those strangers then; they were my brothers in sorrow; all had their "dear Ellas" and "Harrys" and "Tommys" at home; and as one after another they sank down, in their great agony, upon that cabin floor, covering their faces with their hands to weep, I felt the common brotherhood of man, and wondered that in this world of toil and sorrow any one could hate another.

Ella, I will struggle on. Only death can stop me in the search for gold. I *will* be rich, or leave my bones to mingle with the soil of California.

God help *you*, my dear, patient wife. You have some means yet — and I will soon earn you more — if I work like a slave, by the day, *you* shall not want. *You will not blame me, Ella?* With a sore heart, I bid you farewell for the present.

Ever yours,

ALLEN."

CHAPTER XXV.

"Rashly, nor oftimes truly, doth man pass judgment on his brother;"——

THOUSANDS live and die without "*friends*," but who ever heard of a man without "relations."

Some of Allen's relatives did not like Ella. She had not been brought up "in the way she should go," according to their views of propriety; and Allen had not helped the matter, by indulgence. She had helped him to spend his property; and did not know *how* to help him to another; — not a word of *her own.* She had seemed to take it for granted, when living in "taverns," "old red houses," and "garrets," that she had gotten there through mistake; — was out of her proper sphere; — that it was but a temporary correction, inflicted upon her by her Heavenly Father — not a life-time destiny.

True, she had gone through "all the motions;" and acted her varied parts, as well as she could, and to Allen's satisfaction; but, when "weighed" in *their* "balance," she was in many respects "found wanting."

She had not understood the secret of "putting the better foot foremost;" and crying "peace," with an earthquake under the other. *She* thought she had been a martyr for affection's sake; and almost deserved to be canonized for the spirit with which she had met misfortune; but so did not think all Allen's "relations." What was the use of telling "tales out of school?" and talking about "*poverty?*" Was n't it bad enough for *them*, to know that she *was poor?* why tell this fact to the whole world?

And then, her economy was all moonshine. When she kept house, she was too fond of a good dinner.

"She did not like to live on love."

She had never attempted to stitch cassimere, since the day of the famous "pantaloons," at "Hollyville House;" she could not cut her own dresses; and Allen's shirts;—well, if *she* made them, they fitted like a blanket to a bean pole.

Strange, that it should take Ella all her time to keep Harry and Tommy in order, and see to the little household affairs. "My mother and sisters do more," said the redoubtable Banks. "What better is *she* than *my mother and sisters? (Banks is a great man.)*

But, Ella "kept the even tenor of her way;" and if the shirts did not suit, they *were shirts*, and Allen was grateful. If she hired her dresses made, *she did not have many;* if she hired her washings she cooked her own dinners, and took care of her own babies.

She had not *always done this;* but did *now.* It was a grief to Allen, to see her "work so hard;" a pleasure to his cousins; she was happy to please — *them* of course; — or would have been if she had known then, as she does now, *how much they loved her.*

"The exceptions?" Oh, yes, "the exceptions;"

Mrs. Omar and her husband *are* exceptions; they were kind to Ella, in sickness and health, joy and sorrow,—as far as their circumstances would permit. May peace and plenty attend them through life! Mrs. Omar is Allen's half sister

Both Allen and I have brothers, none of whom would like to be called *poor;* but some of them are only in moderate circumstances, with families to provide for; others, have no sympathy with Ella *in her* pursuits, and deem her views about the final education of her children, wild and foolish; hence, she has made few direct calls upon them for aid in the most "troublous times." When she has, a few have kindly responded. She brings no charge against any for what they have not done; she thanks others for what they have. She is writing her own memoirs; not theirs.

CHAPTER XXVI

" Soft, buzzing slander ; silky moths that eat
An honest name."

" WHY does n't Mrs. Lincoln go to California ? " says Banks. " Why does n't she go ?" says his " Mamma ; " Why does n't she go ? " say his five unmarried sisters ; " Why does n't she go ? " says everybody who has no business to ask ; more especially all those persons who envy her for the friends she has won individually, and the gifts her Creator has been pleased to bestow upon her.

In the first place, Ella Lincoln is " better off " where she is.

In the second, Allen does not wish her to come.

In the third, she has not the means to go with.

In the fourth, she would not go if she had.

What a pity that, among the many brotherhoods of the world, there were not another, more important than all, a " mind-your-own-business society."

Ella knows " *why ;* " " the heart knoweth its own bitterness."

How could I with my delicate health and nervous temperament, risk the dangers and sufferings of a journey to California? How could those little boys ; one of them a confirmed invalid ; the other inheriting all *my* weakness of nerve; fainting at the sight of blood; going into convulsions if he chanced to run a brier in his finger; or with the slightest fever; endure the hurry and fatigue, the sights and sounds,— perhaps hunger and sickness incident to a journey to California, either by land or sea.

When I thought of the sufferings those children had endured *at home*, for my sake; during long sad months of illness, when it seemed as if Death himself, with his bow already bent, his aim made sure, pitied them, in their utter helplessness, and turned away his dart. When I thought how they had suffered sometimes since we had no *home;* how they had sympathized with me in the griefs which they could not understand; the apprehensions, which I might not name to them; leaving shadow after shadow, on my pallid brow; — when I thought of all these; I felt that I had no right to lay another burden upon their weak shoulders, to wring another sigh of sorrow from their young bosoms.

And if I had been an unnatural mother, willing to sacrifice the happiness, health, life of my children; to murder them by piecemeal, that "*our cousins*" might be satisfied; Allen, did not wish them with him. He was paying twelve dollars per week, for board; for mere pork and black biscuit; living upon the same *luxuries*, and washing his own dishes when he "kept house."

What did he want of *us*, in that old crazy cabin; with a few loose planks under his feet, deluged by every rain? What did he want of me? to fry the pork and knead the biscuit; then play the agreeable to a dozen hungry miners, in their red flannel shirts, and beards like wild goats? What did Allen want of those two delicate pets, to eat that biscuit and pork, and cry because one was so "puckery," the other so "salty?" Let me read to you what he says.

"Then Banks and his sisters say that you ought to follow me to this distant country; 'that I wish you to come,' etc. Well for *him* that he isn't at this moment in the vicinity of my gun! Who told them more than Allen Lincoln knows himself about his own business? the slanderers! . . . . .

"There are times, Ella, when I forget my very manhood, and yield for a few moments to a forbidden tenderness. My wife! my boys! cries my poor, yearning heart, I *will* go home, or they shall come to me. O, this wretched separation! That is the heart of *Allen the baby.* Then comes back again the heart of *Allen the man,* and says: No, I will not yield to such selfishness. What, cap the climax to my thoughtless wrongs to Ella Lee Lincoln, by bringing her here, with her darling pets, to associate with Mexicans, Spaniards, Chinamen, and Indians,—to share their pillows at night with bedbugs, *head*-bugs, cockroaches, fleas, red ants, musquitoes, and thousand-legged worms? Never! I strike my hand hard upon the rough table, and repeat, never! I stamp my great miner's boot upon the loose plank floor, rocking it like an earthquake,—never! never! never!

"There, don't you see how I can step from the 'ridiculous' to the 'sublime,' which I deem better than the contrary. Never mind what *they say*, Ella; it is hard, but they cannot hurt you. *I* shall meet them ere many months. O, Ella, my wife; how I long to stand once more between you and the cold, censorious world! God keep you!"

Allen Lincoln was one of nature's noblemen; his heart always in the right place, but hardly fitted for the scenes in which his lot was cast; and if he had not, at all times, that business foresight which distinguishes from others the man whose *head* is always foremost, instead of the heart, his wife loved him not the less for that.

There are men, too many of them, who would have said, in reference to having a wife go to California, under like circumstances: "She is no better than I am, let her come. She can cook, wash, and manage household affairs, making my life pass more pleasantly. As for the children, they must take their chance. I cannot turn the world upside down about a couple of babies."

Allen was at heart a true man! But if he had not been, if he had been selfish, and ordered me, — as many male tyrants do, — to the spot where I could be a more available servant, I had not means sufficient at my command to "settle up debts, and pay the passage."

Never, except the day I received the first remittance, had I enough to pay the debts, saying nothing of the passage money. Any one who knows how much it costs to support any family of three, knows that it costs somewhat more than *a penny a day* to feed and clothe a sickly woman and two children.

My literary labors availed but little more than the

mental training which I received. I was not always well enough to write, too often distracted with cares, driven almost to madness by the unkindness of a few who perseveringly persecuted me.

That I would not have followed my husband to California if I had possessed the means, is as true an expression as ever fell from my own, and *more true* than those which fall, generally, from the lips of my defamers.

My bodily strength has never, since his absence, been equal to the performance of such a journey, and if it had been, I would not have thus sacrificed the best interests of my children.

He who holds all destinies in the hollow of his hand, knows why Ella Lincoln is not now in California.

"Judge not, lest ye be judged."

"The Mariette Republican, of this week, contains the parting words of its editors.

"Mr. Ward, who has conducted that journal for seven years, in a manner creditable to himself, and satisfactory to his friends, carries with him the respect and confidence of all.

"Of Mrs. Lincoln, we only reiterate the opinions of some of the best judges and literary critics when we say, that her duties have been admirably performed. May her talents be appreciated, occupied, and paid in future. We hope still to be favored, through the literary journals of the day, with farther, and more elaborate productions from her pen." — *Keyport Herald.*

"We shall miss Mrs. Lincoln from the editorial chair. She has been a bold and eloquent advocate in the cause of truth and virtue. She retires approved and beloved by numerous friends." — *Mellina Star.*

"They have both done well. Mr. Ward, who has edited that journal for several years, Mrs. Lincoln for many months." — *Athens Reporter.*

"We have taken much pleasure in reading her spirited and able articles, for the last two years. Our best wishes go with her." — *Salem Traveller.*

"There are some of them."

Proud Ella Lincoln! Even the Crabbes seemed less crabbed after reading those generous notices.

"Heaven bless their kindly hearts!" said Ella, with quivering lip and dewy eye; "*they* know the value of a good word, spoken in season," and she felt as if she could take the great, cold-hearted world in her arms, and love the meanest soul that lived, for their sakes.

CHAPTER XXVII.

> "Frail art thou, O man, as a bubble on the breaker;
> Weak, and governed by externals."

"BLAME you, Allen? because misfortune has dogged you at every step? Blame you, because every flower you seek to gather turns to ashes in your hands? Never! You, whose whole life has been made up of dreams and disappointments, hope and despair; whose very weaknesses have sprung from a too amiable temper; whose sins, from unselfish devotion to others.

If it be a sin, to have been unsuspicious, trustful, generous, always preferring the comforts of friends before his own, willing to take his life in his hand, and lay it down, if called for, for the sake of the dear ones who look up to him only for support, if to have fallen into the hands of the selfish and vile, who have betrayed and ruined him, be a sin, then Allen Lincoln is a great sinner. If to follow still the phantom wealth, which has deceived him, as an *ignis fatuis* for years, hanging out her false light in the darkness, and luring him on, till he stands, weary and worn, upon the furthermost verge of the middle heights of life, *still poor*, be sin, then, may heaven forgve him! he is as the chief of sinners! But I, his wife, for whose sake he has erred, may not condemn him.

"You will not blame me, Ella?" Never!

"I will have wealth, or lay my bones upon the soil of California." Fearfully has he kept that promise! Alas! there is defiance in the expression — unmeant, yet defiance. Oh, Thou who holdest in thy hand the destinies of all men, take not the poor wanderer at his word!

I had thought the worst was over; that although a cloud still floated here and there, the body of the storm had passed by; that the morning was indeed breaking, and the time was not distant when the broken family circle would be reunited, when we should again have a *home.*

But this letter, after a four years absence, dashed out the newly kindled light of hope. I did not weep over it then; those words were of too deep an import to touch the tenderer chords. Down, down into the chamber of the sterner self they sank, awaking all my energies.

A strange voice seemed to whisper in my ear, "He will never return. Waste no time in tears; a double burden is laid for life upon you; up, and work!"

I was yet owing some little debts, which I had not paid, because the creditors said till now, "Wait, we are not in haste; your husband will return." But now, when I told them that to pay them might never be in my power again — that Allen was *poor* in California, and likely to be, they answered: "Yes, they would like to have that little debt paid, having large liabilities to meet themselves," or some such reason; except in one instance. One gentleman stoutly refused his due, saying: —

"I know Allen Lincoln; if he comes back, he will pay

'John Bird'; if he does not, you will greatly need that hundred dollars, and will be welcome to it."

God himself has paid the interest on that note with unremitted prosperity, to John Bird; and if ever I am able, or my children after me, to pay the principal and the "ten per cent," he will not be forgotten.

All men would be willing to lend, if sure of repayment; few would refuse to be paid immediately in a doubtful case. John Birds are few and far between.

Those "settlings up" of mine were generally conducted something in this manner.

"Good morning, Mr. Cook."

"Good morning."

"How much do I owe you, Mr. Cook? Fifteen, twenty, or twenty-five dollars?"

"Well, I declare, I've forgotten, but I'll see." And Mr. Cook goes to his book.

"Twenty-five dollars and fifty cents. I'll throw off the cents."

(Ella outside). "I am astonished; I thought I'd be sure to *say* enough, but for my life I cannot remember more than fifteen or twenty. Seems to me I did set it down, but it is such a trouble to be particular, when I am half dead with grief and care. He is honest, I know, however, and he was kind to throw off the fifty cents."

Business doing Ella! She has learned a little wisdom since.

My safety was in a tell-tale tongue. I always told Mr. Carver what I had bought of Mr. Cook, and *vice versa*, when I settled, and how much I paid, and as "two of a trade never agree," if one had cheated me, the other would have given me a friendly hint.

I think, too, my forlorn countenance, when I went to pay a bill, was a safeguard; for I was always thinking how soon I might be minus a dollar; and no one with a drop of compassion in his veins would have dealt deceitfully with poor, pale-faced Ella Lincoln. He who would have done so, would have stolen the plate from a church altar.

And now that those little "settlements" were made for the fortieth time, or less, I began to consider in what way I could still lessen my expenses; or how I should earn more than I ever had earned towards supporting myself and children. Mr. Ward had sold out his interest in "The Republican," and retired, and "Mrs. Lincoln," who had nothing to sell, had retired upon her "glory."

I began to consider the propriety of leaving the West, and settling in the vicinity of some eastern city, where I could have easier access to "the powers that be" in literature; and perhaps find some friends among them who would patronize me for sweet charity's sake. I thought, that if I could once see some of those lordly city editors, who had the destinies of poor writers at their disposal, I might, by telling them all about my "ups and downs" in life, so interest them in me, personally, that they would be constrained to advance my literary interests, in preference to those of persons who merely wrote for notoriety's sake.

While the idea of changing my place of residence yet floated vaguely through my brain, I was invited to tea at the house of a friend, and there met Mrs. Dayton, who resided two miles from town. She was a very pretty woman, handsomely dressed, and wore one of the sweetest smiles that ever adorned a human face. I was particularly pleased with her, now that I was introduced to her for the first time, although I had sometimes observed her at *our church.*

During the evening she remarked in my presence, that she was " lonely with no other society than that of her children," (she had but ten,) and that she had " concluded to take a few boarders, if she could find persons whose business would not prevent their going so far from town."

" I would board them cheaply," she said, merely charging enough to cover my expenses. I am so fond of society, that good company would be half remuneration."

" That would be the very place for you and your children," whispered Miss Crow, always ready to help a friend into a dilemma by volunteering her advice, but never quite ready to help her out of it, after the mischief was done. " Such a pretty green yard, and a brook there in the meadow, just deep enough to amuse the boys, and they couldn't drown if they should lie down in it. They could play all day in the care of those large boys of Mrs. Dayton's, and you could write, write, write."

" But winter is coming."

" Oh, yes, then the children can all herd together in one of those rooms up stairs, cracking nuts and building cob houses; they would not trouble you at all."

" Have you been there?'

" Yes; I have seen the parlor. Called one day with a friend when we were out riding. Beautiful parlor! Come and talk with Mrs Dayton." And we moved up nearer.

One week later: —

"I have concluded, Mr. Alton, that it will be my duty to leave my pleasant rooms in your hotel, and board two miles away from town, where a lady has offered to take me for a mere trifle per week, and my company. I mean Mrs. Dayton, who has been a widow three years, and still perseveres in managing her farm — is not she energetic? Having more room than she needs, and being lonely, she wishes a few boarders. The fact is, Mr. Alton, I am not flush of money; it is long since Mr. Lincoln has remitted me any; and I earn but little, hence it seems proper that I should take advantage of an opportunity like this to reduce my expenses. I can pay you now; a year hence I may not be able."

" My dear madam, let not any uncertainty about your funds have any weight with you in this matter. I have boarders in my house who have not paid up in two years; you have never failed at the month's end; I am willing to accommodate you to the uttermost of my ability; I am your husband's friend, and yours." Noble Mr. Alton.

But I occupied in that house two of the most pleasant and desirable rooms; and he was offered more for them than I gave, the very day I entered them; I had not yet become so hardened with poverty, that I could look a man boldly in the face whom I was owing for bread and butter, and I preferred to risk having inferior accommodations, to staying there, and perhaps finally be obliged to wrong him.

I never dreamed of such a thing, at that time, as living upon the courtesies, or charities of others, farther than I could see my way clear to pay them. And yet those *men* who had boarded with Mr. Alton two years without settling, men in business and rich, had no compunctions of conscience in taking advantage of his good nature, and putting him to an inconvenience. I was such an unsophisticated creature! Always jumping off precipices to elude shadows.

I had furnished my own rooms. When I ceased housekeeping and commenced boarding at the New York House, after selecting from my furniture such articles as I needed for my present use, I stored away the remainder, until such time as I should use it again or sell it.

Just as I was in the midst of the hurry and confusion of packing up, and carrying out, the team standing at the door, who should enter unannounced but a certain forlorn widow, Mrs. Malley.

Mrs. Malley had buried a husband and three children, of cholera, only three months before, and to me she was an object of melancholy interest. I lowered my voice, lest perchance some ruder note might fall jarringly upon the mourner's heart, and sat down with her upon the side of a bedstead, from whence the beds had been removed.

"How do you do, Mrs. Malley?"

"Oh, I'm as well as can be expected, after my great loss. But I don't sleep very well nights. I can't. It is so strange that they were all taken away, leaving me a poor, childless widow, all alone in the world, with nobody to care for me. Never was as good a man as Hiram Malley, never. And three sweeter, better children never lived — never." And she wept, and I helped her; for who could think of such a sad bereavement without feeling deeply for the afflicted one? Who with a heart not of stone could have seen *her* tears, and kept her own eyelids dry?

But I felt in a hurry to get out of those rooms, with all my furniture, trunks, band-boxes, et cetera; and although I sympathized with her deeply, I could not help indulging the intruding wish that she would excuse me that time, and come over to Mrs. Dayton's after I settled there and stay all day if she wished, and cry with me at leisure. I could not help wishing that whatever her business might be, she would make it known and depart, for there stood the team at the door, the carpet was taken away, and the dust flying about as often as the boys ran over the floor, both doors were wide open, the fire out, and I wished in my heart she would go.

"Do you take all your things, Mrs. Lincoln?"

"Yes, all from these rooms. I have some stowed away in the garret of the house I last occupied."

"That 's what I came to speak to you about. You see, right away, after poor, dear Hiram Malley died, and the dear little boys followed him, I thought the house was not home to me any more, and so I told the owner he might rent it to some other person, and I sold the few things I had, to pay the expenses of the funerals and the doctor's bills, and I've made my home with my sister ever since. But, somehow, now that I don't keep house, I feel worse than I did before; and my sister says, if I can get a few things to keep house with, I can have her two rooms up stairs, and it will take up my attention to cook, and do the chores, and I'll in a measure forget my troubles."

"It may be better for you. There is nothing like employment when one is afflicted."

"Well, as I said, my own things are all sold, and I thought, as you wasn't a using all yours, and they was all stowed away up garret where you used to live, that I'd like to borrow a few, if it would not be asking too great a favor, — and I'd take good care of 'em; and do sewing for you any time to pay for the use of 'em. It's of no use, any how, for things to be stowed away for the rats and mice to get at them, and destroy them; and furniture sort a cracks when it stands in a dry place, and never looks so well."

Just then Bill Bunce put his head inside and said: —

"Mrs. Lincoln, if you don't go soon I shall have to charge you more; I can't stay for nothin'." And I began to lose all sympathy for Mrs. Malley, and wish her at the world's end. However, I made a strong call upon my better nature, and said: —

"What kind of furniture do you wish to borrow?"

"Well, I thought, if you would let me take the old dining room carpet, and table, and three chairs, and the light stand, and the middling sized looking glass, and the bed and bedstead your girl used to sleep on, and a half a set of your common blue crockery, and a few knives and forks, I could get along."

"Really, Mrs. Malley, I wish to oblige you, and will; but to-day, you see how it is, I could not go over with you to select the articles you want. If you can wait a fortnight, I shall be over in town probably, and will call at your sister's and go with you."

"Couldn't you write a line to the family in the house, and tell them to let me go up and pick them out myself? I would not leave anything out of place, nor take anything but the things you told me I might. I kinder feel so uneasy, and want to be doing I don't know what, since they all died."

Poor woman! I did not wonder. "My paper is gone. Harry, run in to Mr. Alton, and ask him to let me have a little paper, quick." And, laying the paper on the top of the dusty stove, I wrote an order. I felt like crying for my own troubles now, for I did dislike to have my furniture, all nicely packed as it was, disturbed and used by any one. Wouldn't her sister's children scratch the table and chairs, break the dishes, and tramp that carpet into holes? Would not she set her cook-stove in that very room, and do her washing there?" But it was too late to repent of what I had done; so I merely asked how long she would need them, and she answered, "But a few weeks," at the end of which time she would either buy them if I would sell, or replace them.

"Thank you! the Lord bless you for your kindness!" and I was glad to see her depart.

The very next evening she was married — that disconsolate widow — to Tim Hildebrant, a notorious scoundrel, and went off with my property, as I learned a fortnight afterwards. I left others to tell that story. It was not the first time my heart had run away with my head; but this was the last "unkindest cut of all."

I bade them "Good bye" at the Boston House, with much regret. Master and mistress, boarders and servants, had been kind to me in sickness and health. It was emphatically a home, and such a home as is seldom found at a hotel.

During the exposure incident to moving, I contracted a new cold; and, when I found myself at last in Mrs. Dayton's parlor, I was feverish and sick. My furniture was tumbled promiscuously into my room, a back room on the first floor, my bed made, and a fire kindled. But the chimney was a bad one, and the wind "the wrong way" — so said Mrs. Dayton; and it smoked so intolerably that I was glad to have the fire go out. We had a very pleasant cup of tea, however, everything very good; and I said "in my sleeve," "She at least lives well."

Very early we went to bed, and thought, as we lay down upon our pillows, that the wind would change probably, and "all be right in the morning."

Harry and Tommy were not as sanguine of that as myself, however; for I heard one of them say, just before they passed into the land of dreams, "It is a dreadful nasty kitchen," and the other responded, "But up stairs it's worser — not a sign of a carpet, nor nice white quilt, nor anything; and the chairs are as dusty" — and then he fell asleep.

I awoke in the morning with a pain in my head, a sore throat, and was exceedingly hoarse and thirsty. The room was filled to suffocation with smoke; somebody was rattling at the stove, and Tommy crying to go back to the Boston House. Sick as I was, I sprang out of bed, dressed, and started with Tommy for the parlor. No fire had been kindled there, and I ventured on to the kitchen. I involuntarily held up my skirts, as I threaded my way along among chairs, boxes, tin pans and kettles, till I reached the fire, where stood a fat Dutch girl frying some veal, with dishevelled hair, a greasy linsey-woolsey petticoat; above that was visible the upper portion of a coarse chemise, and over that a blue-plaid cotton kerchief. Her hair was tangled, and plainly *unexplored;* but she gave me a chair on the hearth, and expressed sympathy for my apparent ill health. Her countenance was that of good nature and honesty; and, well trained, no doubt she would have made one of the best of servants.

Christine, dirty and forlorn as she was, had under that rough exterior all the better elements of human character.

"Christine, where is your mistress?"

"She's in bed. I gits all the breakfast, then calls her."

"How long have you been with her?"

"Two years — since I first crossed the sea."

"Then you like her — she likes you?"

"Yes; she teached me English; she's good to me."

"At what time do you breakfast?"

"Sometimes I gits breakfast for the family at seven, sometimes eight. Hans Schoefner and Patrick Mahoney eat at six."

Now Harry came in, and whispered, "I wish they'd ever have breakfast, I'm so hungry!" and Tommy renewed his entreaties to go back to the "Boston House." Christine, thinking to please them, took a piece of the veal she was frying, with her fork, held it up before her mouth and commenced blowing, blowing, and, after it became cool, tore it apart with her fingers, giving each of them half. They looked at Christine, the veal in their hands, and at me, until I said, "It looks very good; eat it."

Presently the whole hungry herd of little Daytons came tumbling down stairs, and then "my lady" appeared.

"Good morning, Mrs. Dayton. My room smoked so badly that I took the liberty to find my way to the kitchen."

"All right, my dear Mrs. Lincoln; I hope you will always make yourself perfectly at home. Sorry to hear you talking so hoarsely. I perceived, as I passed your door, that your room is still smoking; the wind is yet the wrong way." And always was, thought Ella.

"Breakfast is ready," said Christine; and then, pretty, graceful, low-toned Mrs. Dayton piloted us into a little darksome place, yclept a "dining-room," where there was no fire, no comfort, that cool September morning.

The children came in after us, before us, and almost

over us, hungry, ill-mannered, and half-dressed, the girls with their frocks not fastened behind, the boys with jackets all awry, and heads like chestnut-burs. Hush! what's that? The four-year-old, tumbling head-foremost down stairs. Christine picks him up. Mrs. Dayton smiles on.

"Coffee agreeable, Mrs. Lincoln?"

"Yes, thank you."

"Little boys have coffee, or milk?"

"Milk, please."

By this time, the Daytons all around the table were in a perfect uproar.

"Give me some meat!" cried one; "Some coffee!" another; "I want some bread and butter!" another; and "You never help me till you've helped all the rest!" another. And, the last complaining throat being at last filled, they proceeded to despatch the provisions with only occasionally singing out, "Bread!" "Meat!" "Coffee!" "*Pertater!*" until, all appetites satisfied, they yawned and stretched themselves all round, and then, pitching through the door, scattered here and there.

During all that *stuffing* process, for I could call it by no softer name, Mrs. Dayton smiled pleasantly, sipped her own coffee very genteelly, and conversed of all irrelevant affairs, seemingly anxious to absorb my attention, that I might not notice the shocking misdemeanors of her ungoverned family.

Harry and Tommy enjoyed the show, and ate with a relish. I, so sick and disappointed, excused myself after a single cup of coffee, and went to my room.

That fire was out again. There was no draught in the chimney; and the room never had been free from smoke, except when the wind was low and "the right way."

Poor me! there I was, sitting in that chilly room, and thinking of the comparative palace I had left behind, wondering how I should get the carpet down, and the furniture arranged,— how I could stay if I did.

Christine attempted to make a second fire; but the more she tried, the more it smoked, the whole blaze rushing out, over and under the stove-door, until, weary and angry at last, she said, "Smoke on, and be d—d to you!" and, kicking the stove like a spiteful colt, away she went.

"My dear Mrs. Lincoln, I will have Christine kindle a fire in the parlor, and you can sit there through the day," said Mrs. Dayton, with her same unruffled countenance. "The wind will go down probably after a few hours; and I suppose you are in no haste about the carpet."

That carpet shall never go down in that smoke-house, thought I to myself, but not aloud. I was beginning to feel very, very sick, and concluded "discretion was the better part of valor" till I should feel better. I sat in the parlor about two hours, and went to my bed, from whence I was removed the next day to an upper chamber, to have the advantage of a little fireplace, where the wind was always "the right way." There was no carpet, the floor swept in the middle, the dirt all swept under the bed; every article of furniture was covered with the dust of many weeks. While I lay there from day to day, the *inhabitants* of the *bedstead* came out often to inquire after my health; and Harry and Tommy discovered that there were walking *idees* on the roofs of the Daytons. O, what a long, miserable three weeks I spent upon that bed! Sometimes my children would be struck by those little untutored savages, when they were out-doors at play; often they tore their clothes, and no one mended them; and they never could eat in peace for the scrambling and noise at the table. At first it amused, now it disgusted them.

Yet Mrs. Dayton, that little, helpless, good-natured nobody, was as kind as her laziness would permit, made me plenty of gruel, asked me seventeen times a day "how I was," and told me how she loved me.

I have never liked good-natured women since. Just four weeks from the day I entered that house as a boarder, the doctor was at the bed-side for the fiftieth time, at least. A board-bottomed chair, covered with dust, stood beside my bed; and I wrote with my finger in the dust, "Doctor, I can neither live nor die in such a hole as this."

A few days later, I left her, fearing it might grieve her sadly; but she received the announcement with perfect nonchalance, smiling when I went out as sweetly as when I went in.

"A soft, low voice" may be "an excellent thing in woman," but, blended with all other kinds of *softness*, there is too much of a good thing.

Peace be unto her! No wrinkle of care will ever mar the outlines of her perfect features. How can she grow old?

CHAPTER XXVIII.

"And, like some low and mournful swell,
To whisper but one word — farewell!"

I RETURNED to the Boston House, to take a little more comfort in the way of seeing good housekeeping, to recruit my strength, and prepare to leave Mariette.

I had not now any important "settlements" to make, and but little money to have "settled" with if I had. I thought that, with strict economy, in some country town, I might subsist for a year upon what remained in my hands, perhaps longer, counting in with my present funds what I should probably earn with my pen.

I had written letters to several friends in New York, Ohio, and Pennsylvania, concerning locations, *schools*, etc.; for now it was time that Harry should commence his education in earnest; and I was anxious, if possible, to place him in a high school, and, his health being still delicate, I could not bear the idea of being separated from him. To obviate the unpleasantness of separation, I determined to seek a neighborhood where I myself could board with him, at the same time giving him the opportunity of obtaining an education.

A letter from a friend who resided at Willowdale, New York, decided me to go there. She represented the village as a little "Eden," where sin never entered;

as "prominent for its healthfulness, and the intelligence of its people;" while the school was the "very best in the world, and the prices low." So I said in my heart, Willowdale will be the place for a poor woman like Ella Lincoln; and I answered my friend's epistle to that effect. And now I undertook the herculean task of "getting ready;" for, although those "*settlements*" *proper* were all "done up," there were yet many things remaining to be done.

All those goods and chattels that Mrs. Malley was pleased to leave for me in the garret were to be sold, and those I had furnished my own rooms with, and some I had loaned long ago, about which I said nothing, because I was ashamed of myself; and it was no light trouble for me to look them up and get them all in the right place, and then find purchasers, and give half of them away at last.

But after walking and riding every day for two weeks, telling everybody where I was going, what for, how long I expected to stay, etc., the thing was accomplished. What goods I could not sell privately, were sold at auction; their paltry price was in my hand, and nothing remained to be done but to kiss the ladies, shake hands with the gentlemen, and turn resolutely away from a place endeared to me by both pleasurable and sorrowful recollections.

Promenading for the last time about the old familiar grounds, I saw the house we had first occupied, the trees we had planted, the well that stood close by the door, the picket fence over which I had often leaned with the first baby on my arm, conversing with friends, or waiting the approach of my husband coming up the street.

Again I seemed to stand there, a young, happy wife, the cool breeze of evening lifting my curls, and stirring them over my temples; the last sunbeams resting on the baby's golden locks, and making them almost as dazzling as themselves. Again I heard him clap his tiny hands and shout as he spied his "papa" in the distance; and then that tall form was beside us. There was the olden undertone of love and kindness, the voice that never chided, the lips whose sternness was for the crowd, whose smiles for the dear ones at home.

Those maples which Allen planted with his own hands had grown tall and stately, and were beginning to shadow the roof; and the tiny mound which he had sodded was there as green as ever. There was the well, and the old trough from whose trickling sides he playfully sprinkled the bright drops into the baby's face. There was everything to remind me that reverses had come — such deep reverses as seldom fall to the lot of any human being. I thought of him as he then stood erect in his young manhood, a tower of defence between us and the cold, harsh world, the life-pulse leaping joyously in his veins, the fiery ardor of a too hopeful spirit yet undimmed by the ashes of regret.

I thought of him as he moved about the apartments, and sat sighing under the eaves of a humbler home, with a melancholy light in his eye, a lip that seldom smiled. I thought of him as he stood bending under a weight of agony that made the strong man a child, gazing upon me and three little children, one a tiny babe, through great, blinding tears, trembling on the brink of the untried future before him. I thought of him as I fancy he is now, a weary-footed, brown-cheeked man, with the wrinkles of life's autumn set prematurely in his forehead — *a monomaniac*, still chasing the phantom which has lured him on through life, as false as the mirage wells of the desert.

"Jesse's grave!" No, I must not go there! I could not have borne the agony which must have seized upon me, wringing the last fibre of my being.

It seemed that *there* I should die; that I should hear his baby voice again, calling me from the place where we laid him long ago; that I never, never could leave him there alone.

It is a forest grave. The shadows of the ancient oaks walk over that lonely cemetery from morn till sunset; wild vines creep over its uneven sod; there are rocks, and underbrush, and wild roses; the birds sing all day in the branches, and a river steals quietly along on the south side, murmuring for our Jesse a perpetual funeral hymn.

So I thought it were better not to visit that little grave on the hill-side, but leave our baby there, sleeping in peace among the vines and wild roses, where the birds and the river would sing to him, and the angels would wake him in time.

CHAPTER XXIX.

"They see not the frightful dreams that crowd a bad man's pillow."

What can I pay thee for this noble usage
But grateful praise, so heaven itself is paid.

One thing must not be forgotten, — that call upon Allen's cousin, to whom I owed but little good will, and much of my misery and poverty. He had avoided me altogether of late, going his own way, buying "town lots," wearing fine broadcloth, and a beaver so smooth that many a hapless fly slipped thereon, periling life and limb. He walked *very tall*, that Jabez Banks, Esq., always stretching himself "the long way of the cloth," as I have heard housekeepers say, when, after shrinking, their cotton factory looked wofully short. He was a little man, with a little learning, a little head, (*but wonderfully long*,) and a heart less than a grain of mustard seed,— who scrupled not to use any of the tricks of trade "during the week," and could read a sermon and pray according to rule, if the minister was not at church on Sunday.

I walked into his office and found him alone. He partly rose, as if to ask me to be seated, then leaned back again, saying nothing. A weakness stole over me for a moment; I almost fainted, when I recollected that I was there to provoke still farther, one who had not scrupled to rob me of money, and then misrepresent me to the world.

That weakness yielded to a stony will, and, after leaning for a few moments against a desk, I said: —

"Mr. Banks, I am about to leave the State, for some months, or years, — *One*, only, knows how long; and I could not, in duty to myself and you, omit to come and speak to you a few parting words." I then reminded him of all the past, of act after act of his of hypocrisy and roguery, and concluded *my speech* by calling him ungentlemanly, and a villain.

He started to his feet, his eyes glowed and burned like two living coals of fire, and, if I had not expected this, should have been frightened, as the hot, heavy artillery of wrath came hissing through his teeth. His last words were, "You shall remember me, madam; aye, I will remind you of this hour when you least expect it. I have wealth; I fear not your feeble malice; friends, and I will buy *yours*."

"Mine are not of the purchaseable order, sir. If I have *one such*, you are welcome to him. Good bye! May God spare you to repent?"

Silly Ella. I had gone into the very nest of a viper, and awakened him, that he might sting me anew.

And yet I was relieved. When a woman has no money with which to buy friends, or frighten away her enemies, it is a pleasure to use her tongue freely. If Ella had passed through the fire of persecution with her mouth muzzled, she would have died long ago. Say what we may of the "unruly member," it is the "safety-valve" of nature, when the pressure is terrible at the heart's core. Did you never read in the books, that more men die of apoplexy than women? May "a word to the wise be sufficient."

"I don't know what to say," said farmer Sutphen, looking somewhat doubtful, very grave, and a great deal sorry. "These sudden changes in the wind are often followed by snow squalls. It may be the best thing that you can do, under the circumstances; but 'distance lends enchantment to the view,' as some fool of a poet says, and I do hate to see you go off there, among perfect strangers, with them poor little boys of yours, to be pushed round, hither and thither, with no home of their own, and you sick half the time. But it isn't so far but you can get back again; and if you get badly used, come back; you shan't want a friend while I live.

"Try and keep above crying and fretting, let what may come, for where's the use in it? If your heart is brimful of trouble, go to God; and if you want money, if I live, send to farmer Sutphen, of Ten Mile Prairie; remember that. Good bye!"

I watched him from the window with a sad, sad heart, as his broad brimmed hat and russet coat mingled with the fashionable coats, and tall, narrow-rimmed beavers of the crowd; and then I sat down to weep away those emotions of gratitude and admiration, which I always feel for one so superior to his kind.

There have been times since then, when I looked around me in vain, for his living counterpart, — when, heart-sick and weary, I longed for his honest counsels, his earnest sympathy. But the sod of the prairie lies heavy on his bosom. When I had been absent one short year, I heard that he had passed away.

Why do the wicked live; they who stand up in the great thoroughfare of life as cursed and withered trees, sheltering no fragile vines, no tender buds, from the hot sun and sweeping storms of the world, while men whose bosoms are fountains of love and benevolence, whose strong arms are forever outstretched to shield the helpless and defend the injured, are cut off in the meridian of life, wringing so many hearts, desolating unnumbered hearthstones?

"Lo! these are parts of His ways, but how little a portion is heard of him? But the thunder of His power who can understand?"

"You go to Willowdale, New York?"

"Yes, Mr. Brown."

"Then you will be almost within the shadow of the land of steady habits."

"Yes, sir, and may be quite there before we meet again. I must fulfil my destiny."

"Well, if you *do* go among the *Yankees proper*, never speak disrespectfully of 'codfish,' or 'baked beans;' and, wherever you may go, always think three times before you speak. Good bye!"

Mr. Brown knew Ella "like a book," as they say. A very hasty "good bye" was that from my respected pastor; but it saved me from a foolish *cry*, just then, when I had no time for such indulgence. I have sometimes been made sick, and unfitted for all business, for a fortnight, by some affectionate friend's injudicious, long-faced "farewell!" It is a sad thing to part with friends; but, when those partings come, each should endeavor, by cheerfulness, to sustain the other, more especially the stronger should consider the temperament of the weaker party. It is better, if possible, when about leaving a community to which we have been long attached, to run away as fast as we can, not stopping to kiss even our favorite "aunty." There are persons who, though really glad we are going, will be sure to come and tell us how "sorry" they are, and conjure up a tear or two, to make us spoil our faces. Fie! run away from them all, as quick as you can, and write your apology to all whom you know to be friends, at leisure.

It rained. Was ever a rainy day more lucky? Only one day more in which to pack our trunks and complete the arrangements for our journey, and now I could finish in peace. It dashed against the windows like a torrent, and stood in great ponds in the road. None but strong men would venture out to-day, and Ella could get down on the carpet and scatter those bundles and garments all around, and have a good time truly. Mrs. Alton had kindly offered to keep the boys down stairs all day, and on this particular occasion I was glad to be without them.

I had been tumbling about over the floor, about an hour, stowing away a dress here, a jacket there; here a scarf, there a collar; here a book, there a pair of old slippers; and still I folded, rolled up, and distributed into those two capacious trunks, glad that I had deferred packing until the last day, for now I was too busy to be gloomy.

My room was up stairs, in front, commanding a view of the street for a quarter of a mile, and as often as my feet ached, from being used as a stool, as they were, I arose and looked out.

"Well done; if there isn't a woman out, this rough day! How her umbrella sways and twists in the wind! She rocks like a foundering schooner. Luckily the gents have so much trouble in managing their own umbrellas, that they cannot see her. My heart! she is the veritable Mehitabel Screggs, and she is crossing the street. What shall I do?

It was not the fashion of the ladies of Mariette to say "not at home" to friends calling at inconvenient hours. We were too honest for that.

Was Mehitabel a friend? In one sense she was. She always said to me just what she meant to say about me to others, *as some do not.* I knew what amount of mercy I might expect at her hands. Of course she did not make the same allowance for my short comings that I did myself, but I readily forgave her candor, which at this age of the world has become a most precious rarity.

I honored her penetration. I might have insulted her by refusing to be seen, but my better self prevailed, and I concluded to admit her. So I dragged and pushed the articles on the floor, with hands and feet, into a corner, and, looking as pleasantly as possible, opened the door.

"Good morning, Mrs. Lincoln. I guess you think I

like you amazingly, to be out in this rain. But I heard you was agoing to-morrow, certain, and I couldn't think of such a thing as not bidding you good bye, so I told sister Mary, I'd just put on my things and come over and *set* a while, as it was the last day we'd meet on earth, probably; for it's so far to New York, that I fear you'll never come back."

"It was very considerate in you, Miss Screggs, to take so much trouble; but I hope you will excuse the disordered state of the room, as I am just packing my trunks, and am short of time." I thought I would not say this time that I was "pleased" to see her.

"O, as for packing,—can't I help you? I'm an old hand at the business. I have a great many cousins, living all round the State, and I visit 'em all, without fail, every year. Travelling's cheap, you know, and it doesn't cost nothing after I git there. One gits so tired of staying right in the same place all the while, it's handy to have plenty of relations,"—and Mehitabel talked on, at the same time deliberately taking off her bonnet,—that tall, yellow straw,—and depositing it in the corner of the sofa.

"Thank you, Miss Screggs, but I need no assistance, and I proceeded with my work. But it was extremely annoying to have those bell-button eyes of hers following every motion, as I picked up this and that, elevating that night-robe, depressing this shoe, and attending to all the et-cetera's of the affair. I began to feel somewhat nervous, and pondered in my heart how I should rid myself of Mehitabel and her never ending tongue.

I thought, too, as I glanced at her occasionally, that I perceived a solemn gravity settling upon her *interesting* countenance, and once I heard her sigh. I began to fear that she might consider it her "Christian duty" to preach me a parting sermon upon vanity, and impropriety of dress, manner, etc. So I said: "Ella, whatsoever you do, do quickly; for if once the text be taken, which was sure to be, — "when have you heard from your man?" she will go on to the end like a race horse. That is not all; she is long-winded, and may go three times over the course.

Luckily I lifted a pink scarf, and shook it out previously to folding, when lo! it attracted her notice, and she called it "pretty."

"Do you like it, Miss Screggs? If you do, allow me to present it to you."

"What, give it to me, out and out? You are very kind, — much obleeged to you. I'll keep it nice to remember you by," and she went to the mirror, trying it on. "Well, it *is* becoming." It looked, on her long, sallow neck, like a pink tape tied around a tallow candle.

She sat down again. One more venture, Ella.

"Miss Screggs, does buff become you?"

"Well, if it isn't too deep, too near a yellow."

"I asked, because here is this buff muslin dress, not much worn, as you see; and I really am not anxious to wear it longer, it not being particularly becoming *to me*. If you will accept of it, I should be pleased to give it to you. Suppose you try it on."

She sprang to her feet, throwing off the old striped

delaine instanter. The dress fitted, except being some inches too short,—a fault easily obviated by turning down the broad hem. Mehitabel smiled like a May morning.

"Well, if that wasn't worth coming after, I don't know what is? I declare, Mrs. Lincoln, you are one of the best women in the world, and I kinder hate to have you go away. Much obleeged to you. It isn't so *very yellow*, after all, and the very thing to wear in warm weather. I guess I'll be going now; I see it slacks up a mite, and may be the walking will be worse, if I stay longer."

My plan had worked like a charm. She arrayed herself again in the delaine, tied up the presents in her handkerchief, mounted old steeple-top straw, and away she went, not forgetting to say that she kissed me *very hard* for good bye.

That was the same "buff muslin" she had lectured me so eloquently upon not many months before. Then she called it a "yellow" dress; now, *I opine, on her*, it became a *delicate buff*. "O, consistency!"

But she went home. That was kind,—and I finished the packing.

CHAPTER XXX.

"To part — what sorrows mingle in that word!"

The arrangements being completed; the "good-byes" spoken; the rebellious heart, that left reluctantly its dear western home, stilled beneath the iron will, and made the slave of circumstances, — nought remained to be done, but to take our seats in a railroad car, and be whirled rapidly away.

No riding out of Mariette now; as Ella rode into it many years ago, in a big stage wagon, in the same dress she had slept in for several successive nights, sometimes in the room with fourteen gentlemen, sometimes on the hay under their feet, with her bonnet smashed as flat as a clam-shell, her hair heavy with the night dew. The strong arm upon which she leaned during that wearisome journey was not around her now; and, in its stead, two little feeble pairs of hands clung trustfully about her for support and happiness. A crowd of memories came trooping wildly over her brain; her heart leaped in her bosom as if ready to burst its fetters; and then all was over; for, with all her weakness and impulsiveness, there was an inner strength, a high, controlling power, that arrested the wild waves of feeling as they rushed to and fro, saying, "Peace! be still!" Yet it was not *her* strength, but His who fashioned her so weak and self-doubting. Staff after staff upon which she had leaned had proved as a breaking reed; home, health, and competence had passed away together; and then *He* imparted to her a portion of his own vitality, and bade her stand at her post, where before she was ready to die.

I left Mariette pledged to one sacred object — the moral and mental advancement of my children. I had no other ambition now than this; I asked not fame, fortune, or friends for my own sake, but coveted all for theirs, that these might, indirectly, give them character and position in the world. I was willing, if necessary, to live secluded and unnoticed, to toil early and late, to wear plain clothes, and hide from the sun and storm under the lowliest roof that civilized man calls home, if, by such sacrifices on my part, I could but further their future interests, and give to the world hereafter two intelligent, upright, and unselfish men, to be blessings to their country, and benefactors to their race.

God himself recognized in me the maternal martyr, took me silently by the hand, and led me forward. Sometimes, poor and sick among strangers, I have been appalled by the difficulties which arose before me mountain high, and, faithless for a moment, said, "It is over! I can do no more!" and then those heights have been levelled by the unseen hand, and all was fair and smooth again.

Away we sped over the prairie towards Chicago. The grass, wet with the recent rain, sparkled as if set with innumerable gems; and the little rivulets, born of yesterday to be kissed away by the sunbeams of to-day, bubbled and smiled as we passed.

Here we rushed past a gnarled old oak or stunted crab-tree, there a cluster of hazel-bushes or blackberry-vines; yonder in the slough grew the rushes. The cattle, frightened at the whistle, went snorting over the fields; and the birds rose in flocks from the grass-lands. We swept on through the heights and hollows, over bridges and through "cuts" in the rocks, all of which amused the little men at my side, but afforded me neither pain nor pleasure; for mine was a weary heart, viewing familiar scenes. Every traveller describes his route; every school-girl keeps a diary of her journeyings, "last fall" or "summer," in the West. I refer you to them and the "Guide Book," and step out of the car, *sans ceremonie*, at the "Tremont" in Chicago, a large, beautiful hotel, comparing favorably with the best in our eastern cities.

Chicago was comparatively a small place when I saw it for the first time, a few years before; now it is one of the greatest marts of the world. I walked up and down its principal thoroughfares, and rode along the lake shore, and thence to all the principal buildings about the city, that the children might see and remember; but they forgot — O, how soon! Children see and enjoy, and go away and forget. Their plastic intellects are easily impressed; those impressions easily erased, except in some instances where their sympathies are awakened, their passions aroused.

I sometimes think, however, that even upon those velvet tablets there is one little corner of a firmer texture, where they engrave their wrongs; and years roll on, bringing no Lethean waters to that guarded spot. Think of it, you who wantonly wrong a little child: the time is coming when his arm will be strong, and yours will have lost its vigor; his voice may yet hold the magic key that unlocks a million hearts; you may speak when none will listen.

Nothing of moment occurred on our journey. We left Chicago when the rain literally "poured," and it poured all day; and then the stars came out, the air was cool and bracing, and we threw open the windows to enjoy it. "See how beautifully it has cleared away!" was passed round from lip to lip in such gladsome, earnest tones, that it was evident the spirits of the passengers had partaken of the gloominess of the weather, and there was now a general "clearing up" inside.

As night approached, we drew a long sigh or two at the prospect of sitting up and sleeping, and then, making a grace of necessity, wrapped our blanket shawls around us, and invoked

"Tired Nature's sweet restorer."

Harry lay down independently; Tommy bestowed his head in my lap. They dreamed, apparently, as sweetly as if resting upon beds of down. I gazed upon their innocent features, fancy shaping for their future a thousand misty forms, mentally pledging myself anew to the work of educating them for respectability and usefulness.

I thought, too, of the motley crowd of restless sleepers occupying the seats around, and wondered that, in a world where our individual interests are as various as our countenances, we have still common hopes, fears, sympathies, weaknesses, and virtues; that all our countless destinies are marked out by one unerring hand; we all meet finally at the gate of death, and lie down and rest together in the arms of our common mother.

Poor wanderers all! stage passengers of the world! We meet; perhaps love each other; the coach stops; we offer the reluctant hand; take different routes; some arrive at home. May we be taking but different routes to the same eternal city! *There* will be happy recognitions, blessed reunions.

"Our Father's house!" More numerous than the leaves of the forest, the drops of the ocean, will be that family of happy hearts. Jealousy and fear will be forgotten; friendship will have ceased to doubt its object; love, that had no voice on earth will freely speak in heaven.

Morning broke over the world. The sunbeams came and rolled away the vapor back against the hills; and still we hurried on. There is a monotony in railroad travelling, a kind of weariness we feel in no other situation; and, long continued, it would be to me as intolerable as the ceaseless round of the treadmill.

A lady alone, or with children, almost perils her life in getting out at one of those refreshment saloons, and finding her way to the table; and then that filling one's mouth with all possible despatch, and swallowing the contents by the way, is death upon a dyspeptic stomach. It is still harder for children, with their keen appetites, living, as they do, almost exclusively in the present, to hear that provoking cry of "All aboard!" just as the meat and potato are mashed up and deluged with gravy, and they are coming down upon them like wolves on their midnight prey.

How often they inquire by the way "how far" it is, "if we are half way there," if we "have got to sleep out-doors any more nights," etc.! How soon after the commencement of a journey their little faces wax wonderfully grave, and they cease to inquire "who lives there?" or the name of this town or that mill-stream! Poor things! the houses, barns, brooks, mountains, chicken-coops, and church-steeples, all mingle together and beckon as they pass, leaving with them no other impression than that of hurrying and confusion.

As I had been advised to do by a friend at Mariette, I stopped the second night to rest; "for," said she, "you will certainly be sick if you don't, and arrive at Willowdale in a forlorn condition indeed. Foxville was one of those smart new villages that smell of pitch and paint, with fussy landlords, who charge every traveller as if they feared another would never come that way; as if they had never heard a sermon, or opened a Bible, and believed death to be an "eternal sleep."

My head was aching sadly. After partaking of an indifferent meal, I hoped we should have a nice quiet sleep, and arriving at our chamber, saw no indications to the contrary. There were two beds with Marseilles quilts, apparently clean; the floor was covered with matting; the furniture of the room was highly respectable.

They are wise about lights, those hotel-keepers; always a night-lamp or a short candle, thought I, extinguishing the tiny thing that the servant had set upon the table, and throwing myself heavily upon the bed. O, what a luxury *is* a bed when one is so thoroughly jaded and sleepy! and this is a pretty good house, if we did not have a good supper, I said mentally, as my eyes closed upon the moonbeams which stole in to share my pillow.

My dreams were not pleasant, and I did not dream long. I dreamed that I was away in a lonely desert, very weary; and, after travelling many a mile over those arid sands, I came to a veritable bed, — dreams are never consistent, — and that bed was cleanly and invitingly spread; it was of the softest down. But ere long I was awakened from my slumber by a prickling sensation from head to foot, and lo! instead of feathers, I had lain down upon a bed of chestnut-burs; and springing out, as I thought, upon the ground, I found myself wide awake upon the floor of my chamber. Touching a match to the bit of a candle that remained, I carried it to my bed; and there — worse than the chestnut-burs of my dream — I saw a legion of uninvited companions. I turned towards the other, and Harry and Tommy were being devoured with like kindness, kicking and flinging their arms, the clothes trailing down upon the floor, their feet where their heads should have been, their heads *everywhere.*

Now I had heard of those pestiferous vermin, that they will not continue their depredations long in the light, so I put down the candle upon the table, and, while I murdered a few of the grandfathers, the rest beat a hasty retreat.

I lay down again, leaving the light, and was soon locked in the arms of a horrible nightmare. I thought myself in the power of fiends, who were tormenting me with briers and needles, pricking every inch of my flesh, and there I lay, utterly unable to move.

"Mamma!" — it was Harry's voice, — "there is something biting us all the time, and we can't sleep any more."

The candle had burned out, and I began to ponder upon the necessity of having another, for with a light we might get rest, and it was only two o'clock; but how was that candle to be obtained?

I remembered to have seen, as we came up, a lady go into a room just at the bottom of the stairs, with a tall candle in her hand; it was possible I might get that; but how? Was that door locked? was any one with her? It seemed the only hope of getting a light, for there was no bell, and I could not go to the bar-room without dressing, — if dressed, I did not like to go there. I started for the room of my fellow-passenger, in my slippers, with a shawl over my night dress, and, stealing softly across the hall, and down stairs, was soon at the door where I had seen the lady enter.

Away down, in the hall of the first floor, I could see a dim lamp. I listened; all was still. I tapped gently at the door, — no answer. I ventured a louder summons. I heard some one spring to the floor; there was a clatter as if a gentleman was hastily dressing, and the door was opened *by a man.*

"What the deuce are you disturbing us at this time of night for? I tell you the stage we go in does n't start till four, — now it's only two. By gracious! old fellow, if you don't take yourself back to your nest in less than no time, I'll —— A woman, by George! What would you have, madam?"

"A sleep walker," whispered his wife, now at his elbow. "You'd better get between her and the stairs, and I'll try to waken her."

I had been so startled and confounded at the great masculine, thunder-tones of his voice, that, for once, I had forgotten the use of my tongue, and stood there as dumb as a brick.

But her presence reassured me, and I explained my errand, asked pardon for the intrusion, and joined those strangers in a laugh at my own expense. They gave me that tall candle, — I was glad it was not burning, — and away I went. It was their own. She told me she never travelled through the country without a little box of candles. I have profited by that information since, always taking with me a sperm candle or two.

Arrived at my room, I slew the nobility and scattered the commonalty, as before; and in the light of that candle we slept, with little molestation, until morning.

The next night we slept in the cars, and at nine o'clock next day arrived at Willow-dale, New York.

The village was situated on a bluff, at the bottom of

which was "Willow Creek.' Well might it thus be named, for never have I seen such a little forest of willows as grew on either side. Some were very ancient; their tops had been cut away, and new branches started from the stumps; others were in their prime, stately and graceful; and all along, between, grew innumerable whips. Just over the bluff was a narrow strip of woodland, which formed a pretty background for the white homes of the citizens; but the village, to my taste, was a comfortless looking affair, standing up in the glare of the sunbeams, with its three churches, three hotels, and half a dozen stores, not forgetting the "Institute" buildings, which, to my mind, had more of brick than beauty,—long and narrow, full of windows, and chalked and pencilled from gable to gable; a sufficient number of pickets missing from the fence to make it look shabbily; dilapidated out-buildings, and other idications that the boys, from time immemorial, had been the executive power of the institution.

And this Willow-dale was the "Eden" to which my friend had directed my steps. An "Eden" without trees. If I had been absolute Queen of America, I would have issued an edict forthwith, that the village of Willow-dale be removed, house after house, to the brook, and set under the shade of the willows, and the Institute carried back to the grove, to be set under the shade of the oaks. Like a horse minus a mane, a hat without a brim, a peacock shorn of his train, is a village without trees. Show me a country house, three years old, without a tree around it, and, unseen, unheard, if the family have usual health, I pronounce them lazy in the extreme.

I do not say there was not a single tree at Willowdale, for I counted eleven, but a general want of them; and yet the town is old.

We were received kindly, but I missed the hearty western welcome. There was more reserve, a wonderful slowness of approach, a kind of manner which said: "*I* am at home here, one of the old settlers, of course your superior. I will wait and watch, and if you behave well, I will be your friend. Where were you born, and where have you been, and what do you think about 'abolition' and 'woman's rights?' What church do you belong to? and are you a member in good standing? They were, all *willows*, those *Willow-dale-ites;* born of the same old roots, watered by the same old current of opinion, shadowing only themselves and their neighbors.

But about our boarding-house. My friend Mrs. Elwood, who induced me to come to this "Eden," had engaged board for me with Mrs. Gwinn, who had a small family, and was just the nicest housekeeper in the country. "This will be the very place for you," she wrote; "Mrs. Gwinn has a horse and carriage, and I have no doubt will be pleased to have you ride out with her often, which will be a benefit to your health and a pleasure to the boys. She is a very pious lady, and her conversation profitable."

So in my heart of hearts I wrote down Mrs. Gwinn

as a little, delicate, soft-voiced lady, with the sweetest smile and lightest step in the State of New York. I had fancied her residence as lovely as her gentle spirit, surrounded with trees and flowers; half hidden in the vines which her own fair hands had trained. Now, I said, those trees and vines will be touched with the yellow and crimson of decay, but autumn will fade into winter, and then we shall have such pleasant sleigh-rides with that nice pony and cutter, — of course she keeps one, — and she must have nuts and apples then, — all Eastern farmers do, — and winter will speed rapidly away; and then will come spring, and spring will deepen into summer, and then we will wander through the peach orchards, and shake the great blue plums from the trees, and gather aprons full of ripe, yellow pears, Mrs. Gwinn and I. — I shall board a long time with dear, little, gentle and generous Mrs. Gwinn, Ella and her boys.

In imagination I forgot to reserve any time for scribbling for the newspapers; almost forgot the main object of going to Willow-dale, — to educate my sons.

That was the "Mrs. Gwinn" of my dreams; to the real Mrs. Gwinn, come, let me introduce you.

A tall, athletic woman, of fifty, in a clean gingham, sleeves rolled up to the shoulder.

"Mrs. Gwinn?"

"Yes."

"Mrs. Lincoln, of Illinois."

"O, yes; the same Mrs. Elwood has engaged board for."

"Take a seat. These are your sons?"

" Yes, ma'am; Harry and Tommy."

" You find me all in the suds."

" I percieve you are washing."

" Yes, I do my own work, — always believe in people stirring about as long as they can. Lazy women are always sickly and sallow; I never knew one of them yet with a mite of health. Besides, it's a duty to work. Whatsoever your hand findeth to do, do it with all your might; for there's no work, nor device, nor wisdom, nor knowledge in the grave, whither thou goest. Take off your things?"

" I will go to my room, if you please."

" Here is your room. Mrs. Elwood insisted upon your having a front one. I could have spared the back one better."

" I *do* prefer a front room."

" You'll do your own washing, won't you?"

" I cannot; but if no arrangement has been made, I will see to it; give yourself no trouble about it."

I thought her black eyes flashed, and the border of her cap shook slightly.

" Well, it isn't *my* business, but I told Mrs. Elwood that, when a woman is boarding, and has nothing to do, it is better for her to do her own washing. It stirs up the blood once a week, and sets it to circulating, and besides, it *saves* a great deal in a year."

" I presume Mrs. Elwood does not realize my feebleness. I have never been able to wash, and never have, although I have experienced many changes, and done other kinds of work."

" Ha! ha! ha! ha! it's the healthiest work in the

world to get up at daylight and go right at it, and finish up by ten o'clock; then there's all the rest of the day to do other things in. But I must go down,—make yourself at home."

"And this is sweet Mrs. Gwinn, that pattern Christian, whose conversation was to be so instructive to Ella,—what can it mean? Mrs. Elwood has sadly misused me. I cannot endure such coarseness; I shall be wretched if I stay here, mused Ella, wondering at the strange destiny which still held my feet entangled, leading me forever among thorns and stones.

But the boys had sunk down into the cushions of the settee, and were looking so sadly, from sympathy, that I brushed away the cloud, and said:—

"Here we are,—a beautiful place, is n't it? and I am glad to find these two large cherry trees in front; they will shade the windows nicely in warm weather."

"That is the ugliest woman I ever saw," said Harry.

"And the crossest," said Tommy.

"O, do not judge at first sight! Mrs. Elwood likes her, and we may. Some persons are naturally bold and plain."

My room was small, barely space enough to pass between the bed and stand, and not an inch left for a table. But there was a little room behind it, just large enough for a bed, which, after much talking, and an extra charge, I secured for the boys. I went out and purchased for myself a suitable table, and was ready to work.

It being the last of the week, I did not attempt to see the teacher of the Institute concerning Harry; but sat down and wrote a few letters to editors and friends, and tried to be happy.

"*Tried*" — and there it ended. As well might I have *tried* to be happy encaged with a tigress. The first time I went down to dinner she said: —

"You're a California widow?"

"Mr. Lincoln *is* in California."

"Then you must be worried about him. So much vice and immorality there. Men may be ever so moral and good to their families here, and when they get there they run into all sorts of wickedness and gambling, and worse things, too. Was he pious?"

"He was *not* a professor."

"Humph! then I wouldn't trust him any farther than I could see him. A man who goes there without the restraints of religion, forgets all moral obligations the moment he gets there. By the way, I don't think there *is* any pure morality without religion. It must spring out of the grace of God in some way. It is a pity for any girl to marry a man that is n't pious. Were his parents pious?"

"They were Methodists."

"Methodists! I don't think much of them. Great many hypocrites in that denomination. They make a great noise and display, but, come to know them intimately, they are backbiters and slanderers, a great many of them. Well, there is but *one right way*, and, bless God, I believe I have found that. *You* don't believe there is more than one church *right*, do you?"

"I believe they are all right, all wrong. All err in some respects, all are right in others. There is no perfection under the sun. Churches are made up of fallible men and women. Only one perfect man has ever lived."

"Why, aint you a member of our church?"

"Yes; but I claim for it no superiority over others."

"Pity the church, if it have any more such members! Pie, or pudding?"

O, Ella! your old pastor, Mr. Brown, gave you, as a parting injunction, the words "think three times before you speak." A pretty time you'll have of it now! See how she flings that chair against the wall, and how her cap border flies back. She'll report you to the sisters! And so she did.

I boarded with Mrs. Gwinn just one month, then made an arrangement with the principal of the Institute to receive me into his family; for I had not been received as cordially by the citizens as I thought my due, and I meant to stay there till I made them sorry. Where people do not love me, I always wish to remain among them until they respect me. I put on my very best manners and went to the "Institute."

CHAPTER XXXI.

A ruler hath not power for himself.

Daily unkindness saps the springs of life,
Slowly, yet surely as the murderer's knife.

Mr. Rood was a Reverend gentleman who had been settled over several congregations, but never remained long in a place.

Always about the time the people were weary of him he was taken with "a cough," and his "health required" that he should rest for a season; and, after a few weeks, being in better condition, he appeared upon a new field of labor, and was popular for a short time.

At last his fame as a transient pastor became pretty general throughtout the State, and wherever he appeared as "candidate," the deacons" shook their heads, and said, "something wrong — either with him or his wife — no use of settling him — he won't stay if we do; and discovering that, although he drew large audiences, he did not draw "calls," he was taken with such "a cough" that he was unable to preach at all, and took charge of the Institute.

He was "Mrs. Lincoln's" humble servant for a few months, and she mistook him for a gentleman.

His wife, like himself, was an educated *nobody;* they had neither common sense nor good humor, patience nor charity.

The first evening I spent in their house I was invited into the parlor. There were present several of the older scholars who boarded with them, a young lady who was employed as seamstress, and the assistant teachers, a lady and gentleman, when lo! they entertained us with strictures upon Mr. Anderson, the village pastor, whom I afterwards found to be one of the best of men, and a pattern minister.

Self-conceited, and without dignity of character, Mr. and Mrs. Rood wished to be acknowledged as superiors, by the community. They lowered themselves, however, in the estimation of the older, graver class, by alternately assuming undue authority over their pupils, and then jesting and playing with the boys and girls.

Always culpably lenient or shamefully severe, the house and school were destitute of the presence of even-handed justice, and those boys who were surprised by a rude shake occasionally when they had not been remarkably good, were repaid for the unkindly dealing by having imperfect lessons "winked" at, and grave misdemeanors dismissed with a single word.

Harry was pleased with the regulations. He had attended the common schools a few months in the West, when health permitted, and was annoyed by the ruder spirits that assembled where schools were composed of the children of people of "all nations, kindreds and tongues," and where the little, delicate child received many a blow from the sons of rowdy fathers, who taught them there was merit in fighting well.

The time was, and not very long ago, when in the streets of Western villages, American citizens would stand by and see boys fight like dogs; yes, cheer them on. I remember to have heard a father say: "I have told my James that if he lets any boy beat him, I'll whip him after he gets through."

All those little villages have grown into cities now; strictly and judiciously governed; and the boys come in for their share of the benefits of corporations.

No village, receiving such an immense influx of population as Marriette for the last four years, is safe without an independent government of its own.

Harry liked the Willow-dale Institute; and a better assorted circle of boarders than made their homes under the roof of Mr. Rood are seldom found.

But did they learn? Hush! not they. Mr Rood taught for money. I sometimes thought he hardly knew one child from another; and Mrs. Rood, professedly the lady principal, curled her hair every day and went to the recitation room, merely playing a part. If some more ambitious than others, knew their lessons pretty well, she did not seem to know they merited praise; the less deserving she dismissed with: "I shall punish you one of these days, if you do not do better."

At home, she was often unlady-like, and a scold. There, when the thousand little vexations of housekeeping came trooping on, one after another, she was angry, and fretted; sometimes she was roused into frenzy.

She was the mother of three children; she alternately slapped and kissed them when at home, almost every hour. She had a little girl for nurse, whom she dismissed very summarily, for accidentally breaking a mirror while playing with the stout two-year-old; and she turned like a tigress upon the only tolerable cook she had, while I was there, because she divided a cake of hot gingerbread among a half dozen hungry boys, attracted to the kitchen door by its delicious flavor.

By the way, the table was just the thing to put one's philosophy to the test. Sour bread, raw beef, codfish and salt ham in homœopathic doses, — poor boys, I pitied them! Many a little lip curled at the first mouthful, many a sweet blue eye turned sorrowfully away. I pitied Ella's boys, but I was resolved not to leave for trifles — and they *grew wonderfully.* Ella turned a longing, lingerling look behind, towards Mrs. Gwinn's loaves and fishes, sometimes; but then I remembered her coarseness and bigotry, and was thankful for the change.

It was a great school, that Willow-dale Institute! Anarchy, starvation and confusion from foundation to chimney top. I knew it from the first glimpse I had of the chalk and pencil marks upon the building proper and out buildings.

I flatter myself I did secure the respect of a few of the citizens of Willow-dale; Mr. Anderson, the pastor, and his wife, I shall ever remember with feelings of the deepest gratitude. They were kind to me in sickness; very sympathizing, and seemed to realize my peculiar situation and its incident trials, yet alluded to it with much delicacy.

Mrs. Elwood, whose over painted "Eden" picture lured me there, seemed to take no warm interest in my happiness. First, "Our Church," next "Our Institute," then Ella — poor, lonely Ella!

While at the Willow-dale School, my feelings became painfully interested in one of the humbler members of the family, whom we called "Albert, The Errand-boy."

Poor Albert was early bereaved of his parents; and after being kindly cared for in the Orphan Asylum of New York, until ten years of age, was "bound out" to a family in the country, where he received daily bread and coarse clothing for the labor of his hands.

At fourteen, he was persuaded to go into the neighboring country, with a man who had engaged to procure a boy to do chores and errands for the Rev. principal of a boarding School."

There was a secret reason *why* his master so willingly resigned him to another, — the boy suffered at times with inflammation of the eyes, and there was danger of his becoming blind at no distant day.

Never shall I forget my first impression upon seeing the little errand boy. A slight creature, with a pale face and shabby gray clothes was swaying to and fro with the wood-saw.

His hands were bare, his feet encased in men's old boots, his cap, minus front and buckram, dangled from the back of his head; and his hair — bush and sea weed! — what hair! Like a tangled mass of flaxen thread, it hung over his forehead and temples, quivering with the motion of the saw, and lifted now and then from his high, pale brow by the rude dalliance of the autumn wind.

"Poor boy!" I exclaimed, involuntarily, contrasting the happier lot of my own pet boys with his.

The old saw ceased its grating sound; a pair of sad, dull blue eyes were upturned to mine.

"What is the matter with your eyes, child? Are you near sighted? "Yes ma'am. I have been near sighted two years."

I did not linger by the little laborer then, but secretly resolving to aid him with my sympathy in future as occasion might offer, I turned away.

An orphan, so frail and dim-sighted! — Ah! Shone that late November's sun that day upon an object more pitiable than the little errand boy?

Day after day, I met him on the stairs, in the yard, or in the street, hurrying as if for life, with bundle, basket or wheelbarrow; carrying clothes to the washer-woman, or bringing home provisions for the family. Evening followed evening, and others rested from their work.

Soon as it grew dark out of doors, the mistress called *him* in to "do chores" for the lazy kitchen girls, until ten o'clock; and when morning came, he arose from a hard, cold bed, to kindle all the fires in a large boarding-house, then do his work at the barn; then, if no other duty offered, saw away again at the everlasting wood pile.

Weeks hurried on, my interest in the little white slave increasing; for still he wore the same hopeless look, as he went half seeing, half feeling, over the frozen ground, or stumbling from cellar to garret, and garret to cellar. I could not enjoy the blessings within my reach, with so sad a picture of wretchedness ever before me.

Christmas; — and a bitter cold morning it was. More favored children were receiving presents from parents and guardians; per favor of Santaclaus; I wished to make glad the heart of the little Errand Boy, who had none to love him; so I gave him a pair of woollen stockings, and mittens, and a nice warm tippet, at the risk of offending his Rev. master and mistress.

Mother, there are white spots on Albert's eyes. Albert looked up — I was sick. The entire pupil of one eye was covered with a film; a tiny speck of milky white just touched the surface of the other.

God forgive me — I prayed that the darkness of death might cover his mental sight, before he should become conscious of his situation.

Bitterly, most bitterly I then felt my inability to provide even life, and lesser comforts, for one so soon to be deprived of the blessing of sight.

Oh, cruel poverty! if ever I realize thy galling chain, it is when I am denied the blessed privilege of holding the cup of plenty to the lips of some poor suffering child.

Poor orphan child! thy story is the tale of thousands!

To bear cruel rebukes in silence; to be whipped and not complain; to eat the very crumbs which fall from a master's table, is the lot of thousands.

Shame! that there should be such sufferers in a Christian land — in Christian families, even in sinless childhood.

That may have been a *home*, compared with some; but such a home as I would rather die, than know would be the lot of my own dear ones; where the sensitive child toils on without the reward even of a smile; his best acts unappreciated and forgotten.

The Rev. Mr. Rood and his family go to church on Sunday, — a fine family — Mr. and Mrs. Rood, their two elder children and the boarders, all dressed in comely apparel, with demure faces, and carrying hymn books.

But where is the little "errand boy?"

At home, in rags, with elfin locks — sorrow in his face — all days are alike to him. Yes, there he sits; the girls are out; at church, perhaps, or gossiping with their friends — he is alone — his hymn book, a huge knife, with which he is preparing vegetables for the Sabbath dinner.

He is in deep thought; thinking perhaps of the mother that long ago laid him softly to sleep, kissing his baby cheeks and singing of the rest for the weary in heaven.

He wonders if she is near him, in all his struggles to subdue himself; — if she weeps over him now, when his young eyes wax dim?

"Mother," he sobs in agony, listening for her voice;

— it is over. A something fanned the air; he heard a whisper, — she has been with him — she loves him yet, and he is comforted. Toil on, young slave; — be strong — be resigned; — govern thyself. God help poor orphans in this stony-hearted world!

Of sedentary habits, I was always the last person up at night in that large boarding-house. Often, during the long, cold winter, putting off my shoes, I stole softly to the eight-by-ten apartment, which, besides holding all the old lumber in the house, was occupied by Albert as a bed-room. I tucked the bed-clothes (their name not legion) carefully about him, then taking down old clothes, skirts and coats from their nails on the wall, and piled them on the bed; then gazing for a moment on the little sleeper's care-worn face, blessed God, that sleep brought forgetfulness. I wondered too, that the Rev. Mr. Rood dared to pray to the God of the poor.

I closed the door, going back on tiptoe, lest I might be detected by the impudent chambermaid, whose mistress might endorse her wrath; for persons harsh and unfeeling themselves, have a strange disrelish for the milk of human kindness in others.

March came, with high winds and pelting storms; the snow lay in large, irregular patches upon the muddy ground.

Other children had warm clothes and dry stockings. But Albert's boots were now worse than skeletons; and he went day after day upon his countless errands; wrung out his saturated hose at night, and put them on in the morning, heavy with mud and moisture.

"The boy is not up," said the fretful chambermaid to her mistress; "and the cook says she built the kitchen fire with her own hands; and I am come to tell you, that I knocked twice for him at the door, and he wont get up."

"Not up?" said the mistress. "Not up?" said the master — "the lazy fellow; I'll see to him," and up stairs he came, pushing the door with violence.

"Albert! Albert!" He started up — attempted to speak, and fell back upon the pillow, with a hoarse, squealing sound. He was sick — sick unto death.

They removed him to a comfortable room; called in a physician, and administered his medicines with regularity and order. In vain! as well might they have cried "fire," after a house had burned down.

"Drink — drink"— he whispered; "Mother — it is so cold — the wood is so hard — the saw is so dull — Mother! — sweet mother! — let me come to you and rest — rest — rest." He soon, poor sorrowful one, slept that sleep which knows no waking. A few kind strangers attended the funeral, and that slight form was laid away at rest; but little did they dream, who buried him, of the weight of agony which crushed the life out of that young heart.

I thanked my God that he was at last at "rest" — that he had gone to meet his mother, where *taskmasters* are unknown.

He slept well. His "errands were all done. The

eyes which had so early waxed dim on earth, had reopened amidst the flowers of paradise.

"It is well with the child;" but for the master, and mistress, there comes a day of reckoning. "Inasmuch as ye did it not unto one of the least of these, ye did it not unto me."

CHAPTER XXXII.

Alas ! sad tidings ; or in flood or fire,
Fate still pursues thee with relentless ire.

A LETTER from Allen, forwarded from Mariette.

"My dear Ella ; — I wrote you in my last that, by dint of toil and self-denial, almost to nakedness and starvation, I had succeeded in raising a sufficient sum to establish a grocery at Georgetown. It was a fine place for that business, and having made many friends among the miners in that vicinity, my chance for doing well was very fair. I erected a little temporary building, filled it to the brim with such articles as are mostly called for ; and then said :—" Strike once more, Allen, for wealth, and the dear ones at home." But I told you all about the store, etc., in that last letter ;" (That letter I never received) "why annoy you by repetitions ? Ah, Ella, I am so loath to leave the past for the miserable present ; if I were not sure that what I might withhold concerning my misfortunes would reach you through another channel, I would just tell you *that store* was on the old spot, this night crowded with customers, and a thousand dollars, the profits of the day, in Allen Lincoln's money drawer. Yes, write you a pleasant fiction, and the last line of the book should be a draft for that " one thousand. " But " murder will out, " so here I make clean breast of it — that store is in ashes. I slept there. At about two o'clock, a windy night, I was aroused by a loud noise at the door, and my eyes opened on an intolerable glare of light. "Lincoln! halloo there, Lincoln! I believé you'd sleep on if h—ll had come up to take you before your time!" shouted a rough voice at the door, at the same moment the speaker bursting in and uttering a volley of oaths — not for your ears, Ella. "On with your jacket, quick, man! or you'll be all blown up in a jiffy! Don't you know the whole town is gone to thunder; and this is the last corner of it? There, give me your pistols; — you secure your money — now for cooler quarters!"

My unceremonious friend was, or had been my room-mate at the hotel where I boarded; a rough fellow, but kind-hearted. Just as we emerged into the street, there was a loud hissing sound, then an explosion that shook us like an earthquake. It was the simultaneous bursting up of a nest of powder-kegs and whiskey barrels, a few doors below; and knowing there was another establishment of the kind still nearer, I thought, sure enough, we *had* better make tracks instanter. I tell you, Ella, I marched out with a long face. Now, do not imagine a fire at Mariette, New York, or any place you ever saw. Just fancy a street; a whole town built up of pine boards, rags, and brown paper; and you will have a faint idea of it. Every third house a tent; a powder-keg or whiskey cask in a hole under every one of them, and a bucket of water a rarity. Well, my old room-mate, John Jack, and I, hurried away. We did not go to our boarding-house—that was among the missing articles; we didn't look up a new one, for they had all "stepped out;" we didn't go to a friend's, for we had none; if we had had, they would have been minus houses; we didn't turn round to help put out the fire; we knew that would be madness; and if not blown up, we should be robbed of our money. So we stepped along to a pretty quick tune of Yankee-doodle. I felt more in the spirit of 'old hundred,' and when out of danger and by a big rock, we sat down to consider, and look back at that burning town.

"There goes *your* store, Allen; by George, it blazes nicely. Why did n't we bring off a host of cigars? it would be so pleasant to sit here and smoke, and take it easy. Yes, there she goes! 'pop goes the weasel!' Look here, old fellow! you may thank my big boots that you didn't snooze on 'till you roasted alive. Why, what the deuce makes you sleep so, anyhow, with all them Mexicans, Spaniards, Chinamen, and cannibals all around you? You ought to have seen *our* big corn crib go down. I helped get out the women and children. My gracious, how they yelled! Pretty nice bonfire after all, isn't it?'

And John talked on. I have given you the style except the oaths, and in my heart I thanked him for his well-meant effort. He knew what a great wave of sorrow was sweeping over the bosom of Allen Lincoln, as he sat there upon that rock, watching the progress of the devouring element, and he opposed to it such barriers as he possessed; forgetting himself, and attempting to make me forget. I knew that his cheerfulness was assumed; that below the surface was deep, deep bitterness of spirit; for he, too, had struggled along against innumerable difficulties, in a strange land; and when, at last, he thought the worst was over, the daylight breaking — that night his all was swept away. He, too, had a wife and children far away; and I had seen him weep over his dear wife's letters. But after all, when the worst came, he was of sterner mould than Allen Lincoln, and he knew it. "I didn't swear at home," he said to me one day; "but since I have been here and suffered so much, it seems to me it is a relief to me to swear; as it is to a woman in trouble to cry often."

Oh, Ella! Ella! Ella! here I am, running on about John Jack! I'm almost wild. When I saw the forked flames sweeping along that street, and taking my all as they hissed and crackled on; but for *you*, I should have put a pistol to my forehead, and there, on that rock, ended the drama of life.

Ella, why am I thus met, at every step, by disappointment and sorrow? Why am *I* not rewarded for all my labor and self-denial by a reasonable share of this world's good things? Why am I the dupe of villains; the sport of flood and fire; doomed to this long, long separation from my beloved wife and children? What *have I done* that a curse follows me through life? Are we, indeed, "the creatures of an overwhelming, never-swerving destiny; pre-ordered to one doom; bound to a wheel that whirls us on until it reaches the point at which we are crushed?"

Forgive me, Ella, perhaps I am very wicked to feel thus, but I will tell you all — all; then you will be prepared for the worst.— And I could not live without your entire sympathy. Be very lenient. — I have never meant to wrong you — but I have — *God knows how much.*

In my money drawer, at the time of the fire, I had fifty dollars, which I saved ; in a belt, around my person, two hundred — the last I send to you, and hope to be able to forward more before you shall need it — I have not decided yet, what to do, but shall keep on trying.

As I have often written you — I write you now — *when I am rich, I will return — not till then.* God bless you. It is because I love you, that I will either *succeed, or die* — Allen.

What could I do, but commit him anew to the care of Him without whose notice not a sparrow falls to the ground, and give up my own strength anew, for the great battle of life.

I had heard from him ; and while there was life, there was hope ; but little hope, however, that we should meet again.

He had vowed to be "rich, or die," in that distant land ; there was ONE who owned all the wealth of the world, and denied it to whom he would. — Shall a man strive with his Maker ?

But why think of Allen ? why sit down in fruitless impotence, reviewing the different features of that wild, strange destiny, whose waves roll on, dashing him forward — backward ; — crested to-day with the sunbeams of hope — to-morrow, one broad waste of inky waters.

Why think of the villains that robbed him at Mariette — the flood that swept away his mills at Yellow Brook, — the fire that came rushing down that street of tents and shantees, consuming all before it, and driving him out, again a desperate and broken-hearted man at Georgetown? — Why think of what he had been; — what he was now; — what he might become? — God is over all. The inner-self grew strong, but the poor, frail body bent once more before the blast. I crushed down all the agony, covered the well of tears; — none knew that I had heard again from Allen — *such news!*

But in vain I said to my right hand, "work;" in vain I seated myself at the table to write; — what ailed me? — the hand trembled, the brain whirled, the feet refused their office — I was sick.

The doctor said, "you are very frail — you write too constantly — as soon as I brace you a little with medicine, you must go out; — must change your habits; — your life will depend upon this. Do not write — I beseech of you as your friend and brother — *do not!*"

He was a good doctor — Doctor Jones — skilful, kind, sympathetic. He came in often, sat an hour when he could, ordered but little medicine, told them to prepare such diet as I relished, to converse with me cheerfully. Slowly I recovered; — for after a time comes reaction or death.

Mr. and Mrs. Rood were not remiss in their attentions during that illness. There is a class of human beings who are very kind when the object is of sufficient importance to attract the observation of the world. They would not like to have had it said, if Ella Lincoln had died there, that she lacked for any little luxury within their reach; — and yet if a veil could have been drawn between them and the world, and Ella *had died*, and had not left abundant means to defray all expenses, *I opine* — well, no matter what — but "actions speak louder than words;" and when I know that people have no regard for my comfort in health, the more they stay out of my sick room, the more I respect them.

Just as the willows along the brook were putting forth their myriad leaves, and the boys sat under them with bright, happy faces, making whistles, I rode by, accompanied by my boys, in a great ugly jolting stage-coach, bound for Pinkneyville, New York. I had noticed, in running my eye over "The Presbyterian," a little paragraph running thus: "Pinkneyville Academy, New York. This old and highly popular institution, has been for the last five years under the care of Alexander Stubbs, A. M., an experienced and competent instructor, etc., etc. For healthfulness and pleasantness, Pinkneyville, compares favorably with any village in the State, etc., etc. For further information, apply to A. Stubbs, A. M., or the Board of Trustees, through Rev. Benjamin Underwood, President."

"Cannot do worse!" said Ella, and to Pinkneyville she went.

She could not say as Mehitabel Scregg's did, when she talked about those "summer visits" among her relations; travelling does not cost much and it wont cost me a cent after I get there; but she knew that Harry had learned but little at Willow-dale and time was precious, and she resolved to find if possible, a better school.

Pinkneyville was thirty miles from the city of New York, and forty from Willow-dale. As we jogged along over the heights and hollows of a State, presenting much variety of surface, we indulged anew in pleasant anticipations.

CHAPTER XXXIII.

"Prettily shaded, neat and high;
Earnests of prosperity."

I FOUND Pinkneyville a pretty town, pleasantly located on a bluff, and shaded with elms and locusts; and hence inferred the general thrift and good taste of the citizens.

No pre-engagement for board, — I had grown wiser; — but we stopped at a hotel, where I deemed it expedient to remain for a few days, and look round for a home.

After a good supper, and a night of quiet repose, I threw open the shutters to inhale the morning air, and was satisfied my moonlight impressions of the last evening had been correct. There was no costly fabric; no imposing architecture; but the spirit of beauty glided among the shadows of those ancient elms, played with the locust leaves and slept in the vines.

Mr. Van Ness, the proprietor of the Washington Hotel, was a gentleman, and his wife a lady; and if it had not been an imperative duty to economize, I should not have indulged a wish beyond remaining with them. But that never-ending necessity for economy ruled the hour; and reluctantly I admitted the fact that we must board in a private family.

"A private family" — "private boarding house" —

always, excepting six, I have never seen anything of the kind. Yet, I have tried *a few;* having *boarded* almost all the time for eight years.

If you wish to enjoy retirement, reside in a city; if you wish a retired boarding-house let it be a large hotel. It is in the country, — at the smaller boarding-house — the affairs of your life are the business of all. It seems so pleasant to have a few take an interest in us personally; — it seems so like a family there, that we unconsciously throw off a prudent reserve, talk too much of ourselves, answer too many questions; and at last, fully committed, repent at leisure.

Mr. and Mrs. Van Ness, of the "Washington Hotel," were very much like Mr. and Mrs. Alton of the Boston House, Mariette. They were so kind to my children that I loved them for that; so unobtrusive, yet respectful towards me, — they seemed so at a glance to take in all the difficulties of my peculiar position, without any outward expression of sympathy, that I loved them for that.

There is in the world a kind of noisy interest which people take in the affairs of the unfortunate; a sort of ringing of bells and blowing of trumpets, about those sorrows which the truly delicate individual prefers to cover with the veil of silence. Oh, those cruel questioners; who ask to wound, and listen, to report; who stretch the poor victim upon the mental rack; then sit and watch the varying color as it comes and goes; and the dew of agony as it gathers upon the forehead; — who love to see the warm glad smile fade out, and the lip that wore it steeped in bitterness.

Mr. and Mrs. Stubbs and Mr. and Mrs. Underwood called. As friends, I liked them. But Mr. Stubbs came in with such a short, quick step, he spoke with such a quick, sharp intonation; his sentences were so precise and pointed; and I thought there was manifest the least possible uneasiness when others were somewhat slow of speech; that I said in my heart, he is high-tempered, overbearing, severe, and woe to the child who hesitates when he commands.

The society at Pinkneyville was superior to that of Willow-dale in intelligence and good manners. When I had been there but a few weeks, I esteemed many of the ladies and gentlemen very highly. They seemed to know that there was a time for all things; and that upon the great dusty thoroughfare of life there was room for persons of all casts and colors; of every variety of taste and opinion. They were generally pious and consistent, each "sweeping his own door clean," not running to sweep his neighbor's. True Christians care less if the stranger who comes in among them be attached to their *own particular church*, than if he love to do the will of "Our Father in Heaven."

After remaining at the hotel three weeks, I removed to the residence of Mr. Rice, one of the trustees of the Academy. He was a good man, and above littleness. Mrs. Rice was a pretty woman, and pattern housekeeper, who went round the house like a bird; economizing without starving her household; and making herself as generally agreeable as any human being could who was too industrious to sit down.

I was pleased with the house and family; but not with my room, which was no one's fault in particular. They had taken me in as a favor, and given me such rooms as they had.

My room was low and narrow, with one window, that in the rear, commanding a view of the kitchen door. It contained all the appurtenances of a bedroom, wardrobes for three, the monstrous trunks we travelled with, and our books. The books were piled in one corner on the floor, and the table was placed against the window.

Do you know, reader, that in some villages it is almost impossible for a woman to secure a boarding place, except in the larger establishments. In many families where they would be glad to accommodate two or more gentlemen, they are unwilling to be troubled with two or more ladies; or a woman with two or three children.

I can see the propriety of their not liking to be troubled with small children; but so long as women do not eat any more, and take up no more room than men, I cannot understand *why* their sister women refuse them place, and bread and butter, at the same price as is paid by men.

One says " No, I'll not have a woman in my way; women notice too much;" another, " She 'll always be wanting something;" another, "if I take her she'll wait upon herself, I can tell her."

I have heard them say, "I don't like women as boarders — I'd rather have two men than one woman, any time." — *No doubt of that.* I have heard them say that "women require more attention than persons of the opposite sex;" which I know they do not get, if they expect it.

Fie! for a few days, it is "Mrs.—" or "Miss — will you have this, that or the other thing," then there is a woful falling off, — the bell is not answered, the chambermaid looks daggers if you ask her to do reasonable service; and if in despair she goes down, down to the subterranean rooms, and there finds the cook absent, and the black hen in the half-stirred pudding up to her second joint, or the cat and her kittens skimming the cream; — why, if she *sees it* — she "prefers tea without cream," and "never eats pudding" for a fortnight — that's all. Tells of it, — never! If she should, she'd better "go to her tent and lie down in despair," forthwith. —Where are you, Ella?

Harry was doing well at school. Naturally amiable, he became a favorite with his mates, was generally master of his lessons, and if guilty of winking or twisting his physiognomy sometimes, not according to rule, he generally eluded the observation of his superiors.

Harry was doing well; and now I thought it better that Tommy also should go to school.

There was not a particle of "Harry," (at least *young Harry*,) about Tommy. "I won't be driven," had been written upon his forehead from the earliest cradle hour.

Kindness could lead him by a silken thread, but harshness could not draw him with a chain of iron.

When a babe, he was as arbitrary as his "celestial

highness," the emperor of China; older, although he never yielded his own rights, he respected, as soon as he could understand them, the rights of others. Through all his infancy he was delicate and nervous; and I watched over him as a sensitive plant, guarding him from collisions with coarse, selfish natures, and gradually gaining over him a stronger maternal influence.

He learned early to appreciate a mother's tender care, and returned my affection with a warm self-denying love. If any other person controlled a single act of his, it was through my direct influence. — If all the executive power on earth had been vested in one mortal man, and that man had said to him authoritatively "take off your hat — I am your superior!" he would have held it on with both hands, looking him defiantly in the face.

The Creator fashioned Tommy; I, Ella Lincoln, received him into my care, to bring up for Him; as a precious and responsible gift.

I knew that in that little bosom was placed a mighty motive-power for good or evil, and it was my duty to study its right direction.

He had learned much at home; or rather taught himself, for he read and wrote seemingly intuitively when smaller than any other child I ever knew, and then he had no disposition to confine himself farther to study.

But now, circumstances being so favorable for him to begin to be mentally disciplined, I said: "We will see, commencing gently." And what I have now written, I ventured to say to Alexander Stubbs, A. M., principal of the Pinkneyville Academy.

"You will pardon my maternal solicitude, sir — I think he will give you no trouble; if he should, you will please send him home to me. I would esteem it a favor if you will not repeat what I have said; only name it to his teacher in the primary department; the children need not know it, to create jealousy and dislike."

"Certainly, madam; it is proper to deal with various temperaments and dispositions in various ways. I understand you perfectly, and appreciate your solicitude for a child so delicate and peculiar. I approve of your course; you may depend upon my co-operation. Good morning, madam."

But the beaver settled down upon his head so hastily; the good words came out so nervously; and he walked away with such a martial tread, I trembled to think of what I had done.

About ten days afterwards, my door was opened violently, and in rushed Tommy.

"Mother, I hate him! I can't help it — I do! Guy! he couldn't catch me; I outran him. You won't send me back, will you? Please let me study and recite to you?"

"What is the matter? why are you here?"

"He struck me — he did!" He was deathly pale, and sank into a chair.

"Who struck you?"

"Mr. Stubbs."

"What did you do then?"

"I struck him back, hard as I could."

"My son, I am very, very sorry."

"I couldn't help it."

"Yes, you could have helped it; but tell me all about it."

"Well, he was in that room; and I had my lesson, every word of it; so I was tired, and lay there with my head upon the desk. He said, 'Get up, Tommy;' we don't allow boys to go to bed in this Academy." Then the boys all looked that way, and some of them laughed; and he came right there and hit me with a book, on my head; and then I——"

"Never mind telling more now; I am going out to walk, come with me."

"Mother, I am not well."

"Oh, yes you are, pretty well; come, we shall both feel better for a walk." And *we did* go.

My time was worth so much to me that I hardly knew how to hear lessons at home; but after that I did, while I remained at Pinkneyville.

Not a word upon that subject was spoken between Mr. Stubbs and myself until the day I left him for another school; then I reminded him of the promise he had so summarily broken.

"But, madam, you will ruin your child."

"If I do, none shall help me."

But I am not gone yet. Harry was doing finely, the place and people I liked, and there I remained until fall.

There is much monotony in country life, more particularly to those who have no home.

When the fruit came, and the blackberries and whortleberries ripened, we made frequent excursions to the neighboring woods; and there was a brook not far away, shaded with tall pines and hemlock: there we went to fish and read — Tommy to fish, I to read. He talked of being a soldier and statesman; a traveller in foreign lands; a sea-captain, a king. I thought of the checkered past, the unrevealed future; of my own abitious dreams in girlhood, never fostered, but rudely met with jests and words of discouragement by a mistaken father. I remembered how miserable I then was to be told *this* or *that* could never be attained by me, little fragile Ella Lee; and now, when I recognized the same spirit in the little bosom before me, I uttered no cold, sarcastic words, but said: "Yes, you may yet become both *great* and *good*. Cultivate first the intellect; learn first the secret of self-government, and in good time you may both teach and govern others."

I dared not talk of the sorrows and uncertainties of life; nor tell him then the story of my own crushed hopes; young life's faded dreams. I saw and respected the fire which God had kindled in that young dreamer's bosom, nor dared to cast upon its glowing face one single cooling drop.

I loved Harry, with his amiable temper and evenly balanced mental powers — he never grieved me; but others loved him too; he had many, many friends. Tommy needed my more tender care because *I, only*, knew him well. *I, only*, appreciated beneath the outward adamant the deep, beautiful undercurrent which in God's good time might go forth as a refreshing stream to purify and bless mankind.

Dear Mrs. Rice, how kind she was. She never looked

like vinegar when Ella came to the breakfast table, after a hot summer night, almost too feeble to breathe; she never rattled the tea set, or overturned the gravy, because the poor invalid's fitful appetite refused this or that, or she called for 'something tart,' three times a day. No, there was many a tit-bit for me alone; the first ripe peach was mine; the first strawberry. Often, oh! how often, she asked 'if I liked something she had not,' and if I answered 'yes,' the next meal, there it was. May she never need a friend, never know the sorrows that I have known, when a stranger and an invalid, conscious that none cared for me.

"My husband has contracted to prepare the 'fourth of July dinner,' said my friend Mrs. Van Ness of the 'Washington,' and I invite you now to come, with your boys, and dine with us. Mr. Van Ness will see you safely to the table, and wait upon you; and although *you* may not care particularly to be there, I am sure the boys will be delighted." Kind Mr. and Mrs. Van Ness.

We went '*to the fourth of July*,' so said the children, as they all arrayed themselves in their best, and marched towards the church, where the Rev. Mr. Underwood made a great speech about 'liberty and union, anti-slavery, the extravagance of American ladies, and the best method of bringing up babies in the way they should go.'

Such an oration! shade of Demosthenes! His lungs were as substantial as a blacksmith's bellows. There he stood, blow, blow, blow, himself as cool as a cu-

cumber, while we were all in the last stage of suffocation.

Think of it! one common-sized country church, scantily supplied with windows; and inside, right in front of the pulpit, is erected a stage for the accommodation of the greater lights, orator, reader, etc.; then the band of musicians in front of that; on either side of the aisle, a square battalion of moustaches, epauletts and feathers; then a promiscuous mass of silks, muslins, gold ear-rings, pea-jackets, pantalettes and babies; not a breath of air except the sighs of disconsolate lovers and that manufactured by the fans; and then think of that interminable burst of eloquence!

Oh, dear; if there *had* been a way of escape! As well might a wedge have walked out of a back-log before the final splitting. But 'nought terrestrial lasts forever,' and just as we were all in danger of losing our patriotism, and wishing 'liberty' and the Rev. orator himself, back into the shades of barbarism, he rounded the last period.

The table was spread under an awning of green boughs, in the rear of the hotel; and amidst the roar of *artillery* and the beating of drums, the long procession marched from the church to the Washington.

"We should have dined at one, now it is past two; that oration was a mile too long," said Mr. Van Ness, as he helped me to a beautiful joint of roast pig; "and a cloud is rising — I fear it may rain."

I cast my eye adown the long row of knives and forks, as they commenced their earnest work, and thought what a little harvest of shillings my friend, the landlord, was reaping now; when lo! there arose a gust of wind, carrying away the arbor, and scattering the guests hither and thither. The dust settled like a cloud upon the unlucky viands; the rain came down in torrents; and tumblers, pitchers, platters, dishes, sauces and gravies, pigs and turkeys; the innumerable items of a 'fourth of July' dinner, were all mingled, and broken, and rolled together like the sweepings in the wake of an earthquake.

The frightened crowd had turned en-masse into the house, until every room and nook was full. There they stood, with dirty faces, and dinnerless, until that shower abated; when they made a forlorn rush for their homes, or the houses of friends.

Behind the kitchen was a wee bit of a room, into which Mr. Van Ness had piloted Ella and her boys as they rushed in with the first wave of humanity; and there they dined, thankful for themselves, sorry for the less fortunate.

A wofully unprofitable dinner was that to my friend Van Ness; and all because the Rev. Mr. Underwood liked to hear himself talk; for if he had shut his mouth after a reasonable time, one table-full, at least, would have dined before the shower.

CHAPTER XXXIV.

Uncertainty, thou worse than real ill.
  Whose every moment is an age of grief,
To real woe we oppose the stubborn will,
  But for thy sickness there is no relief.
Better to meet and wrestle with our doom,
And die or conquer, than in feverish gloom
  To linger on in life.

My health had become as an empty shell. I longed to go South; but had not the means to justify my undertaking so long a journey.

Oh, when life itself seems to depend upon seeking more genial skies, it is hard to be chained to a meagre purse,—to practise a narrow economy,—oh, the heart sickness of uncertainty! Summer mellowed into autumn, yet I lingered there. I sometimes feared that both mind and body would yield to outward influences, and a cold apathy settle upon my energies forever.

"A friend," cried the poor tired heart incessantly—"friends, such as I have had in days gone by." In vain I wrote, read, walked,—there I found no kindred spirit—*there* was no one who loved me for the sorrows I had met, for the difficulties I had conquered; none to whom I might confide the grief now crushing me into the very dust; that anguish hidden from the world, drinking up the very life stream at the fountain head.

"A friend!" God, whose eye is upon every leaf and line of my past history, knows how tenaciously I have sometimes clung to the hand of friendship, but to have it rudely withdrawn; then with what an overwhelming bitterness of spirit I resigned it; — bitterly, yet proudly.

I think of one, who, while I was yet but as a creeping babe in literature, smiled, and took me by the hand, and said, "write on, you are talented, success must ultimately crown your efforts. I am yours, with heart and hand, to speak a good word for you in season and out of season. Let us be friends through life; write me often when you are far away." When the dark hours came, when sick and alone, surrounded by unsympathizing spirits, *I wrote*, — where was *he* then? A few unmeaning words, an empty promise in reply, a dashing envelop, and *he* was gone again.— *Ella was poor.*

Little Jamie Huff, a sweet child in his eighth year, came to my room sometimes with Tommy. I was pleased to have those little ones come in, who were far away from home, that we might beguile away a few tedious hours of their boarding-school lives, by manifesting in their welfare a real interest, and conversing with them pleasantly.

Jamie had large blue, dewy, eyes, and the long heavy lashes swept over a cheek as fair as an infant's; soft and fair, with a faint peach-like bloom. His forehead was very high, and the light brown hair fell lightly over it in wavy curls; his mouth and chin were beautifully moulded; his hands tiny and soft.

He was one of those early-gifted, precocious little ones, who seem to have "not long" written upon their temples, — "not long for earth." Why was he there? the son of wealthy parents, an only child?

For health, pure country air, to be educated away from the noise and bustle, and evil influences of the city.

Then why was not his mother there, to guard his delicate frame from extremes of heat and cold; to see to it that his intellect was not overtasked by unreasonably long lessons; to walk and ride out with him; to pillow his young head on the maternal bosom, when it ached with weariness, or swelled almost to bursting with the consciousness of real or imaginary wrongs?

She was wealthy; her home but a few miles away; and yet she only came to Pinkneyville when the session closed. Oh, yes, she thought to "make a man of him," by thus casting him off upon the tender sympathies of strangers.—"Mr. Stubbs was a good man — a thorough teacher — governed his school admirably— that was the place for Jamie"— all alone. Unfeeling mother! — cold, cruel father!

"Is n't it nice to have your mamma always with you, Tommy; and so kind to you?" he said one day as he came in at noon; for his boarding house was but a few steps from ours. "My mamma is very pretty; and she wears flounces, and ribbons in her hair, but she does n't want *me* with her — she says children are so troublesome. Papa pats me on the cheek when I go home vacations, and says: "Why Jamie, how you grow," and that is all he says. They go to the theatre and to the balls, and have great parties at home."

The bell rang for dinner.

"Come, Jamie, eat with us — Mrs. Rice will be pleased to have you, and I'll go home with you, and make all right with Mrs. Jeffries, where you board."

Mr. Rice being absent, there was plenty of room, and Jamie was delighted to be there.

"Why, what good sweet bread — ours is heavy and sour; and these potatoes are all jammed, with butter in 'em — I wish I could board *here*," — and he ate heartily, talking all the while.

"Well, can't you?" said Harry, liking to hear his tell-tale little tongue.

"I spose not. When mother comes, vacations, things is good enough, and she does'nt believe what I tell her about the sour bread, and old bread puddings — that's sour too. She thinks I only want to go home."

"I thank you," said he, when he had finished, and I went home with him as I had promised.

"I think Mr. Stubbs is unkind to little Jamie Huff, and so is Mr. Burr, the assistant," said Harry.

"Why; how unkind?"

"Well, if he does not have his lessons as well as the rest of his class, he keeps him in nights, and if he does n't get them in an hour, he ferules him."

"Ferules *him* — Jamie? — that dear little creature — as innocent as a babe: and so feeble."

"He does — I am glad you took Tommy out of school; but I contrive to please him, although I cannot like him. Mr. Burr is always *setting him* up against some one; and then he comes in and watches, and the first chance he has to get angry, down he pounces on him."

"Little Jamie Huff is sick; he has a fever, and the doctor has written to his parents."

"Why, Harry!"

"He just lies there crying for his mother, and saying she does not love him, not to come, — and they will be here to-morrow in a carriage to take him home."

"Do you think our Jamie will be sick long, doctor?" said the fashionable mother, as they wrapped him in a blanket and laid him on the bed in the bottom of the coach.

"Yes, madam; very long; till he goes up."— and he pointed heavenwards. She grew death-like pale.

"Hush!" doctor, why alarm his mother?" said the stolid father, "I never believe in borrowing trouble," and they seated themselves in the coach.

"Good bye, boys, Good bye, Mrs. Lincoln, Mrs. Rice, and everybody. If ever I come back, I want to board with Mrs. Rice, mamma."

"You can, dear."

"I handled them roughly," said Doctor Bell as they drove away. "That child well nursed and cared for at home, his little brain not burdened with Arithmetic and Latin, might have lived to manhood — now he is consumptive — indirectly *they* have murdered him. I know them! — they are as heartless as two bricks — that child, only eight, has been away from them two years."

Jamie suffered on three months, and found the *better home.*

Little "Georgie," the doctor's baby, was a sweet

creature of a few months, with great earnest eyes, and a pure brow.

Never was father fonder of a darling boy. As often as he went out he kissed his velvet cheek; and no matter how late he returned, "Georgie" was inquired for — he had not been forgotten during that tedious round.

I had become much attached to Doctor Bell, and his wife, whose residence was next door to that of Mr. Rice, and called upon them often, without ceremony.

"Please Ma'am, the baby's worse, and mistress wishes you to come in and sit with her till the doctor returns."

"Yes, Ann, I will be in directly."

Stillness and gloom rested upon the household; shoes were left at the door; latches softly raised; no voice rose above a whisper.

Spasm followed spasm; the veins stood out conspicuously in the little white neck; the tiny fingers were clenched into the palms of the baby hand; — could that be "Georgie?"

Where was the doctor's skill? was it lost in the solicitude of the father?

No, with a heart full of grief, he was yet the wise physician, but he could not avert God's stroke; the lifted rod must fall.

Slowly it fell, yet with a crushing weight. The child lived on three weeks. The young mother scarcely left it during all that time, for rest or sleep; the father hurried through his daily round to get back to the home sufferer; for the truly good physician forgets none whose lives are in his care, in the selfishness of individual sorrow.

It was a sickly season, and one or more prostrated with fever in every house; but "Georgie" was such a little favorite, he was never forgotten.

Sometimes for a few hours, the spasms ceased, the blue eyes turned lovingly to his natural protectors, and in his own pretty way he asked for food — or slept sweetly upon his mother's bosom. At such times hope revived, and we all thought he might yet live — then a change — a moan of suffering — the contracted limb — and we again despaired.

For three days he had seemed better; sleeping calmly, awaking naturally, eating with apparent relish. The mother who had been apparently resigned to give him up to God, was now encouraged, and doubly anxious for his recovery; and the doctor passed in and out with the olden smile, thinking the little pet would live.

I was alone with Mrs. Bell, and she said, "if Georgie recovers, I am going to take him to see his grandparents, who have never seen him. I sent them his miniature a few days since — dear little one."

A low moan and slight motion drew her attention. She bent over him for a moment, then said, "he is worse — he will never be well — oh that his father would return!"

How soon the fond mother detects the slightest change in the sick babe. It seemed as if some attendant angel whispered in her ear, "the time has come — put on the girdle of your strength — death comes to claim your child."

That night I watched with them alone. Mrs. Bell was exhausted. She felt that strange weariness which steals over the frame when hope first dies out from the breast; yet still she clung resolutely to the innocent sufferer, until we almost forced her from the room. Poor young mother! how wildly she begged to stay, saying, "how can I leave him *now?* — not *now* — oh, do not tell me to leave him *now*."

At last, promising to call her up if any change came over him, we prevailed on her to retire.

We bathed the little restless head, wet the parched lips; nay, even administered medicine after life and death were struggling together for the mastery.

Sometimes, for a moment, the doctor slept; for he was in feeble health, and utterly worn down with fatigue; and then I was alone with death, yet in the least terrific form; — then, except the quick, short respiration of the babe, and the deep hard breathing of the tired man, there was no sound.

Past midnight and a fearful change. He moved his little head, rolled as if in extreme agony; his fingers were so tightly clenched we could not open them.

"How can I see this?" said the unhappy father.

I hoped he was unconscious of pain, — for there are persons who believe the throes of death are but muscular imitations of agony, after the nervous power to suffer is removed.

Past two — and Mrs. Bell was again bending over him. "Can this be our own little Georgie!" she uttered mournfully.

Then came up, with a deep groan, from the tried heart of manhood, "Georgie — sweet Georgie!"

Those sobbing breaths — so far between, had ceased — we felt for his little fluttering heart — it was still. He was in heaven.

We nerved ourselves now, expecting a wild wail of grief from the stricken mother; but in this were disappointed. She gazed upon him in silence for some minutes, then said:

"He is gone — it is God's will, and he knows what is best. Mrs. Lincoln, if you are willing, I wish to dress the little corse myself, and lay it out."

That young mother "laid out" the little sleeper, moving him this way and that, upon the pillows, until satisfied with the position of his head, then called her husband, saying: "Pa, come and see all that is left of dear little Georgie," then calmly turned away.

Many friends were there ready to remove him from the winding sheet, to the coffin; but she herself lifted him from that temporary couch, and placed him in the narrow house, merely remarking, "if it had been God's will I would gladly have kept my child, but He knows what is best."

It is indeed good for us to go to the house of mourning, if there we learn a lesson of submission to our Father's will; for it is a dying world, and sooner or later, the rod of chastisement must fall heavily upon us all. Let us not say we cannot bear it; but bowing submissively to his will, repeat the words of that young Christian mother. "God knows what is best for us."

CHAPTER XXXV.

Roving ever, roving ever,
  Climbing mountains, crossing streams,
Peace we seek to find it never,
  Save in hope's delusive dreams,

WINCHESTER, Pa.

"MY DEAR MRS. LINCOLN — I left Mariette three months since, and have been visiting my friends in this vicinity. My design in leaving the West for a time was to educate my two boys. I have at last 'finished up' my visiting, and settled for the present at this place, where I am satisfied the school is excellent; and, other advantages as a residence equally desirable.

"It would be a pleasure to have you with me; and I think the little folks would enjoy it very much. Let me hear from you upon this subject, if you please.

"Yours, etc.,

"HENRIETTA BURGESS."

"There is a sensible letter; — not a tissue of nonsense about 'Eden' and people who are 'good examples;' but a mere wish expressed, that an old friend might find a home where she is; and her children have the advantages of education, which she esteems as very fair. I like long letters when writers know what they are talking about, but it is a great pleasure to have them stop when they *get through*."

Winchester is a day's ride from New York, — half a day's ride from Philadelphia. I will go there — the autumn is now far advanced, and the sooner the better.

Then came another packing time; another course of "good byes;" another wearisome jaunt for poor, world-weary Ella. But another link was to be added to her destiny by the Invisible Hand; — the strong undercurrent swept her life-bark darkly on; — and seeming to take her own path over the changeful surface-waves, she felt that she was led.

Winchester lies sweetly nestled among the hills, on both sides of the Susquehanna.

We arrived there just as the sun was sinking behind the western slope, and casting a tenfold deeper flood of glory over the gorgeous leaves of autumn.

As we descended the mountain on the eastern side, gazing down upon its white cottages and neat door yards, I was impressed with its great beauty and the stillness of its broad, cleanly streets.

There rolled along leisurely a family carriage, here paced along a lady and gentleman on horseback; yonder played a group of children; farther on came hurrying homeward the well wonted family cows.

"Winchester High School," was engraved in gilt upon the front of a respectable stone edifice; the declining sunbeams reflected upon those large, distinct letters; — they glowed like burning coals; the church spire seemed to flash, and blaze like a long fiery arm; the river glimmered as it rolled like molten lead; and then the sunset glory faded into twilight's first gauzy dimness.

To the lovers of rural life Winchester is a second Eden.

Softly blends its light and shade, brown and green; in chastened grandeur steals along the beautiful Susquehanna; the hills slope gently away until lost in the distance; and we look upon nature unawed by her wilder contrasts, — the heart softened into love for the Creator of such dream-like beauty.

But let the restless, adventurous spirit stand aloof! — there is nothing to charm him in a scene like this; — he would die of ennui. He who listens with zest for the stroke of the builder's hammer, the snorting of the "iron horse," but not for the carol of the robin, should come not hither.

There are men who would starve both body and soul in the midst of all this luxury of nature; who would look out from the windows of their cottage homes, and curse the very vines which clustered lovingly around them; and the stillness which permitted them to hear the buzzing of the tiniest insect; and meet the placid countenances of more contented neighbors with the scowl of contempt.

Are your sentient nerves forever on the rack in the crowded city, go to Winchester and rest, — is your very breath of life the fannings of the agitations around you, *go not* there.

Men have two natures. One ponders, defers, and feels along his way; another fixes high the goal to which he *would* attain, and dashes wildly on, unawed by difficulties or dangers, till death cuts him down as he runs.

But here we are, in the midst of our moralizing, at the door of 'Winchester House;' long, low, cleanly and well kept. No more squeaking of the old stage coach, nor bracing one's self to help the horses hold back going down hill; no more dust in our faces,— now for ablution, a good supper, downy beds, and 'all right in the morning.'

In the morning I learned, to my regret, that my friend Mrs. Burgess was not there, having been called away upon business. Mrs. Fitch, her friend, with whom she had made an arrangement for our board, provided we liked it, calls, and being pleased with her appearance, we go to her home. Here, may our 'ups' be many, our 'downs,' few; and Ella have little to write about.

The principal, his wife, the assistants, students, were all of the better class; the government of the school mild, but firm; the accommodations at the boarding-houses good; and all the influences at, and around the school, tended to one point — the mental and moral advancement of the children. I placed both my sons in the care of Mr. West, the principal, with confidence in his ability and integrity; drew a long sigh of relief; and sat down, *to write.*

Mrs. Fitch was a systematic housekeeper; breakfast at six, dinner twelve, tea six again, without variation. That was the school for me; *laziness* not taught as a science; no cuffing, kicking or starvation; where little children are reasoned with as reasonable creatures, not controlled like brutes, by mere physical force. I was happier now; knowing that my children were well taught and tenderly cared for, half the maternal burden was removed from my poor, weak shoulders. And so we lived, quietly, doing our duty according to our light, no one intruding upon our proper privileges; never, ourselves. designedly encroaching upon the rights of others.

Harry and Tommy had grown astonishingly since we left Mariette; and to me, they seemed already manly and companionable. They were old enough now to begin to appreciate a mother's love and self-denial; to feel for the peculiar trials of my situation; and they made fewer demands than formerly upon my time and patience.

I gently lifted the veil from that *past* which I had sedulously concealed, that they might profit by knowing the rocks which had shipwrecked the hopes of others; and pointed to the future as a checkered map, traversed by noisy, turbid rivers, shadowed by dangerous steeps, flecked with arid wastes. I told them, too, that life has bright, sweet waters, sunny vales, and cool, refreshing gardens, all accessible at times, where the pure and good may rest; that life is a long, long battle, but for all good soldiers there is a great reward; and as weeks and months rolled on, the chords of affection which held us three together grew stronger, more reliable. We felt as *three alone*, surrounded by a world that at best could have for us but little sympathy; we had no hope of happiness but in each others' society; no greater fear than that of separation.

You, who have wealth and friends, can form no just

idea of the love *I* felt for those children, whose every hope for the future seemed garnered up in my frail life. Oh, how precious to me *seemed* that life, I was willing to linger on in suffering, but not to die — not to leave them alone. Too well I knew the common lot of the motherless, and the misery in store for mine, if I should be removed by death. And still I petitioned for 'life,' life' — not for its own sake, but *theirs.*

Letters from Allen Lincoln had become less frequent as months rolled on, and oh, so hopeless, *so* discouraging! One reiterated tale of ill luck, of disappointed hopes; plans frustrated on the eve of fruition; and still that monomaniacal cry, 'I will have wealth or die.' No want of tenderness, no abatement of apparent solicitude for the struggling ones at home; but I seemed to detect in every line and word of his the low undertone of despair.

"Ella, I do not love you less, God knows that. But here is enough for all, and, if I should not finally succeed, my return would be a curse to you. Why go where the chances for success are fewer? Why return to you a disgraced and broken-hearted man, to see others, who have comparatively done nothing, overshadowing my beggar's cot with their stately mansions? Never! the tide may turn, by and by. I will stay here and wait, doing what I can, remitting all that I can spare. You will not judge me harshly, Ella?"

And still those letters grew less frequent, the remittances smaller. But *I* earned a few dollars weekly, and with strict economy, contrived to meet my indebtedness.

No one knew *why* I did not dress and go out; *why* my face was bleaching whiter, whiter, and my figure became more skeleton like, until all strength forsook me; my brain reeled, and I lay down once more, sick almost unto death.

"Want of air and exercise, said one;" 'an overworked brain,' said another; 'a feeble constitution slowly wearing out,' said a third. *I knew! God knew!*

On that bed of suffering, with a feverish pulse and whirling brain, *I wrote for the newspapers.* Sometimes, when my trembling hand *could hold* the pen, with my portfolio braced against a pillow on my chest, I wrote with my paper upon that; when my hand was so unsteady that it jerked hither and thither, making my chirography look even worse than Harry's, I dictated, Harry wrote.

We wrote *humorous* articles, Harry and I; but *we* did not laugh when we penned them. Oh, how little knew they who read, what they were pleased to call those 'spicy,' light-toned articles, in the newspapers, by whom, or under what circumstances they were written. Ella Lincoln's thin, white hand was not there to freeze the smile which the tenor of her words elicited; her colorless lips were not there to say 'a little more,' when the editor enclosed to her that paltry remuneration; her sad-faced children were not there when the editor decided between her and the rich spinster, which of the two he should continue to employ, to say, 'please let the favored one be *my mother*, since you say their abilities are equal, though the spinster be more widely known. Thoughtless readers and editors, the world has many an Ella Lincoln!

We had a fine time, Harry and I, hiding away that portfolio from Mrs. Fitch, who came on tip-toe along the hall, opening the door so stealthily. Just as soon as the door of the room on the other side creaked upon its hinges, Harry took the ink, and I disposed of that portfolio under the bed-clothes, half closed my eyes, and was ready for all questions concerning the effect of the medicine, etc. Very kind was Mrs. Fitch; but I *opine* if she had been aware of the whereabouts of that paper, it would have gone up through the stove pipe *sans-ceremonie.*

" The way of the transgressor is hard." Those mental efforts increased the fever; my brain became seriously injured; the last fibre of my strength failed; and I seemed as helpless as one already dead. The doctor was put to his 'wit's end.' I could not bear 'tonics' nor 'depletion,' had no appetite for food — no strength; and what could he do?

I required now the most indefatigable attention; had frequent fainting spells, or, some call them, 'sinking spells.' I was frightened, always, when that strange faintness was coming on; and the children, who seldom left my room, were greatly distressed by the sight. Oh how they suffered, too!

There was a stout Irish girl in the house, and after Mrs. Fitch was weary and exhausted, she sent Biddy to take care of me, sometimes. She slept on a cot in my room. Well, after seeing me faint once, Biddy bethought her of a remedy. So, I said to her, as I felt that warmth which precedes a fainting fit, 'I'm going, Bridget! — oh Bridget! — gone.' And didn't she marshal a brandy bottle instanter; emptying its contents down my throat as if I had been an alligator.

"Courage! that'll put the courage into you! Drink! drink! d'ye see, its weakness, all weakness. indade ma'am."

I didn't faint 'intirely' that time; but when the doctor came, I was — *oh, how drunk!*

"Very high fever to-night; a hard, quick pulse" — and then he snuffed the air.

"Brandy! do I smell brandy? A drunken nurse; *this won't do!*" and he bent his ear close to my chest, as if to hear the beating of my heart.

"My patient's breath! what does it mean! Look here, woman, nurse! what have you given the patient?"

"It's only a drop o' the brandy, sir, to put the courage into her when she was a dying of weakness sir; that's all.'

"Fool! you have killed her."

"Niver a bit is she kilt shure; it's only for the want of it she's been a dying of weakness these three weeks."

"Woman, what is your name?"

"Bridget O'Flanaghen, sure."

"Well, Bridget, call your mistress, please;" and she went out.

I was very sleepy; had a sort of swimming consciousness that Mrs. Fitch and the doctor bent over me with sorrowful countenances; and then I 'forgot,' as little Tommy said about the sensation of drowning, long ago.

Poor Ella was tenacious of life. Neither sorrow, nor fever, nor the well-meant blunder of Miss O'Flanaghen, had power to quench that little, feeble spark. *She lived*, as some express it, at the very 'door of death' for six weeks; and it was many months before she recovered her usual strength.

Mrs. Fitch and her family, and, indeed, almost all the citizens of Winchester, endeared themselves to me by repeated acts of kindness during that long, long illness. Oh, much of mercy blends with every cup of bitterness! Strangers were as brothers and sisters; my children, for their sympathy and little acts of kindness, grew dearer every day; and God spared me for *their sakes.*

'Sick among strangers,' are words but little understood by persons who are surrounded by brothers, sisters, parents, wives, husbands; little understood by such as have the means to *buy* the services so much needed by the sick. There is no higher christian grace than that of kindness to *the stranger. Almost all kind!* There are those, even at Winchester, who knew Ella Lincoln was 'sick and a stranger,' yet passed her coldly by; who would not have *taken her in* for Jesus' sake, if she had perished with hunger or thirst, — they are the exceptions that prove the rule — Ella has sometimes met *even their* superiors. She 'knows who is who.'

"A real spirit
Should neither court neglect, nor dread to bear it."

"There is a strength
Imbedded in our hearts, of which we reck
But little 'till the shafts of Heaven have pierced
Its fragile dwelling. Must not earth be rent
Before her gems are found?"

CHAPTER XXXVI.

"Hope's at best
A star that leads the weary on;
Still pointing to the unpossessed,
And paling that it beams upon."

THAT long tedious illness left me nervous and sensitive for many months. A word, a look, a line misconstrued in the communication of a friend, often wrung my spirit with intense agony. As I grew slowly better, I longed for change; and to attempt something untried before, to improve my condition.

I felt that the Creator had endowed me with a certain measure of talent for composition; that now he had blocked up every other avenue through which I might have earned my bread; and hence there was laid upon me an imperative necessity to write.

I knew that before a writer could support herself entirely by the pen, she must be far and favorably known; that she must struggle mightily as she climbs; jostled and pushed backwards by rivals; and looked down by those who have toiled their way up the same bold heights, and finally reached the goal of success. And I said in my heart, I may have been too passive, too self-doubting; the world concedes but little, where little is demanded; — perhaps I may not have told my story to the right ones; such as have it in their power to help me in the only available manner.

"O, that I could write a book!" But I could not *live*, while writing it, if I did; who would furnish Ella Lincoln with bread and butter, while writing a book?

A book, a book? why dear me, Ella! you have thought of it now; you have on hand five hundred, more or less, manuscript poems, long and short, grave and gay; written at all times and seasons, from babyhood till now — you have only to write to some kind-hearted publisher, and tell *him* how poor, and sick, and discouraged you are becoming, and that letter will walk right straight into his heart — he will write you a kind, brotherly epistle; offer to aid you all he can, — and he will publish that work of yours — it will sell, because he will know how to sell it — you will "wake up some morning and find yourself famous" — half your troubles ended, and plenty of cash in your purse.

After that, all the editors will be anxious to secure you as a contributor; and your only perplexity will be about the best manner of declining solicitations from them. — Silly Ella!

I had editorial friends in the West, and others to whom I had always gone for advice in the more important events of my life; and I wrote them now, for this was surely an important occasion.

I waited for their several replies before addressing the "powers that be" — prudent Ella!

Within ten days, all those letters were on hand — full of professions of friendship, and promises of assistance in the way of favorable notices, etc, — "yes, any work of" mine "must have an immense sale" "such a general favorite, etc." I had also encouragement from friends wherever I had resided, and credentials forwarded from various places.

Now roll up the MS. and send it to the publisher — *let that book appear, and "astonish the world;"* — or rather attract the attention of the few whom I desired to please. Money was not then my object. I looked forward to the future, for an indirect remuneration.

Manuscripts and credentials, I sent first to "Lafever & Co.," Philadelphia, accompanied with one of my own unsophisticated, silly letters, telling the whole story, as if I had known them all my life, and knew that they would take interest in me personally, for "sweet charity's sake."

Very gentlemanly was "Lafever & Co's" replying immediately; not with a short, crusty, "I won't do it," but many "regrets, that on account of pressure of business, just now, it would be impossible for them to undertake the publication of those poems, which they liked very much, etc. — had "their best wishes for success," etc.

My specimen manuscripts were returned, as I had requested, through the politeness of a friend. Ella was very nervous. She wrote "De Hart & Co, New York." Two weeks, and no reply — well, it would have been kind in them to answer, as I had stated that I was an invalid, and barely able to sit up. They might have replied, and given me the advice I solicited, at least; might have dealt with me as they would that others should have dealt with their own dear ones under like circumstances.

I wrote again, and was answered. It was a kindly, gently worded letter, — such as the true brother writes to the suffering sister, whose body and mind are both prostrated by disease, heart and soul in every line.

They never publish light literature or poetry — they thought that generally understood.

But, unwilling to discourage me, and earnestly seeking my welfare, they had taken the liberty to forward the specimens I sent them, to Brinkerhoof & Co., Boston, who dealt principally in poetry and lighter literature!

They offered to do "anything within their power for the advancement of my literary interests, — in the way of good words, etc;" and gave me such information concerning the expenses and hazards of book publishing that I relinquished the idea of a literary venture at once.

Enclosed was the reply of "Brinkerhoof & Co." short, crusty, and business like.

"Dear Sirs: — We cannot undertake to publish the volume of which you speak," etc. Respectfully, etc.

I have since learned that poetry is poor capital, both for author and publisher. One of those days, however those poems of Ella's will appear, though her share of the profits may be *Glory and a Garret!*

I was not sorry I had written De Hart & Co., for it was a pleasure to find them *gentlemen;* and afterwards they kindly secured me some work to do for a city editor

If I had been in usual health, I should not have made an attempt of that nature; or, if having made it I had been unsuccessful, I should have brought all my egotism to the rescue and said, I know the poems are respectable; and by and by they shall be published.

As it was, although no one's fault in particular, the disappointment was a cruel one. Such repulses, not then understood, added to the weight of sorrow for which there was no earthly balm, threatened the very springs of life — and but for God's mercy would have unstrung the intellect forever.

We had been long at Winchester, boarding at the same excellent HOME; performing the same daily round of duties with no new difficulties, no serious discouragements. Ella continued to read, write, sew on buttons, and stitch up rents; the boys grew *out of* their clothes and *into* intelligence; — their lives were all surface, *hers* all under-current.

Mr. Harris of the New England Branch of Peace, had long been a kind friend to me. He had placed my articles in his columns in the most favorable light; spoken of me often to his readers as a talented contributor; paid me liberally; — and written me kind, brotherly letters.

I knew he was a gentleman; there was so much delicacy in his expressions of sympathy; so much of respect, blended with the tenderest compassion for an invalid stranger; a mother struggling against an adverse tide for the support and education of her children; — I knew he was a good man, the first epistolatory line of his I ever read.

An editor may do much to advance the interests of his writers by judicious praise; by placing their articles conspicuously before the public; by cheering them on with private approval, and paying them promptly and liberally.

On the contrary, an editor may retard the interests of any writer, by keeping her articles long on hand, while he publishes others of not greater merit; by praising others and not mentioning her name; by sliding in her contributions at last among patent "Pill" advertisements, "Strayed Cows" and "Houses to Let."

If a writer possesses only medium talents, it is in the power of the editor of any popular journal to lay for her a foundation for future success, or to forge for her the first link of a hard, cold chain of circumstances which will fetter her energies to the dust.

So reasoned Mr. Harris as he put away Ella Lincoln's first appeal for sympathy among the letters to be answered by his own hand at his earliest convenience; thus should reason every editor who has *a heart.*

Mr. Harris knew that Ella Lincoln was poor, that her poverty had hindered her promotion. He knew that, if by her own desperate energy, she should struggle up the hill at last, many who seemed not to see her now would offer her the hand of fellowship at the top; and he resolved now when she was but half way up, that he would prevent her from falling back to her first position, and then he wrote her thus

"DEAR MADAM:—I have long desired to be of more service to you as a friend than I have yet been able to be. Now if it should meet your approbation, I have a plan which I think might promote your interests and my own, and I trust the gratification of my readers.

"Mrs. Jared, the present assistant editor, being in delicate health, and the time for which she had contracted to remain in the office having nearly expired; she will probably discontinue her valuable services soon.

"I have engaged no one to fill her place, and if you would like the situation, I should be most happy to see you here with your family, as soon as it may suit your convenience, etc. Be so kind as to reply immediately.

I remain,

Most truly yours,

Mark Harris."

I was yet feeble, often being obliged to lie down and rest through the day; and at first I only regretted that it was so utterly beyond my power to accept of so desirable situation. But the temptation to reply in the affirmative was strong; the wages a great inducement; and I thought it barely possible that a change of climate might benefit my health. After much useless reflection, I concluded to submit the matter to the kind friends with whom we had so long resided.

"Shall I go, Mr. Fitch?"

"Is Mr. Harris young, or elderly?"

"I presume he is middle-aged, sir."

"Is he a married man?"

"I recollect in one of the humorous editorials something about the little branches,— I supposed that meant children; but they may be the property of Mr. Harrison, a reverend gentleman connected with the office. It is probable, however, that *he is* married."

"Does he know that your health is delicate?—how many hours' labor per day, will he expect at your hands? You can endure but little; remember that."

"He does know I am frail—I am to enter the office at eight A. M., and leave at five P. M.; an hour for dinner."

"Fie, it will kill you."

"But think of the salary; how much better than the fluctuating pay for stories and essays. Oh, I am willing to be very weary every day; to work when my head aches; if I can get a good regular salary weekly, that will support my children and finally pay all my debts!"

"Distance lends enchantment to the view,—what would you do with your boys?"

"That's a hard question. What I am earning here will go farther toward our support, than will my salary there, if I take them, board there being enormously high. I dislike, too, to remove them from this school, which is so excellent. Harry might remain, and Tommy go with me; and then it would be hard to separate the brothers.

"Well, Tommy cannot be left, he won't stay of course; so young, and never having been separated from you—but if you choose to leave Harry, he is old enough, and to stay alone will do him good. I will look after his welfare as I do after that of my own children; but about going, I will not advise you—the road runs both ways."

"Yes, indeed, I shall go with you," said Tommy, "for who would take care of you if you were sick?"

"I shall not be sick there, probably, the change of air will be beneficial; and if I should be, Mr. Harris will see to it that I do not suffer. But I am willing, and wish you to go, if you are inclined to do so, indeed, if Harry is not willing to remain here alone, I will stay, or he shall go."

Harry did not reply then, and we dropped the subject.

A few days afterwards, I said "now I must decide, and answer Mr. Harris."

What was my surprise when Tommy said, with all the firmness and dignity of manhood; "Mother, if you think it would be better for both brother and me to stay here at school; and if you will not *need me* to help you there, I am willing to stay; because it will not cost so much to live here, and it will be better for me."

I looked at him in astonishment. It seemed but yesterday since he was a tiny creature, clinging to the neck of his 'mamma,' and was indulged in every whim of babyhood. Now here he stood talking of what would "be best for him," and addressing his "mother" with all the confidence of one who had already learned to reason and govern himself. Tommy, the nervous, sensitive, as some were pleased to say, "spoiled child," who at Pinkneyville "struck Mr. Stubbs back again."

Oh, *I knew* then that after all my solicitude, all my care, he would not disappoint me; that if I lived to see him a man in stature he would be a man in spirit.

Harry, always quiet, governable and good, was manly and reflective beyond his years ; Tommy, once as impetuous as an unbroken colt, had grown reflective too; I was proud of them — and again away down in the depths of my maternal heart, I resolved anew, that death only should quench the ardor of my exertion in their behalf — Ella Lincoln, so frail that friends hardly dared to expect her life from year to year, devoted herself anew to the education of her children. No true mother rests satisfied with doing less — rather would I live out but half my days, and leave my boys behind, educated and honorable men, than to look back from three score and ten upon those children doomed to hopeless mediocrity, by my own selfish neglect — there is my view of a mother's duty — I will perform it *all*, God being my helper — and if, after all, they prove false to themselves and me, my hands will be guiltless of their sin — let them look to it ; fearful will be their responsibility if they break a mother's heart.

I wrote Mr. Harris that I would come. I did not then fully resolve to leave Tommy behind, but went about making preparations for a long absence, thinking that if even at the last hour, if he should express a wish to accompany me, it would not be too late. I even had his clothes prepared with reference to taking him, in case he should thus decide.

I said to him often, "if you go, my son, you will have many things to sell or give away to the school boys; your skates, balls, story-books, fish-pole ; every thing you play with here, it will not be convenient to take so far," and he replied as often that he did not wish to go. I knew it would be better that he should remain, but never said to him "I prefer to leave you;" I could not have been so cruel.

That long dreaded morning came at last. I was ready. I committed both my dear ones, without reserve to the care of their beloved teacher, and said to my friends, one and all, "be kind to my poor lonely boys, when I am gone"— and then, "Ella, be strong!"

Whatever they may have seemed to others, to me they were beautiful and sprightly boys, affectionate, talented, giving high promise of future usefulness. They were *mine* only — my all. Through years of loneliness, grief, and toil, I only had clung to them — they to me.

When so young that a cup of cold water trembled in their little feeble hands, they had held it to my lips in sickness; when other children slept, they, poor babes, had lain down by my side, in their clothes, watching the movements of my restless hands, listening to catch my faintest utterance.

"Mamma, you won't die, will you?" they would say, their sweet blue eyes swimming in tears, their little throats choking with emotion, "you wont die, and leave us alone — there would be no one to care for us if you were gone — you will be better to-morrow, wont you?"

"Hush, brother! let us be still; may be she will sleep, and feel better."

They had shared all my griefs, disappointments, wrongs; could I leave them now — leave them there among strangers, to ply their little life barques along alone, with no surety save the eternal Father's promise that they should not lack bread? Long and weary would be the distance between us; sickness might come; one of us be laid in the grave. Many circumstances might arise at least to keep us long, long separated — how could I go?

One wild, bitter gush of anguish swept over my heart-strings as a flood; *one moment* of anguish, then all was over; the everlasting arm was beneath me; the still small voice whispered, "I will keep them." Crushing down the strong maternal yearning to be with them — I hurried away.

There is an acme of human suffering, and the evil which does not kill us very soon, we learn to bear with patience and submission. Yonder rises the cloud in frightful blackness; we hear the sullen roar of the tempest; the big drops fall upon our uncovered heads; we bow down with sickening fear, praying for a place of refuge. But when all is over; when the fury of the storm is sated with the desolation it has made; when the earthly possessions in which we had garnered up our hopes are all swept away by the remorseless tide, we look calmly out upon the track of that tempest, feeling that no danger could move us to such agony again.

Better is a sad certainty than a deep, secret, withering apprehension! I sometimes think that the fact of my having out-lived such great calamities is an earnest of better days in store; that God has preserved me through all trials, that purified and made wiser, I may be intrusted with some nobler and more perfect work.

CHAPTER XXXVII.

Oh, memory! why this bitter taunt!
  Oblivion — would thy wave
Could wash away the forms that haunt
  Us ever from the grave.

My route lying through Woodville, New Jersey, I stopped there to pass a few days with a friend, who was very dear to me, having been one of the companions of my childhood.

I was surprised and pleased to meet Peggy there; — dear Peggy of the olden time; who rocked me in the cradle, and gave me good advice every Saturday night, about keeping the Sabbath, then more on Sunday about behaving properly through the week.

She had not *faded;* her large dark eyes had not lost their benevolent expression; her lips wore the same peaceful smile.

But I observed that the crisped hair beneath her lawn cap was sprinkled with gray, and a few additional lines traversed her high, full forehead.

Peggy had found a home with one of her relatives in another town; but she came to Woodville sometimes to visit the old neighbors, who were all happy to see her, and as often as she left them, invited her to came again.

"'Pears to me," she said, "you have grown old amazingly fast! That western wilderness did n't agree with you. I thought it would n't; I never believe it 's right for folks to stray off so far away from where they've been born and brought up. It is n't nat'ral, nohow. Folks used to stay at home and see to their own business, and be thankful that they had enough to eat and drink and wear — now they go all over the world, like a lot of jack-lanterns, lookin' for they don't know what. Well, I did all I could to keep you, but you know what the sayin' is, 'Young folks thinks old folks fools, and old folks knows young folks is!'

"I had a sort of warning that your goin' would n't end well; and, sure enough, it 's all come true; there 's your family all split up, and divided, and scattered, like chaff before the wind, and you've even left your own children, to go to Massachusetts; — that I don't approve of — did n't they cry? I 'spose they've got a church or two out in Illinois, by this time, and a Sunday school — hav n't they? I tell you how it is, *Miss Ella*, where there's no meeting-houses, the Sabbath is broken every day; and where there's no Sunday schools the children grows up in ignorance and uncivilization."

I was glad that Peggy was in one of her *imperial* moods, for I was somewhat amused, and that helped me to stay back the tears, that were fast rising in their living beds; and I did not wish to treat my friends in the parlor to "a scene" that evening.

Peggy did not know *all*, or she would not have *wondered* that I had "grown old amazingly."

"My life is lingering in its prime,
If life by length of years be told;
If sorrows mark the flight of time
I'm death-like old.

"The numbness and the damps of age
Have chilled me many years too soon;
I faint, while yet my pilgrimage
Is in its noon.

"The lightning from my veins has fled,
The visions and the rapture high, —
All, all are gone, and in their stead
Cold ashes lie."

So thought Ella, as she struggled mightily to subdue herself; and felt that she would like to be alone to weep.

With a look of maternal tenderness, those large dark eyes had settled upon her countenance; the sable arms closed lovingly around her; and she pillowed her head once more upon the bosom where it had often slept, free from sorrow and racking cares, long ago. The fountain was unsealed, — the waters flowed, — then came relief and peace, — that peace which is born of the consciousness that God is behind every cloud, still guiding — ever pitying the sorely tried.

Just as the sun went down behind the mountain, Peggy and myself entered the low gate of the old graveyard. It was fuller now than when I saw it last. Many a new stone had been added to the long rows of brown and white, and I recognized familiar names, as we threaded our way along through the tall grass to the old family corner.

Ella has a poem of hers somewhere, on that old village church. She gives you the closing lines:

> There the earth doth kindly spread
> Shelter o'er a mother's head,
> There a sister found a tomb,
> Life just budding into bloom,
> And a father's weary eye,
> Closed for age, is sleeping nigh,
> There my parents' parents sleep;
> There their brethren silence keep,
> Still doth bloom the sweet wild rose,
> Where they all in peace repose,
> And the grass is rank and tall
> O'er the buried forms of all:
>
> Memory — memory, close thy book!
> What availeth it to look?
> Soul! the living claim thy care —
> God will watch the sleepers there.

"It seems but a little while," said Peggy, "since I saw even the oldest of them, busy and smiling, as they came and went to see my master and mistress, and the little children at the old homestead; — and there they lie. Even that lily-bud, Miss Carrie, that grew up so pale and white, and seemed to sink down so weary-like into the first chair that offered, I hoped would stay a little longer — but she grew whiter — whiter, every day, until it seemed as if every drop of blood in her body was gone — only a few blue veins showed in her neck, and her thin hands looked so wax-like — and all one month she was up and down, up and down again on the bed, — and one night she called me to her, and said, 'Peggy, I feel strangely — I shall die soon,' and then I called the family, and, as they gathered around the bed she said: 'I am almost there — they wait for me — home, home! —' and she was gone.

"All that was since you went away, Miss Ella."

"Yes, what of my father? tell me how he died."

"Well, master was a good man, and loved his family and was kind to the poor; but some said he was cold and self-willed — I never thought so — he just did what he thought was right, and if other folks did n't think so — why who was to judge between him and them?"

"Well, he was old when he died. The young folks had all married and gone away to the city, and there he lived alone, with just me to keep the house, after Miss Carrie was gone, — and the hired man — nobody else but the company that called sometimes, and the relations that staid weeks when they came, to keep him *cheerful like;* — and he had strange turns sometimes, and was kind-a suffocated in his chest; and I said to him: 'Master, we must all die — I hope you will live a great many years — but if the Good Lord should call for you, is your lamp all trimmed and burnin', and are you ready to go?'

"And he always answered, 'Yes, Peggy, when it is His will I trust I am ready,' — but he would n't see the minister — he said 'what man can stand between my soul and God?' And one night, just as he finished his tea, he fell back in his chair — and died.

"Then the children came to the funeral — and after a little time the property was divided, and the old homestead sold, and my home was broke up for this world.

"But there is another, away up yonder — where that steeple points — and we shall all go there by and by — home, sweet home!"

As she spoke, her sable finger pointed upward, and her eyes closed in devotion — she uttered a few low words of prayer, and then we turned away.

The old homestead, we passed it on our way back to my friend's. That low, white house, with the trellised porch, and the green blinds, has stood sixty years. It has been repaired and re-painted many times, since my dear old grandfather presented it fresh from the builder's hands to his beloved daughter; the green grass in that wide door-yard has been trodden by almost countless feet, and the flowers along the borders have been planted and tended by almost innumerable fingers.

That garden fence has been many times rebuilt, and the old brick walk has been broken and trodden into the earth — and re-laid — making it new again. It was a very fine house "in its day," but now is, like Ella, old fashioned.

The panes in the windows are small, the windows are smaller than those of the more modern dwellings around them; the doors are narrower and have fewer decorations; and the roof patched here and there, looks brown and weather-worn.

There is an air of comfort and luxury about it which

time has not destroyed; many of the old trees remain, and the brook still meanders through the garden and grounds; and there is the little fish-pond away where the willows used to be — but the willows were old when Ella was young, and they are gone now; and a row of young locusts stand up in their place. The old pear tree that stood by the garden gate is broken down — that too was old when Ella was young. The grape vine that hung over the arbor, making it dark and cool within, has died out, and a wild honeysuckle grows in its stead. The purple morning glories, that grew by my mother's bed-room window — that were replanted for her sweet sake, and tended year after year, when the sod lay heavy upon her bosom — they are not there. The tall cherries still interlace their branches over the garden walk; but some of them are old and ready to fall, and the robins that sit there and sing, seem not so beautiful as those of long ago.

The hand of the stranger has opened the door, and Peggy, who knows her, says:

"This is Miss Ella Lee, that went away long ago. I wanted her to see the old house, and the room that was hers, and her mother's bed-room, and the old back room where her sister and so many have died; for the Lord's ways are wonderful, and she may never see the homestead again."

It was quite dark now, and as the polite and sympathetic stranger piloted us through the rooms, I started at the sound of our own footsteps, and our own shadows as they glided along the walls.

The carpets and the furniture were all new, the old

book-case full of leather-bound, standard works, was surperseded by one of modern style, filled with cloth covers and modern *nonsense;* the old piano-forte, with slender feet, carved and gilded exterior, by one of heavy modern fashion; the old family pictures, thc portraits of the loved and lost, had disappeared from those familiar places, and the fixed eyes of strangers looked down in their stead.

Ella Lee's room. It seemed lower and smaller than it did long ago. But the latch of the old door was the same, and the very creak of its hinges familiar; the windows on the south and east looked forth over the same landscape

I sat down in each of them just where I used to sit, and looked out upon thc olden scenes, — *olden* — yet oh, how changed!

The moonlight streamed in through the shrubbery and glimmered on the dew upon the grass; lights danced in the village windows — and Ella left the homestead, *never to return.*

Home of my childhood,
  Oh, faded from my view,
Nor quicken the anguish
  I would not renew.

CHAPTER XXXVIII.

The sunlight glowed on pavements smooth,
  And granite fabrics high,
And all throughout that busy mart
  Was life and energy.

"CARRIAGE, Sir?"—"Carriage, Madame?" "United States House"—"American Hotel" etc.

"Carriage, Madame?"

"Yes, Sir, take me to the United States." "That is right here at the depot. I'll call a porter for you."

"Thank you, sir."

Room "106," second floor—tea sent up, and all things agreeable;—but I felt deeply the loneliness of my present situation, and retired to spend a restless night, and think of the past, and the untried future before me. Why was I here; so far from all my loved ones, in a strange city in Massachusetts; where but a single human being took interest in my welfare, and that one not personally known to me? Had I come here to prosper, or to sink into still deeper poverty; to find friends, or be wounded by neglect? Many hours of the night had passed away when I fell into an uneasy slumber, from which I awoke at day-break, with a severe nervous headache.

I had not arrived as soon as I was expected by Mr. Harris, who politely sent a friend to meet me at the depot, for two days in succession; and now, how unfortunate, he was out of town. But the Rev. Mr. Harrison, who was connected with "The Branch of Peace," called upon me at the Hotel, also the two brothers-in-law of Mr. Harris, and this somewhat relieved me of the oppressive loneliness one feels in a strange Hotel.

After Mr. Harris returned, he secured for me a room in a first-class private boarding house, where there may have been some two hundred boarders; — the number seemed large to me, after a long residence in the country, where twenty in a family was considered a houseful indeed.

It was with reluctance that I entered a house of that character, as I was out of health, low-spirited, and disinclined to go much into society. I was averse to being questioned by strangers, for I knew that my heart-history had a "preface" upon my forehead, which honest nature had written there, in despite of all my efforts to present to the world a smooth, blank sheet.

They were kind to me there, the host and hostess, and the few boarders with whom I became partially acquainted.

But I declined all invitations to go into the parlor, and evaded all conversation at the table, — not that I underrated the kindly efforts of the host, hostess and boarders, to while away those hours which seemed to them passing so gloomily away; — but from a sheer, hopeless ennui; — a sinking of the animal spirits, a kind of silent aberration, a home-sickness which almost crushed me into the grave.

I attempted to commence my labors in the office, but without success: my brain was stupefied, bewildered, I could not *think;* I went out and returned, alway mistaking my way; I did not notice my own seat at the table; — I was wretched; — wretched; — and could not rally, could not bring reason or necessity to the rescue. Thus passed three weeks, losing all my time.

The fourth, I said to myself, "Ella, thou canst not return, it is too late; thou canst not live without wages; thou art too poor — for shame, Ella; faint-hearted, cowardly Ella; cast off this incubus, and be up and doing, for the sake of the dear ones dependant upon thy care" — and Ella was herself again.

A few weeks later, found me as busy as a bee, reading dusty manuscripts, and proofs, and scribbling editorials.

Mrs. Harrison was there, Editress of "The Ladies' Budget;" dear, kind Mrs. Harrison, whom I afterwards found as a sister, whom everybody knows so well, that to say much in her praise would be fulsome flattery; — her Rev. husband was there, and a number of persons of both sexes in various departments of the establishment.

I did not like to be exposed in that office to the gaze of every person who came in; I would have given *my fortune* for a screen between me and even the persons employed in the same room; but what could I do? — It is a cruel destiny which drives a woman of such habits, tastes and temperament as mine, out into the face of the great, staring world; to earn her bread, as it were by working on the highway, for what but a public thoroughfare is an editor's office?

I asked Mr. Harris as a favor, to give me the most retired position in the room, and he gave me a desk in a recess, for which I was very grateful.

In the furthermost corner from me, sat Mrs. Harrison, next, Mr. Harris; next, between him and me, Mr. Harrison. The office was large, handsomely fitted up with desks, etc., and a mere casual observer would have said we were all very happy, and there was no life like an editor's.

And there is none! — So thought Mr. Harris; harassed with cares, pestered with intruders, beset from morn till night with solicitations for employment and pay, from the poor and suffering whom he could not aid; and glancing now and then at those ponderous books which told the tale of "loss and gain."

So thought Mrs. Harrison, as she toiled from day to day over that never ending "Ladies' Budget;" with weary heart and aching head; and so thought Ella, doing the best she could, with no hour unoccupied from sabbath to sabbath again.

Oh! if every reader could know the solicitude, toil and expense, connected with every issue of a newspaper, he would prize that little weekly messenger more highly, and pity every soul whose handi-work was in every line.

Mrs. Harrison, yet in early middle age, was a veteran in editorial business; the pride and pet of her husband, and all who knew her well loved her for her gentle nature, her ardent piety, and unassuming manners.

Few persons of her fine talents bear their honors so meekly, few are so companionable — so ready to hear and help all who stand in need of kind words or deeds. She pitied Ella, with her pale cheek and care-pencilled brow; — and Ella went to her at all times for the counsel and encouragement she so much needed.

But the time came — all too soon for Ella; when Mrs. Harrison discontinued the "Ladies' Budget," and accompanied her Rev. husband to a field of labor far away.

For her sake, Ella was glad; for *her own* sake, Oh, how sorry! and for the sake of all who had learned to love her through her gifted pen. But she retained an editorial position in "The Branch of Peace," and Ella was still privileged to commune with her through the pen.

Oh, the troubles of an editor! Reams, bushels, haystacks of manuscripts, which have been accumulating for years, and still they come.

Ho! you scribbling "Jose;" or "Susy;" "Uncle Ned," or "Aunt Deborah," do you suppose *that* sheet of fools-cap, which you are now folding and directing in your best manner, will ever find its way into that newspaper for which you design it? sure you have not wasted your precious time, and all that ink? — what right have you to expect that veritable article of yours will fare better than the hundreds already "accepted;" to be published sometime before newspapers shall cease to be?

"These manuscripts are some of them very ancient," said Mr. H., opening the drawer which displayed all styles of folding, rolling up, and directing. I have no doubt but that *some* of them may be good; and, if your are willing, we will re-read and select the most valuable from the mass, with a view to future publication.

It seems too bad to have treated really worthy authors in this manner, but what could we do? so much sent in, and but one little sheet to publish it all in; — few *do* really write well; those who *do not*, expect the same favors and pay.

Some boldly dash off a note and send it with their MS., demanding ten or fifteen dollars; others leave all to our liberality — which is worse — and some ask room for theirs, as a favor; while we sigh over yesterday's pile, there comes another, and to-morrow, another, and we toss them aside in despair for future consideration; — that *future* never comes.

I read manhood's bold chirography; woman's gossamer lines; the blots and erasures of the unpractised school-girl; the ungrammatical sentences and misspelt words of the aspiring youth; sonnets, homilies, comic essays, stories, — translations — accompanying notes, etc.

"Dear Sir: — I trust you will pardon the liberty I take in sending my first effort, etc."

"Mr. Editor: — You will oblige me by publishing the enclosed sketch, and sending me five dollars — send four copies to my address, etc."

"Dear Sir: — I am very poor, the widowed mother of four children; there is but one thing I *can do* — *write.* I do not profess to be a superior writer, but to have fair newspaper talent. Friends tell me you are kind to the poor; — hence I take the liberty to send you my first MS. Oh, befriend me, sir, as you would that God should raise up friends for you in your greatest need; publish and pay for my articles," etc.

"Mr. Ed. — I am a mere boy. I wish to write for a newspaper in order that I may help myself through college. By paying me a trifle for this article, you will greatly encourage and oblige," etc.

Timid school girl, it is long since you penned that first song; aspiring boy, may you have reached the goal of success years ago; presumptuous man, demanding "five dollars and four copies," — poor widow, appealing for sympathy and help, — your paper is faded and yellow; the dust lies heavy in every fold, — years have passed and no response; WE estimated you differently, yet treated you the same — you have gone your different ways — God only knows your destiny — scattered here and there over the earth; — doubtless some in the grave.

Ah, many a sensitive spirit has been wounded by *our* neglect; many a poor widow, whose pen was her only hope, has watched for the weekly coming of our Journal with feverish anxiety; — while there, in that deep, deep drawer, has lain the crumpled MS., its identity forgotten.

The bosom of every editor is made the repository of tales of suffering which would melt the heart of a stone; while he has but one alternative, to deny others or ruin himself.

Some *are* cold and even cruel to correspondents; others reject their communications with dewy eyes, and think of those crushed hopes with a sigh, amidst cares and vexations as numberless as the sands of the sea. Ella has a fellow-feeling with all poor contributors, but never envies an editor.

Ella put many a dislocated distich into joint, and wrote editorials after ten P. M., as a penalty; and Mr. Harris was always pleased to do all he could to encourage modest worth, even though it *did* cost time and labor.

Months rolled on; I received many kind and courteous letters from persons corresponding with our Journal. I received letters, which came from the homes of poverty and sorrow, like a low, dismal wail; — full of anguish which I *felt* but could not mitigate, —thrilling appeals to *me* for counsel and aid — ME — myself the very sport of misfortune; — how could I bind up the wounds of others, with none to minister to my own?

But I gave them my sympathies; those suffering ones — I told them how *I had* struggled, was struggling still; and commended them to Him upon whose strong arm all might lean. I thank them for their confidence; love them, though personally unknown to me; they are my brothers and sisters of the heart. When life's "weary watch is o'er," we shall meet and know each other in our Father's house.

I had left the larger establishment and taken an attic room in a widow's house.

It was high, and the stairs seemed — oh, how long; but when I reached my chamber, it was pleasant, and still, and, when evening came, the stars looked in lovingly at the windows, and the gentle ocean-breeze played in the folds of the curtains.

I looked out upon the stars, sometimes, at the still midnight hour, thinking of two young sleepers far away, and the strong man who had bidden them "good night," and lain down to rest in distant California.

I was comparatively happy. Letters from Winchester were satisfactory, the children were well, and improving rapidly in their studies; I was enabled to remit them more money by this self-denial on my part — which only consisted in climbing the stairs; — and I was retired; passing in and out as a shadow unquestioned. My bed was beautifully clean; the furniture convenient; and none of those worse than "Egyptian plagues" which infest the city boarding-houses, were pleased to dwell with Ella Lincoln so near the moon.

There, angels bright
 Came down at night,
To watch my pulse's play;
 Their shadowy wings,
 In circling rings,
Went up at break of day.

CHAPTER XXXIX.

> "To hallowed duty
> Here with a loyal and heroic heart,
> Bind we our lives."

MRS. HARRISON, editress of the "Ladies' Budget," and assistant in the "Branch of Peace," had long been absent.

I sat down from morning till evening, writing, reading manuscripts, reviewing books, reading proofs.

I had asked as a favor of Mr. Harris, that he would allow me to do all that I possibly could, and increase my salary in consideration of my having assumed such varied duties.

It was necessary at that time for Mr. Harris to have his work done by the fewest possible pairs of hands; and he may have allowed me to assume more work to do than he would have done under less perplexing circumstances; and more than I could accomplish with justice to his interest.

But I was content; saying in my heart, "it is for the sake of my own dear children that I toil; I am happy, if by my unwearying industry I can shield them from ignorance and imposition.

It was pleasant to know that, far away in that valley home, *they* were well cared for, by their excellent teacher and numerous friends. Every week I enclosed to them all my wages, except barely enough to pay my board, and boarded where I was merely comfortable, with a poor widow who, like me, had seen "better days." I sought no luxuries, purchased no new article of clothing, for appearance' sake; indeed, when I first met the cold, searching winds of a New England winter, I looked sometimes at the long rows of furs and cloaks in the shop windows, and envied those whose duty did not forbid them to buy.

I coveted no society, obstinately refused all invitations from my hostess to "go into the parlor," and wrote — wrote. At eight A. M. every day, I entered the office, and, allowing myself but half an hour to dine, remained there at my desk until five P. M., sometimes six. Seven was our tea hour, at the boarding-house, and I invariably arose from the table and walked directly to my room. Then I took up my pen, and kept it running until eleven — always eleven, — sometimes twelve.

Yet, still weary and worn as I was, adding a new care-mark to my tell-tale countenance every day — knowing that by this bold outrage upon the rights of nature, I was shortening my journey to the last resting place, I was comparatively happy. I thought only of my children — still my children; — and for *their* dear sakes was willing to forego the last league of my own life's journey.

Mr. Harris went about the office without the accustomed smile; his hand trembled as he wrote; he gazed abstractedly out of the window, or into the fire; and I knew that he was suffering intensely, but did not divine the cause.

Many persons came in, and went out to return soon again, and there was an unexplained confusion about the establishment that greatly troubled me. More than ever before I longed for retirement — a home — a place where my pale, thin face would not be constantly exposed to the rude stare of the stranger.

"Sold out" — "suspended payment" — "compromised with creditors" — "failed," — so said rumor. I only knew that some difficulty had occurred, but did not know the exact extent of his misfortune. I was aware, however, that his present trouble was not the result of indolence or want of economy, but of the common mischances of business.

His expenses had been enormous, his receipts not in proportion; others did not meet their obligations to him; the crisis came; no friend happened to have both the ability and generosity to assist him, and he met the common fate. So I suppose; for the same event happens to thousands yearly all over the world — why not to Mr. Harris?

It is hard. He has a lovely wife, and little dependent family, accustomed to luxuries and indulgence; it is hard, because some who have suffered through his misfortune will charge with him unkindness, others with dishonesty. He suffers intensely, for he is sensitive and refined; temporary wrinkles gather upon his brow, his lip quivers; a great wave of sorrow is sweeping over him. May God temper the wind to the shorn lamb!

He suffers; but he is young; he will, ere long, surmount *that wave*, and ride on to prosperity and happiness, guided by the experience of the past.

Mr. Harris and his amiable wife have the deepest sympathies of a large circle of friends.

But Mr. Harris is only *one* of many sufferers. In that editorial room are several persons suddenly deprived of their salaries, and many also in the printing office. There is the foreman, Mr. Primble; he has finished his work there; his salary is discontinued: and he must look for a new home.

Mr. Primble has a lovely and talented wife, and a little family dependent upon him — God keep them; and to all whom Mr. Harris has given employment, whether they have or have not families!

When we hear of the suspension of business in an establishment like that of "The Branch of Peace," if we have not a personal acquaintance with any of the parties concerned, we hear it as we do the thunder afar off, with but little emotion; but when we not only are acquainted with sufferers, but are ourselves under the cloud; when the "flash and the clap come together," we view it in a different light.

Ella Lincoln was accustomed to sudden reverses; she had virtually "taken the bankruptcy" every Saturday night, year after year; but she had not yet learned *to like* these sudden flaws of fortune; her nerves had not become less sensitive from receiving such reiterated shocks — perverse nerves!

I was turned out of employment into the streets of a strange city, without a dollar, not knowing where to go, or what to do.

Always feeble, always weary, I had not sought to be known; not anticipating an hour like this, I had not cultivated the friendship of city editors generally, and was personally acquainted with only two. They expressed sympathy, but offered me no work; and I did not ask them for it; I was too much grieved, too proud.

Should not their own *generous hearts* have suggested the propriety of their giving me employment until I could have time to make other arrangements. Rather would I have starved than ask a favor where I had reason to suppose it would be granted grudgingly!

A literary lady who had professed some interest in my welfare promised to interest those editors who were her personal friends, in my behalf. Of course I cannot *doubt* that she was sincere in her professions of regard; as I have never seen her, or so much as received a kindly message from her since. *Perhaps* her "numerous cares" have prevented her from seeing or writing me since she "felt for" my "peculiar situation," as she is boarding at a first-class hotel, and "has n't a child in the world."

I addressed two editors in distant cities; personal friends of long ago; and received such pathetic epistles in return, that if I had not been short of time, I should have wept over *their* troubles, not mine. They had on hand "such an overplus of matter;" "so many contributors engaged for the present year" that really they did not know what to say; and one of them "regretted that I had not applied at an earlier date." *I* did not regret that the present misfortune had not occurred at an earlier date; it seemed even now too soon.

Some offered to employ me at insulting prices; some offered me the places of correspondents who would discontinue after a few weeks or months, if we could agree upon terms.

Mrs. Harrison interested herself, unavailably, in my behalf. In her reply to the communication which announced to her the recent change of editors in the "Branch of Peace," she said: "the whole fraternity will take you by the hand; how can it be otherwise? What noble-hearted editor *could* refuse to assist a woman in circumstances so peculiarly afflictive?" Kind hearted lady; she judged of the fraternity as an unbroken chain, forgetting that its separate links are composed of metals of various degrees of hardness — she judged others' hearts by *her own.*

As a class, I have a higher respect for editors than if I had not been in situations to see and appreciate their labors and trials. I respect many who have employed me, some who have not. There are a few in the city where I am writing who have not been in circumstances to assist me pecuniarily. Such have still given me the friendly hand, and fraternal advice; and influenced others, more fortunately situated, in my behalf.

When I consider how hard they work; how almost incalculable are their weekly expenses, and then think of the pitiful price which they receive for each particular newspaper, I am astonished that so many do contrive to live, and some prosper. As a class they are not cold-hearted, though in some instances thoughtless in their dealings with the sensitive and refined; but a few of them have hearts like *flints* — would they were *fewer still!*

Now, thought I, if I can get something else to do, some employment for the day time, I can write at night, almost all night, and attend to the other business again next day.

Not knowing where else to apply, I went to an Intelligence office and left my name as one in need of employment; "any respectable employment."

There now, on the big book of the intelligence office, was written the name of "Ella Lincoln," the village belle of years ago; whose every want was anticipated, every whim gratified. "Ella Lincoln;" *think of it!*

Life is not all dark, but by and by it is crossed by a golden thread of sunshine.

Frightened by the coldness of those to whom I had first applied; confounded by the tone of the replies which came up from beneath those piles of "manuscript" — so heavy that they had crushed out compassion from the hearts of the poor editors upon which they lay; wondering and grieved at the apathy of all of whom I had thought better things, I sank into a mental stupor; a misanthropic spirit seized me; I forgot the *blessed few* — "the exceptions," and looked upon the great world of hearts as one illimitable stone heap.

Ella, is that you? are you not ashamed of yourself? — where is your hitherto indomitable perseverance? Remember, your children have no hope but in your success! — up and work for your life. God helps only those who try to help themselves.

How *could* I call upon those stranger editors; tell them the story of my griefs and wrongs; and appeal to them for aid. Were there not persons in the city whose interest it might be to tell another story; *who* would indorse my report? Would they not think it strange, that one who professed to have written so long for remuneration; who had lately been associated with a prominent Journal, should have difficulty in getting immediate employment? Why was not she employed by the *new editors* of that Journal? If *they* thought her talented; if they believed she had been true to her trust? It was a natural question — how could I blame them?

A friend who took an interest in my welfare said to me one day: "Why do n't you write to Mr. Downham, of the new firm at "The Branch of Peace?" He is a good man, a Christian; and whatever he may *say*, the others will *do*. Ask *him* for employment. Tell *him* that indirectly, himself and partners have injured you as a writer, by dispossessing you of your situation; leaving the matter a mystery to your friends abroad, and standing in the way of your obtaining the same kind of employment. *He* has a heart; that Mr. Downham!"

I wrote Mr. Downham, stating to him frankly my circumstances, telling him of my utter destitution, that I was here a stranger, without a dollar, etc.,— that my children were away in Pennsylvania without a dollar; that my connection with "The Branch of Peace" had been very unfortunate for me, as it had ended; I told him all that I thought necessary to enlist his sympathies in me personally, and as a writer, whom he had *indirectly dispossessed of her salary.*

I appealed to him as a husband, brother, Christian; I wrote an impulsive, earnest letter; such an one as comes from the heart of every woman so sorely tried.

The reply was kind, gentle, manly, brotherly; closing with, "May you ever look to me as a friend."

In that letter he promised me a little work — a little pay. "Three columns, more or less, of short articles, at five dollars per week," for an indefinite time.

Now for that amount of short articles, *bona-fide editorials*, I had received from ten to twelve dollars always; but "five" would pay my board until I could do better; so I accepted the offer, with a warm-hearted "thank you." Every one, who knows how to write them, at all knows that four short, pithy, condensed articles, either grave, or witty, in one column, are better worth ten dollars, than are four columns of story matter worth two. It is more trouble, more labor, to "get them up." But in our arrangement, "sketches" were prohibited.

"Sketches!" why, were not they to have 'sketches' from the pen of the renowned Miss Cross-bow, the far-famed Mr. Hilltop? 'Sketches from the pen of Ella Lincoln!' Who ever heard of *her* as a story writer? Her talent lay in a different vein, if *she had any*, which was at least questionable. Strange that the readers of 'The Branch of Peace' had ever tolerated 'Ella Lincoln;' indeed, very strange that she had had the audacity *to write at all;* that Mr. Harris had patronized her; that Mrs. Harrison had condescended to appear with her in the newspaper.

I read Mr. Downham's letter with a grateful heart.

'Respected my talents, was pleased with the manner in which I had discharged my editorial duties; *had* thought, on account of the strength of the editorial corps that, very reluctantly, he must dispense with my services. But this appeal!' *well, it overpowered him*, and *his letter overpowered me;* overpowered my better judgment. Silly Ella! I thought it came fresh from the heart, *one heart, not many;* that it had but one reader, and was strictly confidential; a private letter. Ah, me!

I heard of its *fac simile* a day or two since, and Ella's reply. The original of his *was* fresh, but the *copy* is stale and worn. Can mine have been fingered by clerks, pandered by curious eyes? Alas! it went forth as a dove; will it yet return to me a viper? Of this, more anon.

Now, Ella, courage! try again. What, make my debût in another publisher's office, to be received coldly, or make a bad bargain? No news from the 'Intelligence Office.' Well, probably they would not want me in a store, because the man at the desk could not recommend me as experienced in measuring tape and cambric; as a gentleman's housekeeper, because *he* did not know I had kept tavern — I forgot to tell him *that;* as a chambermaid, because I did not look strong enough to lift a blanket; as a cook, because I so resembled *starvation*. That man at the counter *knew*.

"Is this the office of 'The Old Mortality?"

"Yes, madam."

"Editor within?"

"He is not, but will be in presently; take a seat."

" Mr. Howell ? "

" Yes, madam. "

" Mrs. Lincoln, late assistant editor of ' The Branch of Peace.'

Mr. Howell said not *a word.*

" By the late misfortune of Mr. Harris, former editor of ' The Branch of Peace,' I am reduced to necessity, and have not yet secured so much work as I need. I thought it possible that *you* might furnish me with occupation until I could make other arrangements."

" I know you as a writer; like you very well, but don't need you — can't employ you, madam ; " and Mr. Howell scribbled, scribbled.

" Good evening, sir. "

" Good evening, madam. "

" Pie crust abridged ; a perfect old steel-trap ! " said Ella, going home. " No more publishers to-day ; my nerves are all unstrung. "

" A letter ! whose chirography ? Don't know. Oh, from Mr. Thomas, a dissenting glergyman. I recollect now. I addressed a note to him three days since, having heard he was benevolent, asking him to befriend me."

" My dear madam, yours came, etc. I regret your misfortune, etc. Situated as I am, there is but little that I *can do*, except in the way of giving you good advice, and making you known to others. If you need me, call upon me. Anything within my power I will be pleased to do, in the way of assisting you. Mr. John Wilkes, of the ' Daily News,' is a good man, and liberal ; if you will mention my name to him, I have no doubt but that he will find a way to help you. I am most truly yours,

RALPH THOMAS."

I wept over that letter. A heart was there; a heart with the will and the power to help me.

No matter if there was a deep snow, and my boarding house was a mile from his office. Not a thing worth minding, that the wind was cold and searching, lifting great snow-drifts and whirling them in my face; no matter if I had to borrow a fellow boarder's furs and moccasins, to prevent my freezing to death! I walked resolutely to the office of the 'Daily News,' hope buoying up my spirits, and making my step as elastic as a child's.

He was not within. I retured, not at all discouraged, but grieved at the delay. I wrote a note, stating that I had called; the object of that call; and appealed to him for sympathy and aid. Dropping that into the Sub. Post Office, I calmly waited the result.

"My dear Mrs. Lincoln," — I could read no more just then. The lines twisted, rolled and danced before me. The words were all underscored and italicised. The capitals loomed up like steeples.

He had never seen my face. No man had said to *him*, 'Respect her for my sake.' I was 'dear' to him as a suffering sister of humanity; as such, he gave me heart and hand.

No wonder that I wept, wept tears of joy and gratitude. God's image yet remained on earth, and earth was beautiful.

I brushed away those tears and read:—

"If you will be so kind as to come to my office, on Saturday, between the hours of twelve and two, we will have a little conversation about your affairs."

"Be assured, that whatever may be in my power towards the advancement of your interests, I will do most cordially, etc.

With a deep interest in your welfare, I remain,

Very truly yours,

JOHN WILKES."

When 'Saturday' came, I did not forget 'between the hours of twelve and two.'

I found him there, a youthful personage, tall and graceful, with a world of thought upon his high, white forehead, a world of feeling in his clear, blue eye.

"Mrs. Lincoln, I am very happy to see you, etc. You wish for more literary employment?"

"Yes, sir."

"There seems to be but little that a lady can do in a daily, so much of the work being done in the night; but what you can do conveniently, you may. Here is a subject upon which I had thought of writing myself; I think you would manage it better, and if you please, *you* may write the article; I will pay you now."

He handed me a bill.

"But what if the article should not please you, when finished?

"Oh, I am confident it will."

Now I knew that the writing of that article was mere moonshine; that he did not need it; that he himself could have written it better. I knew that he only took this delicate manner of bestowing the money which he feared I much needed.

I merely thanked him for the employment, and rolled the stone resolutely over the well of tears, unwilling to wound *him* by giving vent to emotions which struggled for utterance. Heaven bless him!

Mr. Wilkes gave me a letter of introduction to a friend of his, whom I found a *gentleman.* When I say "*gentleman,*" I mean something. *A man* who is willing to suffer inconvenience to befriend a woman in distress; who does not say *one word* when he thinks another; who does not cough and "hem;" and twist in his chair; and tell her "how highly he respects her" just to pass away the time, until he can get his "courage up" to tell her that he will do nothing for her.

Mr. Barnard, of "The Stripes and Stars," is a gentleman. He looked at Ella Lincoln's pale, care-worn face, dewy eye, and pitied her for the great sorrow which had darkened her life.

Mr. Barnard promised me employment; and has made that promise good. I *knew he would*, at the first glimpse of that fine, benevolent countenance. And yet *he* was not "hard up" for "contributors."

He had "Alps on Alps" of manuscripts in that office. Heaven bless *him*, also — may he never taste the cup of poverty — never want a friend!

Another letter, commencing with: "My Dear Mrs. Lincoln" — expressing sympathy, promising to use influence in my behalf.

A letter, like the voice, has an undertone sometimes;

a low whisper of kindly feeling, distinct from the written words; and we read, and re-read that letter, until we seem to have known and loved the writer long ago. Such was the one before me. I felt its true fraternal spirit, sweeping over my bosom-strings, like a sweet strain of melody, melting my soul to tears — sweet, grateful tears!

Another, " Most Truly Yours," from one whose high position rendered his friendship doubly valuable.

One, two, three, four — Ella was *rich* now! Thousands who move in the gilded circles of fashion, have not *four* friends. Many, who had been mine in prosperity, had looked on coldly while I struggled with the adverse tide, saying insultingly, " God help you!"

Yet now — now, when a cloud of darkness, tenfold more appalling than before, had settled over all my prospects, almost putting out the light of hope, God had raised up friends for me.

CHAPTER XL.

"May speak thy mind;"

Oh pray that the shadows
Though darkly they fall
On mute retrospection,
The handmaid of all;
Though far o'er the future,
Their wings may be cast,
May fade into brightness
And glory at last."

I WAS anxious to please Downham & Co., of "The Branch of Peace," and to continue to write for them until the time had expired for which my own personal friends had subscribed for that Journal, on my account.

I had suggested to Mr. Downham, the propriety of his explaining to his readers the reason why I had so suddenly ceased my editorial duties; and he replied that "there was no necessity for such an announcement; that my articles would appear under the editorial head; and it would be better *for me* that things should remain as they were;" — *kind Mr. Downham!*

I contributed the stipulated amount of MS. weekly, for a few weeks; then observing that it was not used, I did not furnish the usual quota. I thought in *my humility*, that those gentlemen had never been pleased with me, as a writer; but, in their overflowing goodness of heart, had paid me the sum of five dollars, weekly, in the same spirit that they would have put a slice of cold ham into a beggar's basket; and it being necessary that I should earn as much as possible, I wrote for other papers, thinking that at some future day, if in more favorable circumstances, I might refund to them the money which they were overpaying now.

I received a hint from them, *and a loudly spoken one*, that the full amount of MS. was expected weekly, to be used or not as they pleased; and they were pleased to say at the same time, that they were satisfied with my articles, etc."

"Then why do you not use them as you engaged to do?"

"That is our affair;" and they said a few words which wounded the sensitive nature of Ella, while at the same time it aroused all her pride, and led her to utter something more than "sugar-coated" phraseology in return.

Downham & Co. differed from each other in their literary tastes; and both, from Ella; and although she used her versatile talents with the greatest allowable license, she failed of pleasing either. She began to wonder if she *could write;* if she *ever did write;* and if she could not, and never could, *why* she had received a fair share of compliments from editors and friends; and why her articles had been somewhat extensively copied, which is a pretty good criterion by which to judge of a writer's success.

For the first time in a long newspaper experience, the propriety of one of her articles was questioned;

half of it printed, the remainder thrown away; and many "straws," unobserved by any eyes save hers, indicated to her the direction in which the wind was blowing.

But, pressed as I was for time, I gave but little heed to lesser incidents, and wrote on; for the hopes of THREE seemed chained to the energies of one right hand.

"Have you seen the new Prospectus, in the Branch of Peace?" said one of our boarders, putting a paper into my hand. It read thus: — "The far-famed Mr. Northern-light writes for this Paper; the accomplished Miss Morning-star writes for this Paper; sweet, playful, bewitching Daffodil writes for this Paper; and numerous other gifted contributors, under various nom-de-plumes, write for this Paper." Not a word of Ella Lincoln.

I was not quite annihilated, but *felt* the flagrant insult offered me in those very columns in which I had labored so long, and, some were pleased to say, successfully; I knew it would be read, and *felt*, by numerous friends. But alone, poor, and unprotected, as I was, I saw at once that my only policy was to "suffer and be strong."

Men, in their business-transactions with men, may do things honest and honorable, which appear in a different light when their dealings are with unfortunate women. Men *who are* MEN, will not persecute any woman, until she is constrained to utter "hard things," then stereotype those hasty, heart-wrung expressions, for the rude stare of the world.

Ella "loved Rome more than Cæsar;" a weapon

was pointed at her heart; and her only alternative was to level her own piece at him who held it. Ella is not writing a romance, herself the heroine, and representing herself as without a fault; she writes the history of living flesh and blood, and of a strong, earnest nature, in whose cup of life the Father blended every element which tends to make up a human character; of one peculiarly fitted for trials and endurance; claiming no mental superiority, but *soul enough* to honor or despise; to appreciate a courtesy, or resent an insult.

"Downham & Co. paid Ella Lincoln five dollars per week for manuscript, which she promised, but has never furnished." So says Report.

After Downham & Co. use *all* the manuscript which Ella has put into their hands, giving her articles an honorable place in their columns — if Fortune favors her sufficiently — she will refund to them the amount of money which they may have overpaid.

But so long as the names of the present proprietors shall remain at the head of its columns, Ella Lincoln, who has, in days gone by, secured numerous subscribers for the 'Branch of Peace,' will never say to another friend; 'Take it for my sake.'

She cannot point to Downham, personally, as a pattern of generosity, and say: 'Respect him for my sake; he was kind to me in misfortune;' because he first led her to confide in him as a friend; and then, when her literary reputation was in a measure in his power, he depreciated her as a writer, *in the estimation of some of his readers*, by a covert, cowardly insult.

Some, not all. Ella has numerous friends, who understand and *appreciate those favors she has received of Mr. Downham.* Some have discontinued the 'Branch of Peace;' to others, it no longer comes as a welcome messenger; and more than a few would willingly see it sleeping in peace, with a new 'Branch' rising, Phœnix-like, from its ashes, with the name of 'Mark Harris' on its forehead.

Mr. Harris, the former editor of 'The Branch of Peace," seems already to have found, again, the highway to prosperity. Mr. Primble, the former foreman of the 'Branch, etc., is associated with him in business. I was in the office of 'The New England Mercury, which they edit; and there I saw the faces of several of the former employees of the 'Peace," all wearing the smile of content; and apparently viewing life on the brighter side again. Mr. Harris has proved *true to me as a friend.* I came down from my attic months ago; and am pleasantly situated, in an excellent family, relatives of Mr. Primble. I remain a widow of the heart, mourning my *living dead,* with but little hope of a future earthly reunion.

My children remain at Winchester, cheered in their loneliness by the sympathy and care of those persons who have them more especially in charge; and receiving the kindest courtesies from that excellent community; to many of whom we owe more gratitude than words or money could repay.

We have a few relatives, and many friends, to whom we are indebted for acts of kindness, both in earlier and more recent troubles. God bless such as have souls, and pity all who have *none!*

CHAPTER XLI.

CONCLUSION.

"He that writes,
Or makes a feast, more certainly invites
His judges than his friends; there 's not a guest
But will find something wanting or ill drest."

"An autobiography! Oh, Ella!" some will say; "it is a shame for you to go back into the high-ways and by-ways of the past, and bring out its joys and sorrows for the rude gaze of an unfeeling world; to *talk* of the poverty which has dogged you like a shadow; the unkindness that has stung you like a serpent; of your faults, and follies, and the weaknesses of your dearest friends. Some will charge you with untruthfulness; some say you *cannot write;* others, that you add your *mite* to the list of "trashy works," fit only for the bonfire, to *make money.*"

That *is* the thing, *money! money*, for the comforts it purchases, the rest it allows to the weary, the home it provides for the homeless, *money* to educate the young, to feed the poor, to comfort the afflicted.

But not all *money*, not all a willingness to wound those sensitive friends who would not have my somewhat eventful life reviewed by curious eyes; who would not have my faults and weaknesses the subject of remark and criticism.

No, not *that*, or *this;* I have, here and there in the

wide, wide world, brothers and sisters of the heart; I meet them in my daily walks; I commune with them in my dreams. They are here. I know them by their mournful eyes; the mystic haze of sadness wreathed around their temples; the net-work of care upon their foreheads; the quiver of their thin, pale lips; the restless movements of their vein-traced hands. They are *there*. I seek in vain for their fleshly portraits in the halls of memory; I know not if their foreheads be snowy or brown; if their eyes be like the eagle's or the dove's; if their locks are like midnight, or chestnut, or silvered by time. But I know that they are *there*; for there comes to me a low under-tone of sorrow in every breeze; they have spoken to me through the pen; they have read and understood the words traced by my earnest hand.

Seen or unseen, I love them, and long to whisper words of comfort and encouragement amidst the cares which press so heavily upon them; I will tell *them* the tale of my own outer and inner life, that they may profit by my short-comings, and avoid them; I will tell them how *I* have persevered in the onward path, sustained by one high purpose; never, in my darkest hours, utterly forsaken of God.

I will tell them to struggle on, true to one holy aspiration: seeking the happiness of all around; educating themselves for life and heaven. I will entreat of them to cling to their little ones; never to "put them out," lest their young lives be turned to bitterness by cold looks and unreasonable commands; to cling to them while existence lasts, lifting up their own weak hands between them and the world, with one prayer upon their lips continually: "Let not these go forth to ask for sympathy among the mammon-worshippers, who will underrate in them the noblest gifts of Heaven."

I will tell them, never to bow their foreheads to the dust, underrating themselves because their inferiors accept of menial service at their hands. I will say to them: "Though your earthly relatives may look on coldly when your last hope grows brittle as a spider's web, the Eternal Father looks down and pities you; Jesus forgets you not; and although the night may be yet dark, the morning waits in the distance to burst its fetters in a flood of glory.

For the sake of all the poor and sorely tried, whom I love but cannot see; or, seeing, cannot otherwise bless, Ella Lincoln will write this Book.

"What is written is written." There are some who will condemn both the book and the author. Was there ever a book or an author without faults which might be magnified and over-colored by ill-nature?

I trust the good and generous reader will judge me leniently; if persecuted by those of an opposite character, I will try to be resigned, remembering "it is good to be afflicted."

www.ingramcontent.com/pod-product-compliance
Lightning Source LLC
LaVergne TN
LVHW010153110826
845151LV00002B/505

* 9 7 8 1 4 2 5 5 3 8 2 3 1 *